THE MISADVENTURES OF A VET

Rana Preet Gill

ISBN 978-93-52011-82-7
Copyright © Rana Preet Gill , 2019

First published in India 2019 by Inkstate Books
An imprint of Leadstart Publishing Pvt Ltd

Sales Office:
Unit No.25/26, Building No.A/1,
Near Wadala RTO,
Wadala (East), Mumbai – 400037 India
Phone: +91 22 24046887
Email: info@leadstartcorp.com
www.leadstartcorp.com

Disclaimer: The Views expressed in this book are those of the Author and do not pertain to be held by the Publisher.

Editor: Shilpi Sinha
Cover: Ashwini Jadhav
Layouts: Victor Patali

Dedication

For Mr Ramesh Vinayak sir for making me
a part of Spice of life

About the Author

RANA PREET GILL is a Hoshiarpur based Veterinary Officer working with Animal Husbandry Department, Punjab.

She contributes to English newspapers: Hindustan Times (Spice of Life), The Tribune, The Hindu (Open Page), Deccan Herald, The New Indian Express, The Hitavada, Daily Post and Woman's era.

She has written a novel titled 'Those College Years'. Her second book was a compilation of her pieces in several newspapers and magazines titled 'Finding Julia'.

She is active on Facebook, Instagram (dr_rana_preet_gill) and Twitter (@drranapreetgill).

This is her third book.

Acknowledgements

To my parents, Mrs Harjit Kaur Gill and Prof Karamjit Singh Gill for inculcating the habit of reading in me.

To Ms Yojana Yadav for always being so kind and loving, Mr Arun Joshi for the encouragement, Ms Priyanka Singh for accepting my middles, Mr Sumit Paul for his time and effort in going through my manuscript.

To Sehar, Varun, Roopi veer ji, Puneet di, Deepti, Amarbir and my in-laws for their support.

To my editor Ms Shilpi Sinha, Project manager Ms Naina Solanki and Leadstart Publishing House.

CONTENTS

THE PROLOGUE

"Rhea di, I have brought you a special cream. Trust me, it will make you fairer and you will glow like a night bulb."

"I am already fair, Kanu. I don't need any cream and the marriage will be solemnized in the day. There are going to be *pheras* at the Gurudwara."

"I still can't believe you are getting married. Does he know, you are crazy?"

"Kanu, I will kill you if you used this word in front of my husband. I am not the same girl, who was your roommate at the University. Things have changed. I have become more mature. Well… hmmm...kind of! I am a respected Vet now. Last year, I got lot of coverage for the work I am doing with PETA (People for Ethical Treatment of animals). So just shut up and mind your own business and come to the marriage, dressed sensibly."

"What are you going to wear for the wedding, Rhea di? And did you buy the lingerie for the wedding night. If not, I can buy for you or try shopping online. Zivame is giving a 50% discount. In fact, buy some pieces for me also."

"I don't have time for all this. So many guests in the house. I am sick of all these people. Why do they have to live in my home?" Rhea registered her disapproval.

"Oh! Poor Rhea di still has encroachment issues. By the way, they all have come to celebrate your wedding, stupid senior. And buy something nice for yourself. Don't wear those boring bras and torn panties you are so used to." Kanu chuckled

"You disrobed me to see my panties. I knew that something was wrong with you. See, I knew you had lesbian traits as well!"

"I saw them hanging on the wire one day and I was so embarrassed to admit to other girls that these panties belong to my roommate. Yuck!! That was the most disgusting day of my life. Don't make a fool of yourself on your wedding night. For God's sake, buy some decent stuff." And with this Kanu hung up.

Look at the nerve of this girl. Telling me what to wear. So, what if she has a husband who drools after her and wants to make love to her every night. That doesn't mean she can get so preachy. I wonder if she uses all her exotic lotions and potions on him as well.

Buaji came flopping around and gave Rhea a jolt.

"Rhea beta, the beautician called up at my number, so many times. What are you doing? They are waiting for you. Remember to get full body wax, manicure, pedicure and diamond facial."

"But Buaji, full body waxing is so painful. Can we skip that? Rest is fine."

"No, beta. You must look pretty and hot at the same time. Chalo, chalo don't be lazy. Get your act together and move. Go on your scooter."

"Can anyone drop me to the beauty parlour?"

"Everyone is so busy. Please help yourself. Remember, God helps those who help themselves!"

And she shoved a reluctant Rhea out of the house for the painful yet necessary salon activties.

Wow! Buaji has that one liner handy. I don't know if I will be helped this time. All this is making me so nervous. Do I have to get married? Damn!!! Why did I say yes?

Part 1

The Marriage

1

MARRIAGE AT GURUDWARA

Rhea had finally said yes for the marriage. After rejecting many guys her parents paraded in front of her, she finally found one who had a hazy resemblance to the love of her life.

"So, you said yes to this marriage because he looked like the one, you have been dreaming about. We have been discussing your hazy visions." The cousin who was getting Rhea ready, pinched her bottom and winked at her.

"Can you please stop asking silly questions? Who told you all this nonsense? Me getting visions, this is crazy!"

"Everyone knows that. All of us know that you have been having visions of your future husband. And this is the reason that you are in thirties and getting married late. Otherwise, why wait for so long. Nahi!"

"Who is spreading lies about me? I never said anything about visions. Did I??? I said I never met the guy whom I found suitable."

"Well, you need to have a heart to heart chat with Buaji. She is feeding everyone all this silly stuff. People have been asking why Rhea waited so long to get married."

"Damn Buaji!!! Why is she so nosy all the time? She could have said that I was waiting for the right person. What's all this vision and dream story? I could never understand her completely?" Rhea was holding Penny, one of the strays, she had been petting affectionately.

"Fuck Buaji! Penny, meri jaan I would miss you. But then you are not so small, or I would have smuggled you inside my lehenga and we both could have got married at the same time."

"Rhea di, are you crazy??? Don't you dare take a dog inside the Gurudwara! Who does that? I have never seen a bride hold a dog in her lap and kiss it. Rhea di…. Are you listening???? Stop kissing the damn dog! The lipstick would come off. I don't know why you are getting married to a human when your heart is brimming with love for canines."

Buaji chimed in with the cousin.

"I agree Chutki. Rightly said! Wah ji wah! You are such a beautiful bride! Haye haye! Kutte nu chad de, beta ji (Put the dog down). It will spoil your lehenga."

"No, don't shove it away. Penny is the love of my life. Let it stay, please! I want him to be the best man at my wedding." Rhea wailed while someone took away the dog from her lap.

"Dogs are not allowed in the Gurudwara and there are no best men at our marriages. You talk sensibly! After a lot of pleas, you have agreed to get married and now for God's sake don't spoil everything, you brat!" her mom rebuked her mildly.

Rhea's self-professed love for the strays had taken hold of her more strongly the day she started practising as a private Veterinary practitioner in her hometown Nurpur, and her collaboration with PETA meant she got a dog shelter constructed in the city. Some days she would bring some of the inmates to her home as well. This caused lot of problems at domestic front and she would be admonished all the time, but her parents had reconciled to the fact that their daughter is unyielding. So, they grudgingly partook of her enthusiasm, albeit, not with the same gusto.

"Apne viah wale din taan chad de, these pestering dogs. (Leave the dogs, on your wedding day). Take them back to the shelter someone. Bhabhi ji, you should not have chosen Veterinary for this girl. I told you to give donation of 10 lakhs and get her admitted to DMC, ohi apna wala Dayanand Medical College, Ludhiana. Pammi's son pursued MBBS from that institute and he is married to an MBBS Doctor now. Very nice. At least, we could have called her a full-fledged Doctor. Now she is only danger dactar. I mean dangaar (animal) dactar."

"Please Buaji, don't say anything about my profession. I am a successful Veterinary practitioner and I am proud to be one.''

"Aho ji, nale pun nale phalian. Keep on putting the injections and keep on making moolah." Buaji said with a glimmer in her eyes.

"Do your in-laws know that you are crazy about animals? Did you give them a sample of your affections or they will receive a jolt when you will put a stray pup in your mother-in-law's arms saying, "Lo Mummy ji, tuhada potra (grandson)."

Everyone doubled up with laughter listening to Buaji's light banter. Rhea smiled meekly listening to all the talks half-heartedly. And somewhere she was getting irritated by everyone having fun at her expense.

Can't they just disappear? I cannot take all this anymore. Get lost everyone. Just fuck off!!!!

Her dad came running, heaving breathlessly "We will be late for pheras (wedding rituals). Come on everyone, get in the cars. Anand Karaj has to be performed before 12 pm."

The women in the house were dressed in choicest of finery; embroidered lehengas, embellished anarkalis and Patiala salwar suits. The razzmatazz dazzled her, making her edgy, as she wanted to run away from all the chaos.

"Chalo kudiyo, chalo, get going. We should not be late." No sooner were the words uttered by Buaji everyone made a mad scramble. There was a collective rush as all of them jostled to make a quick exit.

"Rhea is going in which car? I want to sit with her. I got her ready." An excited Pinky commanded everyone's attention.

"You only adjusted the palla. She got ready at the beauty parlour. Don't try to take credit for something you never did in the first place. Liar! And when Massi's daughter got married you accompanied her and hogged all the limelight. This time I will sit with the bride. My turn this time" a firm opposition cropped up as Chutki was beaming with pride, all excited about her triumph.

Both the girls looked at each other with venom spewing at the corners of their lips.

"I am the first cousin. I have all the rights to be with the bride. You are a distant relative." Pinky persisted.

"You always want to sit with the bride. Do you think this will improve your matrimonial prospects? The way you are getting rejections from the prospective suitors, there is no way you will get married in near future!"

"How dare you say that, you bitch? I will slash your tongue." Pinky looked at Chutki with a blind rage as if she wanted to gouge out her eyes, that very moment.

"Mummy, suno what she said? Tuhandi Bhua di bhen di nanan di kudi is abusing me. Fuck you!"

"Mind your language, I am telling you. This is going too far. As if I don't know about you. You ran away with that boyfriend of yours and came back after spending two nights."

"Who told you that?"

"Ahaaa… look who is talking? Wadi aayi sati savitri? (She thinks she is the pious one?) Don't you dare cast your not-so-virgin shadow on Rhea di. Stay away from her."

"Oh! As if she is a virgin. Everyone knows about her boyfriends."

Rhea's ante pepped up seeing her name being discussed in all this.

"Stop discussing it. I am the bride. You cannot say anything about me. It's a bad omen."

"Rhea di, tell her, you are a virgin. Tell her in her face." Pinky reprimanded.

"Sweetheart! Pinky dear, let it go. It's my wedding day. Why get into a detailed discussion? Don't create a damn scene! Virgin, pure...who talks all that stuff these days. As if it matters to anyone." Rhea whispered, getting closer to her as she stood stubbornly resolute, crossing her arms against her chest, firm like a warrior.

"You are my Rhea di! You are pure and honorable. How can this immoral girl say you are not virgin? We are going to resolve this matter now. Right now. Say it, you are a virgin and only then we proceed for pheras (marriage vows)."

All the murmuring came to a halt as everyone was looking at Rhea with an amused expression who was feeling uncomfortable, continuously under the glare.

Chutki sensed her desperation to escape an answer and came to her rescue "You don't have to answer it. We all know that with so many boyfriends, no one could afford to remain a virgin."

"No, we will sort it out now! Give an answer to her." Pinky firmly clutched on to Rhea's arm now.

"Let it go. We are getting late for the pheras. Koi fado Pinki nu (Anyone please get hold of Pinki). She has gone crazy."

"I won't let anyone go from this place unless she apologizes to Rhea di for casting aspersions on her character." She pointed her finger at Chutki now.

"Oye, kudiye band kar eh drama. Virgin ya not virgin, Viah toh baad ki farak pena. Kyun ji (Stop this drama, girl. Virginity will not matter after marriage). Someone, please, move her aside."

Chutki came in all her sartorial elegance and assaulted an unprepared Pinki who fell on the ground with a thud.

"You are jealous of Rhea di. You are jealous because she is more beautiful than you and you do not want her to get married."

Pinki got up, stroked her head and made a lunge at her opponent catching her unawares this time.

"Arre ruko, tusi dono. I am getting married. Listen to me, girls." Rhea panicked when she saw them getting out in fisticuffs, kicking each other despite the heavy lehengas they were wearing for the occasion. She was saddened to see such a bad start where her relatives were unable to maintain the dignity of the occasion and rained a volley of choicest abuses in their mother tongue on each other.

"Rhea di, you stay out of this! Let me tackle her. What does she think of herself?" Pinki shrieked.

"And you think you are the lady don of your pind. Gawar! (Illiterate). Look at you! You have smudged your face pink with excessive make up, looking like a clown. Hahaha!"

"And you think you are Miss Universe! Look at the cheap lehenga you are wearing. I know you bought it from that nukkad wali shop in Rainak Bazar which sells second hand pieces. Wadi aayi beauty queen!"

"Damn! Don't spoil my wedding day by petty fights. You both can sit with me. I will drive the car myself. You both along with Mama, Papa can be easily accommodated. Now stop it! All settled." Rhea made a fervent attempt at reconciliation.

"Rhea di, I don't want to sit with her. I will sit in front with you."

"No, Rhea di, I will sit in the front with you."

"Had di ni tu, you bloody bitch!"

"Satnayas ho je tera, Kidde pen tenu." (May you rot in hell)

The body blows again rained on each other and when Rhea tried to intervene by placing herself in the middle, she got shoved as well.

"Mad girls, why are you pushing me? I am the bride!"

"Oh, sorry didi, by mistake. Let me help you. Okay, you go with the bride. I will come in another car." Pinky finally decided to be the amicable one to end this fight.

"No, I don't want to go with her. I am going with my mom. Fuck you and fuck the bloody bride!!!" Chutki ran away as Rhea looked helplessly at the nerve of the girl who had come all the way from Bathinda to be part of the festivities only to tell her to be fucked off.

"Look at her attitude! She doesn't want to go with you! She doesn't want to go with the bride. An imposter! A crook she is!" Pinki lamented at the rebuff. After all she was making sincere efforts to make amends.

"Rhea, everyone is waiting in the car. Come fast!" A hurried call made her nervous and edgy.

"Forget her! Forget everything Pinki! They are waiting for me. Please help me get up. Quick! Damn! This lehenga. I am not able to get up. Come on, hold my hand."

"I am so sorry di. Let me help you. The lehenga is very delicate. Please be careful while getting up."

She warned Rhea but inadvertently stepped on the chiffon

fabric while trying to pull her up with all her might.

"Damn! Girl you are standing on the lehenga and stop pulling me like this. It will get torn. Step away from it you idiot!" No sooner had the words escaped her lips, there was a sharp sound of the perforation, by the subsequent push and pull.

"Awwwww, you tore the lehenga. You tore the damn fucking lehenga! I told you not to step on it and then you are pulling me with all your gargantuan might."

"OMG! Rhea di, Buaji will kill me if she sees this. Please for God's sake don't tell anyone." Pinki shuddered at the sight of torn lehenga, her eyes wide with the fear and loathing she would receive from the family for doing this blatant act of idiocy.

"You are an idiot! It's all your fault. First you started this virginity drama and then you stepped on the lehenga. I am about to get married. Where will I find a replacement in such a short time?" Rhea thundered and brought a visibly shaken Pinky on the verge of tears.

She mellowed down when she saw Pinki crying. She composed herself and tried calming her down.

"Pinki, don't cry sweetheart. Let's concentrate on the solution. It's so nerve rattling. Everyone has gone crazy. The tear is not big. I will adjust the dupatta and see that it doesn't show. Can you get me a few safety pins, so I can cover it nicely?"

"Wait for me here. I will get them from my bag. Don't go anywhere. Just stay here." Pinki scampered away, maneuvering her way deftly, picking up her dress nimbly in her fingers.

Rhea, crestfallen occupied the chair, fidgeted with her dupatta and felt dejected at the happenings.

Damn! I cannot cry. My eyeliner will get smudged. Why is all this happening on my wedding day? Why me?

Buaji came running all the way to Rhea, poked her gently and narrowed her eyes.

"It seems you do not have any intention of getting married right away. Everyone is waiting for the Princess to sit in the car. The bridegroom has already reached the Gurudwara."

"Buaji, just a second. I want some safety pins. Wait!"

"You look perfect girl and stop fussing over your looks. Aaj kal ki ladkiyan, too conscious about looks '' with this she held Rhea's wrist and dragged her towards the car.

"Buaji, listen I want to tell you something. There is a problem. Where is mom?''

"Arre, what telling something! Don't be a run-away bride like Julia Roberts. Are you getting all nerves? Chalo, ji chalo this girl is shying away from marriage now. Jaldi chalo to Gurudwara or she might run off to her brood of dogs." Buaji laughed wildly, as she draws a kind of sadistic pleasure by connecting Rhea with the canines.

She was trying to hide the tear that now covered most of her midriff with the heavy dupatta.

"What are you doing, Rhea?" Buaji thundered. "Stop fiddling with the dupatta. You will tear it. This is such a beautiful chiffon lehenga, I chose for you."

"Buaji, don't you think you should have chosen something sturdier for me. Something stronger since I am a Vet and I'm a little rough in my dealings."

She encircled her in a big jhappi and lovingly kissed her forehead. "I know you act like animals who surround you all the time, but marriages are special and sacred. I wanted to choose the best for you. So, this delicate and priceless lehenga for you, my darling."

"Buaji, you are smudging my make-up. Let me go."

She knew Buaji had that genuine affection for her at heart even though she kept on making fun of her, but that was her nature and she had been the happiest to know when this alliance had been solemnized. She undertook all the effort and scurried every shop in Ludhiana to buy the most expensive and the most delicate fabric for her. Rhea only wished it had been a little tenacious.

The wedding venue, the Gurudwara was in middle of Nurpur town where the cavalcade had reached and was now causing a traffic jam. The road was narrow and busy at all times of the day. The constant honking of cars and jostling of pedestrians was proving to be a nightmare for the baratis. Buaji shoved Rhea out of the car and kept on propelling her forward, till she reached the gates of the Gurudwara.

She had consciously put her hand on the dupatta keeping it in proper place to hide the tear. Her mom and dad along with her brother, Rajji were waiting at the entrance of the Gurudwara for her.

Bhai ji came running along, "Oh beeba, you are late. Jaldi karo. Only half an hour left. The other party has to go for pheras at 1 o'clock."

"That's all right, Bhai ji. But make sure not even a single phera is missed. We don't want a half-baked marriage." Buaji started giggling as Bhai ji responded.

"Na ji na. Pakka viah karange." (Don't worry. We will make a solid alliance).

"Just give me a minute. Mom, there is something I want to tell you."

"Na, mera bacha don't say no to marriage now. We will be ruined if you say no at this moment. Nothing will happen. Say 'Waheguru' and get married."

"Ma, why are you not listening? The fucking lehenga got torn and I am holding this dupatta to cover the tear. Do something or when I will sit for pheras people might see my red panties underneath."

"Haye, haye, siyapa! What have you done? Didn't you wear the black petticoat I gave you instead of this light colored one? This fabric is so damn transparent and fragile. I told your Buaji not to go for this one."

Rhea's future mother-in-law appeared with her set of women relatives and looked at her with a perfunctory smile.

She was a bulky lady with a huge frame. Her complexion was milky white, and her eyes shone like gleaming orbs. Her skin was sagging and although she didn't seem to be the kind of person who was bothered by her appearance, Rhea knew she was quite a beauty in her heydays. She had met her a few times before marriage and every time she went before her she felt ripped off by her overpowering looks.

And now when she stood before them, Rhea could only mumble a measly 'Sat Sri Akal Mummy ji' which went unheard and she was completely ignored as the lady chose to address her mother directly making her seem silly and unimportant on her wedding day.

"Ki gal bhenji, viaah nahi karna? (Don't you want the marriage to be solemnized?) Our boy has been seated before the Guru Granth Sahib for an eternity, and your daughter looks so diffident. Should we take the barat back if your girl is not interested in marrying?"

Rhea was stunned at the harshness of the words. She could not believe that her future mother-in-law was so powerful of creating a damage with her words. In the few meetings before marriage, she has appeared very agreeable towards her and loving but today on the day of the marriage her hidden bitterness surfaced glaringly.

Her mother smiled, bowed her head and folded her hands and said in all compliance, "Nahi, nahi don't say like this Bhenji. Just mother and daughter talk. We are coming right now."

Her mother looked at her with a pained expression and a sense of helplessness. She escorted Rhea to the designated spot in front of the Guru Granth Sahib (the holy book designated as the eternal living Guru) and whispered in her ear, "Your dignity is in your hands today. Save it. If something goes wrong your mother-in-law will never forgive and will taunt you for the rest of your life."

With the forceful words, she along with Buaji escorted Rhea to the place where the bridegroom, Abhi was sitting. He winked, making her shudder. She smiled despite the predicament and the continuous strife in her mind.

His hazy and almond eyes were captivating and held many promises. He looked enchanting in his turban and beard which he would shave off after the Anand Karaj (wedding rituals). This was the first time Rhea was seeing him in a turban and he made a very handsome sardar. And though she was unsure of the marriage vows they were going to exchange in the presence of the august Guru, a million emotions tugged at her heart and made her dream that this would turn out to be a wonderful alliance. If only she knew at that precise moment that her mother-in-law would turn her life into a living hell, she might have run away but than she did not know what future held for her.

She forgot the hesitation momentarily and plonked herself besides her would-be husband with an uneasy grace. Her gaze was intercepted by her mother-in-law's hovering eye and she hastily lowered her eyelids drooping them down.

Oh please! She should not come to know about the tear in the lehenga!

No sooner Rhea sat cross legged alongside, the tear in the fabric grew a bit more obvious. The dupatta had to be firmly held in place to cover it up and a pale shadow of something red underneath was quite evident. She had to hold it nice and firm if she had to hide the gnawing tear that ate into the flimsy fabric of her lehenga and was intent on making itself more embarassing.

But nothing could escape the hawk eyes of her mother-in-law who came in hurried steps and maneuvered her carefully.

"Is everything okay? All well with the lehenga. Why are you pulling the palla in front of you? You are spoiling the grace of the lehenga. Leave it."

"No, Mummy ji, let it stay. I am fine."

"Arre, no. Let it go, stupid girl! It must be given a free fall. The grace of this lehenga will come only if you let the palla fall on one side."

"No, I am not letting it go Mummy ji. I will fall from grace if I let go."

Rhea pulled the palla from Mummy ji's hand but not before she saw the tear and recoiled in horror.

"Tu fateya lehenga payeya viah wale din, pihte muhe tera (You wore a torn lehenga on your wedding day, shame on you!).

Bhai ji came forward with brisk steps, "Mata ji, eh nu, saas wala drama ghar ja ke kar leo. Duji party ne aa jana te viah dhariya reh jana (You can enact this mother-in-law, daughter-in-law drama at home. The other couple will be coming soon to get married and this marriage might be left in haste). He had brought two muslin cloths which he wore around the neck of groom and bride. Then taking end of each fabric he tied a firm knot.

The knot that tethered two individuals to each other for a life time. It signalled an indication of their companionship forever. Rhea wondered how much compatible and comfort giving relationship it would turn out to be, but she made a promise to make an honest effort to make this marriage successful.

With great discomfort and an effort to salvage her

remaining grace, Rhea completed the pheras keeping the palla holding it firmly in front of the tear. After every phera she could see the admonishing gaze of her mother-in-law. She would crane her neck back to hear the whispering amongst the female relatives, getting more conscious.

Bhai ji who was standing next to her after completion of the third phera could not help himself and remarked.

"Beeba, viah karan aeyo ho?" (Daughter, have you come to get married?).

"Hanji, baba ji"

"Pher concentrate karo. Ether odher ki chatiyan mari jande ho. Ethe cheating da koi scope ni (Concentrate on getting married without looking around. There is no scope of cheating in this place).

Rhea looked at Bhai ji in complete shock.

"Bhai ji, tusi kine viah karande ho din wich?" (How many couples do you get married in a day?).

"Ah hi panj sat viah kariye de aa ji (I get married around five to seven couples every day).

"Sariyan nu free di advice dinde ho ya menu special treatment de rehe ho (Do you give free advice to everyone or I am the special one, receiving it?).

Bhai ji hurriedly moved aside to make way for them for the fourth and last phera.

Rhea could not escape the angry stare of her mother-in-law and the whispering amongst the women some of which wafted down her way.

"What was she discussing with Bhai ji? Are brides supposed to converse during the pheras?

Soon after the wedding vows were completed, her mother ushered her away from the prying eyes of the relatives and made her change into a not- so ornately decorated lehenga.

"This is all I have got right now, Rhea. You will have to manage with the only one I have."

The bridal party moved towards the marriage palace with hush- hush whispers about the torn lehenga, giggles and disapprovals.

"She wore a torn lehenga at the pheras. Look at her! What was she thinking?"

Rhea's eyes brimmed with tears as she followed her husband holding his hand walking, albeit a few steps back wondering at the strangeness of the situation.

"Why did I say yes to this marriage at all?" the mother-in-law lamented albeit only in her thoughts.

"Why did I choose a Veterinary Doctor? That teacher who taught in the government school was good enough. What shame this girl has brought upon us? She wore a torn lehenga. What will people think of us now?" she ruminated and got sad as they left the Gurudwara and proceeded towards the marriage palace.

At the palace, the atmosphere was more vibrant as most of the people were gorging on the delicacies and varied assortment of food. Rhea was crestfallen and looked a little dull and drab in the lehenga procured by her mother in a jiffy. She was not able to pin it up properly, so the dupatta kept on falling every time she moved her shoulders. The top was a tad too loose and the neckline kept on plunging. All the time she was conscious and kept on adjusting her bearings.

Her mother-in-law kept on gazing at her with penetrating eyes, making her more conscious and nervous. While she sat frozen in time posing for photo ops with her husband, the old lady did not come even once and made her presence felt. Neither did she let any female relatives come to the fore and talk to Rhea.

After it was time to part ways, Rhea's mother came and

spoke to her in hushed tones, "Your mother-in-law is pissed off with the whole tear in the lehenga thing. She was babbling to her relatives about the same. I wish your marriage had ended on a more positive note. But there is nothing we can do about it. It just happened. Take care of yourself. And be strong. The way you have always been."

****

At the time of bidai (departure), leaving her home was a painful experience for Rhea. The rituals were performed but in a low-key manner. Her mother felt lost and slightly out of place. Her eyes were moist, and she had been making lot of effort to maintain a veneer of happiness but deep down she shuddered at the hardships her darling daughter would have to go through to make herself a part of that family.

Rhea's luggage had been deposited in the car and she hugged everyone with misty eyes. Her mom, dad, Rajji, Buaji, Pinky (who finally appeared from some hidden corner) and the gaggle of female relatives surrounded her.

"Rhea di, I am sorry for ruining the wedding day." Pinky whispered taking her in a half embrace.

"It's okay. People will forget the faux pas soon enough. Let us not talk about it anymore."

She hugged her mother tightly, enveloping her arms around her, encasing her in a bear hug, holding back her tears and murmuring words of comfort, "I will be fine, Ma. Don't you worry!"

Her mother-in-law saw the mother daughter camaraderie and rushed towards their side.

"Chalo ji chalo, late ho gya." (We are getting late)

Rhea grudgingly let go of Ma and soon she was ushered into the car.

While the car drove away from Nurpur, her mind was

flooded with memories, of a happy childhood, a carefree existence in a protected environment and of unbridled love and affection showered by her parents. She wondered if she would be able to feel the same warmth at the house of her in-laws.

It was a difficult change for her to move to Ludhiana to complete her Veterinary degree. She was never able to gel with other girls. But for the past few years, she had been working in her hometown. Her mother had fussed over her, feeding her all kinds of stuffed paranthas, taking extra care of her, pampering her wheareas her dad has supported her in all her endeavours, provided her the emotional support and freedom. Life has never been so good. She loved her parents, she loved her job and she loved Nurpur. It took her years to say yes to a nuptial alliance. It was only once she entered her thirties that she succumbed to pressure of her parents and relatives to get married.

And now, once again, she was getting plucked from her hometown and being placed in an alien environment.

Sitting in the car along with her husband, her thoughts veered around her job. She had been working as a Veterinary practitioner for the past many years, her practice had soared giving her many faithful clients. She also got in touch with some flagbearers of PETA and they had constructed a shelter for the stray animals. She even got honoured by the local SDM for her work. Life has never looked so satisfying and marriage was not on her cards but once she entered her thirties her parents started pressurizing her even more and finally coaxed her into meeting Abhi. And once she met him, she could not say no.

He had been gentle and funny (the one thing she loved the most about men) and in that first meeting his repository of jokes enthralled her and she fell in love with him. He was tall, fair, having a medium build. He had charmed her with his humble demeanour and gentle talk. They discovered so much in common in the very first meeting. The subsequent ones strengthened her belief that he was perfect for her, someone who would listen to her and would understand her compassion and concern for the animals, so she ended up saying yes to him.

She looked at him with a careful eye but he was intently looking outside.

Damn! He is not even looking at me. What's he thinking?

She moved her hand and placed it carelessly next to him to touch a little. Then she lifted her hennaed fingers, stroked the palm of his hand. He looked at her longingly, squeezed her hand and smiled impishly. How she wanted to nestle in his arms? She wanted to kiss his honey coated lips right now, in the car, with her mother-in-law staring at her, maneuvering their actions.

The memory of the last time they kissed still lingered fresh on her mind. He had come with his parents and her dad asked Rhea to show him her room. It was the first time they had kissed. His hands moved gently over her back and his lips nuzzled her neck before he gave a passionate kiss on her anticipating lips. She has reciprocated enthusiastically. The kiss lasted a long time before someone knocked on the door. Her mother had come pussyfooted sensing the danger. She did not give them enough time to explore more of each other.

Mummy ji, in the meanwhile coughed a little. She had been sitting with the driver, watching them get cozy in the rear-view mirror and this was her indication to Abhi to let go off Rhea's hand.

He sensed his mother's discomfort, reluctantly shoved himself away and used his arms to move himself a little away from her. For the rest of the drive, he did not even look at his wife, which she found rather odd.

He is my husband now. In any case, he will make love to me in the room.

* * *

2

A NEW HOME IS CALLING

After a long and tiring drive, they reached Pathankot. Dusk had descended, and it was difficult to remember the narrow alleys through which the car moved in a serpentine motion. She had been twice to her future home which looked immaculately maintained to her. Her mother-in-law was a finicky woman who took great care in arranging things, keeping them in a perfect and apple-pie order. The color scheme of things looked ideal to her. She wondered, how someone as imperfect as her will fit in an idealistic home.

As the car came to a halt after innumerable twists and turns, Rhea's heart churned with mixed feelings. She felt strange in the alien surroundings. Her mind became a vortex of emotions, she felt overwhelmed at the strangeness of the new life she would have to adjust to. She missed her home, her parents, her job, the dog pound. She was missing everything and it all came to her in that instant and she felt terrible.

She alighted from the car and started crying. "Na beta, rona nahi. Ehi ta zindagi hai kudiyan di" (No child, don't cry. This is what a girl's life is all about). An elderly woman hugged her, comforting her as she took her in an embrace.

"Ek tain drame ni khatam hunde aaj kal dian kudiyan de!" (These young girls are too dramatic!) her mother-in-law muttered under her breath standing next to her. She did not provide her any consolation or comfort but kept on her diatribe in muted tones. But she made sure Rhea listened to every word uttered by her.

Wasn't mother-in-law supposed to act as a mother to her? She assured my parents she would treat me like a daughter. Where has all the love and regard dissipated? Why is she being so nasty to me while I haven't even uttered a word yet?

"Chalo chalo, let's start the ceremonies if this rona dhona is over?" (Let's start with the ceremonies if she is done crying?)

****

After a long time when all the ceremonies were over, someone escorted her to a room. She felt damn tired as she sat alone thinking about the rituals that were a part and parcel of the marriage.

Such elaborate rituals! Do they guarantee you happiness? Do they ensure that you will be treated well at your in-laws house and taken to be as part of the family? If not, then all these ceremonies are a charade. If you are going to burn your daughters-in-law for not bringing enough dowry, if you are going to harass them because they are more independent than you want them to be, if you want to shame them because they are unable to bear a son for your clan, don't marry your sons. Let them stay single. Do not bring daughters-in-law to your home for the sake of an heir? Welcome them as if they are your daughters, cherish them, love them, respect them and make them part of the family.

But daughters-in-law are never daughters. Rhea understood this on her wedding day. She was sad and pensive in her room, chock-a-block with stuff. And then it suddenly came to her mind that her own bags were not there.

OMG! Where are my things? Did they leave them behind?

She scanned the room to find that her American Tourister bags were missing. The anxiety, the insecurity all came back to her, flooding her senses. She paced out of the room and saw a group of ladies, sitting, chatting amongst themselves.

"Has anyone seen my bags? Where are my bags?"

"Ni kudiye kede bag? (Girl, which bags are you talking about?)

And they started giggling and whispering amongst themselves.

"Eh dangaar doctor aa na kudi? Ehna nu hor koi kudi ni mili? (Is she a Veterinary Doctor? Didn't they get any other girl for their son?)

Her mother-in-law came hurriedly to find out the reason of commotion.

"What happened?"

"Mummy ji, my bags are not here. Please tell me they are safe."

"They are in my room."

"Thank God! Please put them in my room instead of yours."

"Okay, I will ask someone to do that." she replied without looking at her.

"Aaj kal diyan kudiyan bahut tej ne. Unhe sochiya saman sahuriyan ne chori kar liya" (These modern girls are very sharp. She thought the in-laws stole her stuff).

Everyone laughed heartily as a voluptuous woman cracked an innocuous joke at Rhea's expense.

She lowered her head and fidgeted for a while for she did not know what to say. She could hardly utter a word and felt mortified standing in front of them.

Damn! Where is Abhi? Where is my husband? Why has he left me all alone here?

She retired to her room and wondered why she was all

alone.

Is this how the newlyweds are treated by their in-laws? Why all of them are sitting outside and no one even asked me to be with them. Where is my phone? Damn! I have nothing to do. I need a book to read but then they are in the bag and it's in Mummy ji's room.

"Drink this milk", Mummy ji came into the room and handed over a tall and inviting glass of milk to her.

"Where is Abhi? I haven't seen him for a long time. Please tell him to come to the room."

It was for the first time that she took Abhi's name since they got married. It sounded strange to her own ears. His name evoked a desire in her and she smiled coquettishly.

She was glad to be given something to drink. She had eaten a few morsels for lunch which were not enough. While her husband ate heartily oblivious to the whole lehenga fiasco, she sat depressed cursing herself for being a part of the slugfest between her cousins.

With the glass of milk in her hand, she realized how hungry she was! She drank it in one gulp. It tasted sweet with a hint of kesar and almonds in it.

It tasted like that milk badam drink, Rajji was so fond of. Her elder brother who used to take her out on long summer days to their favourite ice cream and confectionary shop. He always used to have a milk badam while she used to choose a kulfi with faluda, her favourite. He would let her take a swig from his own drink, taking a little bite of her ice cream in return. They would smile and after finishing the treat, he would pay the money and they would make a move back home. He would hold her hand and make her cross the road and even after they have reached the other end he would not let her go. He would encircle his fingers around her hand and she would grasp them firmly. And they would go hand in hand, from ice cream shop to home, savouring the taste and flavor of the ensuing sweetness that would linger on their lips for a long time. They would never talk on their way back home. She would often think of her next visit to the ice cream shop and wonder that she would try something different. But then every time she went, she would inadvertently end up asking for the same old flavour.

Rajji had always been so caring, so protective. She missed him, she missed the occasional swigs from his milk badam. She missed home. She missed her family.

Where is everyone? Where is Mama and Papa and Rajji? I don't want to be here. I want to be home. Get me back to where I belong to! Where is my home?

****

Meanwhile, Mummy ji came treading heavily and demanded, "Where is the milk?"

"Oh, I drank it. Can you please give me something to eat? I didn't have dinner. Actually no one asked me also. I was just sitting there like a perfunctory head of a state on stage observing all the proceedings in a desolate manner, oblivious to the festivities of my own marriage."

"Haye, haye, half of the milk was for my son, you idiot! And don't you dare use this impressive language in front of me!"

"Mummy ji, I did not realize it was to be drunk in partnership. You did not tell me so. And where is Abhi? I have no idea he would come asking for his share of milk? In fact, you should increase the daily quota of milk since I am here now."

She smiled gleefully and wobbled her eyes at Mummy ji in all her innocence. But in her heart of hearts she was wondering.

Did she call me an idiot? Did she? Or it was one of my illusions.

After bombarding Rhea with insinuations, Mummy ji went out of the room in a huff. She hung her head low and cursed the old lady with all her might.

Why she didn't show her true colours while we were coming and meeting them? She will roast me like a kebab with a volatile temper like this.

Abhi finally came to the room. He smiled as his eyes shone with excitement. With a broad frame and a chiselled jaw, he looked perfect. His cheeks pitted into dimples at the right places and whenever he smiled, his smile broadened to meet the contours of those dimples.

"Where were you? Do you know it's a crime to leave your newly married wife all alone, that too on the wedding night?"

"There is so much work. So many relatives to be taken care of. Let me go for a quick shower. I will be back soon."

He emerged from the washroom after a long period and kissed her lightly on the cheek, "Why is my pumpkin so sad? Are you missing your parents?"

"Your mother, Abhi, why is she so rude to me? We just got married. Isn't she supposed to be nice and soft spoken with the new bahu?"

"Oh, don't worry. She will be fine. It's because of the lehenga you know. Just pissed off with you because things were not perfect. And the one you changed into was not up to the mark. Otherwise, she is a very sweet lady."

"And I thought you did not care about all these things. This is so embarrassing. But it was an accident. The fabric was so delicate, my cousin inadvertently stepped on it and it got torn. I know it was a big blunder, but it just happened."

Abhi placed his arm lovingly around her and gave her an impromptu kiss. His hands gently glided from her shoulders towards the roundness of her breasts and he fumbled for a moment, trying to find a way inside. His fingers impatient, slithering, navigating their way into unchartered territories.

Rhea pulled his fingers away, kissed them lightly, placed her head on his chest and smiled, trying to inhale his fragrance. Suddenly she panicked, "We should lock the room from inside. Someone might come. So many people at your home today."

"This is your home also, sweetheart. And no one is stupid enough to disturb us. It's our first night together, after all."

Abhi lifted her chin upwards and looked affectionately in her eyes, lovingly stroking her face as he placed a deep kiss while engulfing her in his arms.

"Wait, let me change and this jewellery hurts." Rhea was trying to get away but Abhi with his firm hold was entwining her more into his arms.

And suddenly there was a loud bang and the door of the room was wide open as Mummy ji arrived flapping in all her finery and grace.

Rhea panicked and slumped in Abhi's arms while he plonked her on the bed and stood ramrod in front of his mother.

"Hanji Mama, what happened?"

Rhea gathered her frail form from the bed and tried to make a feeble attempt to stand up.

"Beta, what's the hurry. You are man and wife. There are so many guests at home. Why don't you attend to them first and later you can make merry with your wife? Baaqi, it's your wish. Now since you are married, why would you listen to me." She fumed, fretted and left the room.

Abhi's demeanour took a quick U turn and he glared at Rhea.

"See, I told you we should lock the room" she squirmed and fidgeted uncomfortable in her lehenga.

"Shut up! And do what Mama says". He stormed out of the room and she was left grappling with the absurdity of the situation.

But Abhi never shouted at her before marriage. He seemed to be the most charming and affectionate guy she has ever met. What has the marriage changed? And how can he shout at her for no reason? She was unable to accept this huge shift in the behavior of the people around her.

Perhaps it's the strain of the marriage or the torn lehenga that has made people so bitter this very day. She tried to mollify her fears.

Although a tad disappointed, she ushered herself into the bathroom, changed her lehenga and wore a bright yellow suit with matching dupatta. She removed her jewellery and carefully placed it in a wooden hand-crafted box gifted by her dad.

She missed her family so much. She has never been shouted at but since her arrival in this house she has been a victim of unwanted rebukes and insinuations.

If this is going to be the fate of this marriage than I am going to be unhappy for the rest of my life. But before passing any quick judgements I need to make a serious effort to mingle.

She moved out of the room into the kitchen and put on the best of her smiles. Mummy ji was cooking something along with other relatives.

"Mummy ji, it's midnight. What are you making at such an odd time?" she questioned.

"Beta, the food served by your family was so lacking in taste and quality that we did not eat anything at all."

Her eyes burned with shame while the few ladies standing in the kitchen giggled. Speechless she came out and sat on the sofa wreathing with an insane desire to hit Mummy ji. Her eyes had resurrected million dreams of being loved and cared in a new family. Those dreams seemed hazy to her and she lamented her choices.

How can she insult my family like this? It's too much. I want to bang that tawa on her head. Yes, I want to hit her if she said one nasty word to me.

"Here is your phone. Your family has been calling you."

As soon as she was handed the phone, it rang up. It was Buaji on the other side.

"Rhea beta, did you reach safely. Are you fine?"

"Yes Buaji, I am good." She could barely speak. The words seemed to have struck in her throat and she could not find her voice.

Buaji sensed something was wrong. She pressed her for more details. "

"What happened, bachhe? Speak up. Did anyone say anything to you?"

"Please give the phone to Ma. I want to talk to her. Please Buaji. '' she made a desperate plea.

"Hanji, Rhea beta. Are you okay? Did anyone say anything about the lehenga?" Her mother inquired longingly, hoping her to respond favourably.

"Ma, why did I say yes, for this marriage? It seems they brought me only to hurl abuses at me. My mother-in-law is being very nasty. Do something!"

"Rhea, calm down. Do you have people around? Someone might listen. Everything would be fine. It was an awkward incident that could have happened with anyone. Please don't blame yourself for anything. Your mother-in-law is one dogmatic lady. You need to find a way to tackle her."

She tried to calm her, but she knew Rhea would need strength and lots of effort to keep up this marriage alive. She clucked her tongue expressing her disapproval but there was nothing that could be done now.

She shut down her eyes, holding back the flood of tears which threatened to dislodge the border of a comfortable and a protected life she had built around her daughter. A wall of love, care and comfort that has shielded her away from any harshness. For the past few years since her arrival from the University after completion of her degree, she had sensed a change in her. Though she had desisted from asking any questions she had known all the way that something changed her life. She grew even more protective and showered her darling daughter with incessant care and affection.

Buaji placed her hand on Ma's drooping shoulders and for a moment they both shared a comfort in the knowledge of shared concerns. Buaji kept quiet and stroked her hand all the while mumbling, "That girl is stronger than you think. She would be fine. Don't worry."

****

Rhea after attending the call made a move towards her room. She looked at the ladies who still had not exhausted their share of wedding songs and regalia and were still living those few hours of frenzied and constant activity.

They were still in the wedding finery and were living the moments of affectation and surrealism. Perhaps they are still wondering where are the cameras for which they had pouted so gleefully. But the marriage was over. The marriage in which they had little or no interest, for they were only present for showing their attires and the wedding paraphernalia and the food on which they gorged mindlessly.

How much entertainment and enthusiasm they are exhibiting? As if there is something inherently beautiful about marriages that they figured out right now, which they are celebrating with much gusto and flair. Were they as happy at their own wedding day as they look now? Did they acclimatize and make peace with themselves? How difficult it is to leave your home, your belongings, every single thing that you have maintained a contact with! And start everything from a scratch, making a place in a home where you are perceived as an outsider and treated like one.

She changed into her sleep wear. There was no sign of Abhi yet and she fiddled with her phone for some time and decided to call it a night. She checked the time again and again. As if the ticking of the clock would bring a propitious outcome any moment. It was 2 am and she was tired and exhausted.

She turned to virtual media for some succor and turned her Facebook on and mindlessly flickered through the images. She wanted to update her wedding pics soon to get all the wonderful comments from people so far removed from her life right now.

Except Kanu, her ex-roomie, no one made the effort to come. How adorable she looked flanked by her husband and her son! Mesmerizing in fish cut lehenga with that hen-pecked husband of hers, who kept swooning at her all the time. Kanu seemed really happy and what was that she had on her face that made it glow so much. Must have found a new concoction or devised one. God bless you Kanu! Rhea murmured and closed her eyes. All those moments spent sharing, caring and fighting emerged before her eyes while they were together in hostel. How much they used to fight and call names to each other? Everything seemed so distant to her. Everything that she shared with anyone in the University.

Even Mani, her classmate and her clinics partner did not come. She got caught up with an emergency case that came up at the last moment that made her change her plans. Mani, Oh Mani! Are cases more important than marriage of your partner in crime?

She smiled at the memory of the big bountiful dog chase. Mani was one person who was as passionate as her when it came to their profession, so it was acceptable. She knew she would have come, had Rhea goaded her more. Though physically present Mani would have been far removed mentally, all her thoughts wired around her case, so Rhea did not insist. She knew that cases were her priority. Her dedication has made her the top Veterinary Doctor of Ludhiana city. The same passion that fuelled a clinician in her did not let her settle into the routine chores of domesticity. Mani was still single.

She kept on thinking about her friends from the yore while thoughtlessly scrolling down Facebook. A kaleidoscope of smiling faces, cherubic people presenting themselves as the perfect couples, the perfect lovers, over spilled on her Fb wall. If life is perfect anywhere it's on social media. You see the kind of pictures that make you rile with inferiority complex.

How is it possible that everyone is leading a picture-perfect life and is intoxicated with that surreal happiness? Everyone but me?

And she wondered if people were living dual lives after all. And here was Ranbir, her ex-flame and classmate with his pretty wife. Both enveloped in a bear hug, appearing like conjoined twins.

How many pictures do they get clicked in a single day?

Rhea just wondered. Every other day they are clicking themselves in weird positions and splattering the pictures on social media making everyone jealous.

She wondered if all the love that chimed on Facebook resonated in real life.

Damn! This is my wedding night and I should be out there making love with my husband while I'm here on Fb swooning over my past crushes. What the fuck is wrong with me?

She cursed herself and extricated her mind from the wayward desires. After all, Ranbir is married and fathering an infant daughter.

It was 3 am now and still no trace of Abhi. She was

exhausted. Her eyes would not stay open and she pressed her palms upon them trying to comfort herself. How could she sleep before he comes? How long she should wait?

And finally, she nuzzled herself on the bed and no sooner had her head hit the pillow, she was chartered away to a different realm. A world of dreams!

She dreamt of Ranbir holding and guiding her towards the Anatomy lab while she dithered in her steps making every effort to make herself free from his grasp. And he was yelling, "Rhea, we have to dissect the carcass, or we will lag behind. You are such a lazy one."

And she was wearing the same torn lehenga and a knife in her hand which she was wielding like a powerful warrior. She was brandishing it in front of Ranbir, challenging him to use his might to get her into the lab. For she will not go, what might happen. She will die like a brave one, killing him but she won't dissect a single cadaver from now on. He extracted a sword from somewhere and now they were in the middle of a war like situation where he was shouting with all his might, "If you won't do it, we must fight and the one who wins gets the dead animal as the prize to be carried home."

They were in the middle of this fearsome battle and she was about to make that ultimate lethal move that would cause that terrible blow when suddenly she heard someone shouting her name.

"Rhea, Rhea wake up!"

She woke up with a jolt and saw Abhi peering at her intently with sleep deprived eyes.

"Please make tea for me, Rhea. My head is splitting. Please meri jaan." And he kissed her lightly on her baby-soft cheek.

She woke up bleary eyed. "Did I just sleep? What's the time? OMG! What a weird dream it was! Horrible. I was in the

Anatomy lab and someone was pushing me, and I did not want to do the dissection. Crazy dreams!"

"Haha, professional dreams if I can say so? Now hurry up and get me tea. Wedding time is crazy. I had no idea it would entail so much effort and care. I am tired as hell."

Abhi was so sweet to her that she completely forgot that few hours ago he yelled at her for no reason. She wanted to discuss the matter but decided to wait for the opportune moment to bring forth the topic for discussion. Meanwhile, she struggled to get up from the bed. She felt sleep deprived and shaky and without proper nourishment making tea for her husband at that moment seemed a gigantic task to her.

She went to the kitchen and fumbled for the lights. The kitchen though small was very immaculately maintained by her mother-in-law. She had no idea where the required things were placed. It was so calm and quiet at that hour. It seems after making dinner in the wee hours ladies were cooling their heels off.

With great effort, she located the essentials. She was still thinking of talking with Abhi about a lot of topics. One of which was his mother's nagging nature and her sharp barbs acting like little pricks on her conscience. And how she spoke to her mother rudely at the Gurudwara. She was sure she could talk to her husband and make his mom understand her point of view.

She made two cups of tea and took to the room where Abhi was sprawled out on the bed.

"Where were you, the whole night?" She questioned.

"I was making arrangements for Taya ji and family at the local hotel. And then they didn't let me come as we were chatting till late. They had come all the way from Nanded. I am meeting my relatives after aeons."

"I felt so lonely Abhi and Mummy ji was so harsh with me

and you also shouted at me for no reason. That's not fair."

"Listen Rhea, first of all stop complaining. We are not dating, we are married and secondly if my mom lovingly says anything to you it's fine, accept it. She is like your mother now."

"But Abhi, I am a qualified Doctor. She can't talk to me this way for no reason. Moreover, she hardly knows me. She should give me some time to adjust in the family."

"You will be fine, sweetheart. Nothing to worry. You are a part of the family now. Don't spoil your mood. We will go somewhere for a few days. Tell me where you want to go?"

"But Abhi, she should not have complained about the food as well. Does it make a valid point to put such grievances in front of a newly married daughter-in-law? Not fair!"

Abhi moved away from the bed to occupy a nearby chair now. The tea cup was dangling in his hand precariously.

He brought it on the table with a force that it spilled some of the tea.

"Stop complaining, Rhea! This is the problem with overeducated women like you! Did my mother say anything to me? Not at all. She was appreciating you so much in front of the relatives. She said my bahu is a doctor. And here you are. All full of complaints and negating my mother when she is trying to make this bond stronger."

He stormed out of the room and the cup kept rattling on the table while she fumbled for a cloth to clean the little drops that smudged the bed sheet. Her eyes were moist, radiating heat and she tried to get rid of the solitary tears that encircled her eyes. Though she tried with all her might, she could not hold them back and buried her head onto a pillow. The love and affection that was evident in his husband's voice moments ago, suddenly evaporated and the words scarred her conscience.

She composed and collected herself and the tea cups and

went towards the kitchen. She washed and kept them near the wash basin upside down with little drops encircling the rims, hanging on to them in a determined manner. And with an elongated swoop they got detached from the cup now flopping on the floor, spreading on to a trickle and losing their essence. She sighed and looked at the tiny droplets getting lost in this amateur struggle to stay connected but eventually losing out the battle rather disgracefully. In a matter of minutes, the cups had dried down and were looking sparkling clean and she wiped them nicely with a towel and kept them in the cupboard.

3

A BRAND NEW DAY

The next day started with a new promise and a new hope and Rhea assured herself that everything would be fine and her fears of being an outsider in the family are whimsical and she is over reacting.

May be that's how things move! Perhaps, all brides are treated once in a while without any love and compassion by their in-laws.

She was heartbroken and dejected but, in the morning, she decided with all her might that she would try her best to make a good impression and use all her persuasive powers and charm into extracting the love and goodwill, she was entitled to.

She chose a colorful perky blue suit with gota patti that sparkled in all it's finery exuding a charm making her fall in love with her own image. She kept on standing in front of the mirror peering at the youthful burst in her vigour and the litheness of her taut body while her cheeks turned pink.

She was not the same girl who dressed clumsily in her mother's clothes all the time but over the years she has carefully crafted her own style and poise. She had been able to carve out a separate identity for herself by becoming more conscious about her looks. A job meant that she earned her own money and her parents never demanded anything from her, so she was able to spend the way she wanted to. A considerable sum was spent on clothes and matching footwear. She dressed in a beautiful manner every day.

Meanwhile, Abhi came in and saw her standing in front of the mirror with glazed eyes. He shook her, and she gained her composure. Extracting herself from the past memories she replied, "Yes, what happened?"

"I am asking you the same question, sweetheart. We are getting late. Mehta uncle has invited the whole family for lunch."

"Yes, I'm ready. Let's go."

The Mehtas were counted amongst the richest in Pathankot. They owned a lot of factories in nearby Himachal and were good friends of her in-laws.

When she arrived in the living room, everyone was ready and set to go. She wished her in-laws in a barely audible voice. Mummy ji gave a perfunctory nod and a perfected smile and gestured her to sit beside her.

"How are you, beta ji? I know I was a little rude to you yesterday but don't mind. And don't ever say anything to Abhi. Janania diya galan wich bandeya da ki kam! Hai na ji. (Men should not be included in all the womanly talk). You understand what I am saying na."

"Yes, Mummy ji. I got your point. I would never say a word to Abhi."

"But you toh said na. You were complaining about me. I heard it with my own ears. What do you think? That you would live in my home, breathe profanities against me and I would not come to know." She hissed and narrowed her eyes.

Rhea felt the hatred in those eyes bore into her and averted her gaze. It was difficult to seep in so much of negativity.

Damn, she was listening to us! The podgy little woman was standing right outside the door when I was talking to my husband.

Her chain of thoughts was broken, as Abhi came inside and declared that the car won't start, and they will have to extend a helping hand by giving a little thrust.

Rhea and Mummy ji rushed outside to be the first one to oblige Abhi. Rhea was wearing pencil heels and she could hardly walk gracefully. In her excitement to be one step ahead of Mummy ji, she tried walking fast.

"Mummy ji, It's okay. You stay here. I will give the much-needed push to the car."

"Aaj kal diya kudiyan!!! It's better you stay here, and I will do the needful." And Mummy ji walked hurriedly past her, elbowing her.

Mummy ji can't score a brownie here. She can't be the one who can give the car the much-needed push. I am the one who should be out there helping my husband.

Amongst all the jostling and 'me first', Rhea dithered, unable to maintain her balance, she slipped and fell over Mummy ji. This led to a minor mishap as both of them fell at the entrance of the house.

"Kudi ne marta meinu (she killed me). Oye Abhi! Help me!"

Abhi came running and started tugging at Mummy ji's outstretched hand for help.

Rhea kicked her heels away, but she could not control the laughter that emerged after she saw Mummy ji flayed on all fours, cursing, grumbling and howling at the pitch of her voice. The household help Kimti too came rushing outside.

Kimti was in his mid-fifties, agile and athletic, but he appeared far young than his age. He was of Bihari origin and has been living with the family for a long time. He was considered a part of the household structure as he has seamlessly moulded himself into the contours of the family. He lived in a solitary room at the back of the house that was designated to him. She did not see him in the marriage at all, but she knew all about him from Abhi. She has not been able to interact with him much, but she knew she needed to win him over.

He rushed to Mummy ji and supported her bulky frame coaxing her to stand but she could not and was now all over Kimti as if canoodling with him.

Rhea stifled a laugh, seeing Mummy ji and Kimti nuzzling a chemistry of their own, oblivious to the rest of the world. She was shrieking in pain, unable to bear weight on her right foot and it occurred to Rhea that she might be having a fracture.

"We should not make her stand. She might be having a crack. That will create more problems. We should call an ambulance."

Abhi immediately dialled the local hospital. An ambulance arrived shortly, and a stretcher was taken out. Mummy ji was put on the stretcher and Papa ji along with Kimti sat beside her in the ambulance.

"We will get her X ray done to access if there is any fracture. You and Rhea can go and attend the lunch. No need to worry. We both are there for her." Papa ji instructed Abhi.

Abhi held Mummy ji's hand and started crying but she had stabilized and told him to get off the ambulance.

"Mehtas are very good friends. You cannot miss the lunch. If there is something wrong with the car, call a cab but go you must. Don't worry about me."

"Mummy ji, I am sorry. I got a little more enthusiastic about helping Abhi." Rhea apologized.

Mummy ji ignored her completely, closed her eyes and lolled her head on one side. When Rhea made another attempt at conversation, Papa ji waved at her. That served an indication for her to keep quiet. And the ambulance drove Mummy ji to the hospital as she lay on the stretcher in her shining red silk suit that she specially chose for the occasion.

Abhi waved back, teary eyed. Rhea waved, a little exultant

with sparkly hues in her eyes.

And now it's only us. And we can talk and chat our heart out.

The moment the ambulance was out of sight, Abhi initiated the ignition of the car and it roared exhaling a lot of smoke.

He kicked his hands on the steering wheel in exasperation, mouthing invectives at the car.

"Damn! This bloody car. After all this drama, it has started."

Rhea sat on the front seat and flinched uneasily at her seat at his volatile show of temper. She tried to assuage him, "It's okay, Abhi. Let's hope it's not a fracture. She would be fine soon."

"It's your fault, Rhea. All your fault. If you had not tripped and fallen over her, everything would have been fine. You planned all this!"

"It was meant to happen. How did I know I was about to fall? You are acting funny. If we all know what was in store for us, life would have been rather easier. But it's not. Let's attend this lunch and then we can drive to the hospital and find out what is wrong with Mummy ji?"

"No, we are not going anywhere. You deliberately pushed my mother and now you plan to enjoy yourself."

His eyes were glowing like embers now. She saw a man who was completely besotted with his mother. Who could not see anything beyond her? Who was naïve and could be manipulated easily. She also loved her parents a lot, but she wasn't blinded by mad love that overpowered Abhi to such an extent. And precisely at that moment she felt that she was more reasonable and mature in the ways of life. She made a reluctant effort to get out from the car but Abhi stopped her.

"Let's go. Mama will be upset if we did not go. I don't want to hurt her when she is recuperating in a hospital bed."

They drove wordlessly and soon the infectious gloominess caught Rhea as well and her mind got infested with the same morbid thoughts debating the usefulness of a marriage. She wanted to get married, but she delayed it long enough on one or the other pretext. And now all her premonitions seem to be coming true. She shuddered at the thought of losing Abhi and decided to work on salvaging her nascent marriage.

They arrived at the Mehtas all prim and proper but with gloomy faces. As they were ushered inside, the hostess remarked, "The newly marrieds! Why do you look so sad and gloomy people? Cheer up. It's been only a day and you already seemed to be tired of each other." And she laughed out loud at the candour of the remark.

They looked at each other perfunctorily, dishing out their own version of hopes and dreams and the shared narrative that has entwined them in the lifelong companionship.

The luncheon went well, and they came home lost in their own thoughts. After dropping Rhea home, Abhi got up to make a move for the hospital.

"Arre, where are you going? Take me as well ." She ran after him as she saw him leave.

"No, you stay here. You pushed my mother. You wanted to kill her." He snarled, and she backed off.

She squirmed at the volley of words and took a few steps back horrified at the allegations hurled at her.

How can he be so mean? I did not push his mother. And why did he say, 'my mother'. She is supposed to be her mother as well now when they are married. How can he blatantly accuse me of something I never did or never tried to do? It was after all a little accident! And it could have happened either way. His mother falling on me. And me ending up having a fracture.

She went to her room and flopped on the bed and curled

herself up for some comfort. She covered herself with a sheet and lay there for a long time when she heard a soft knock on the door.

"Rhea beta, what about dinner? What should I make?" It was Kimti outside the door waiting for instructions.

When did he come? Wasn't he there at the hospital?

She tried to ignore him and lay on the bed without making any movement, but he kept on knocking.

Finally, she got up, her hair all dishevelled and her make up all smudged. The eyeliner spread by the intermittent crying, gave her a monstrous look and she scared herself by looking at the splitting image of her altered appearance in the mirror.

She opened the door and Kimti looked at her in a strange manner.

"I thought you were in the hospital. When did you come back?"

"I came back with Papa ji to get some clothes of Bibi ji and then he instructed me to stay with you to help you with dinner. Don't take it all upon yourself. It was bound to happen. Kismat as they say it. Do you like Aloo Gobhi? I make it very yummy. You would absolutely love it."

"Really! You do! You mean I don't have to do anything. You will make all by yourself. But I have toh seen Mummy ji doing all the cooking." She finally smiled and felt better interacting with Kimti.

He comes lowest in the pecking order, but he is super nice to me. Isn't that amazing? And finally, he considers me to be a part of the family.

"She cooks because she loves it so much. I came to their home, long time back as a kid when Bibi ji's father brought me from Bihar to help in the fields as a labourer. It was a hard job and I ran away one day only to be found again and thrashed by her father. He was a very violent man, I must tell you. The beating that he gave me that day was very sound, and I could never forget it."

"Did you ever try to run away again?"

He smiled. His eyes shone thinking about the possibilities he could have delved into, but he nodded his head.

"No. He could have killed me that day. I decided to stay put but I told them I could not work that much. They employed me in their home as domestic help and Bibi ji's mother was really nice to me. When Bibi ji got married I must be around fifteen. They sent me along with her and since then I have been part of the family."

"What was your age when they brought you from your native village in Bihar?"

"I must be seven. I guess. It's a vague idea though I am not sure."

"And your parents let you go!"

"Yes, they did. They were paid handsomely and with so many mouths to feed, they were left with no choice. But I have no regrets. I have lived a good life. I regularly send money back home to my family and I visit them every year."

"Are you married Kimti?"

"Yes, I am and don't remind me of my wife and kids now. I would definitely tell you about them. Let me get back to work. Abhi will demand dinner when he comes home. Pray he brings some propitious news."

****

Abhi arrived home late evening, tired and devastated.

As Rhea predicted, Mummy ji ended up with a simple fracture in her right foot.

"Simple fracture is good. It would heal early, Abhi. Don't

you worry."

He glared at her.

"You mean to tell me, fracture is good. This is your take on my mother getting injured."

"No. I mean to say, simple fracture is good. Since the over laying skin is intact and there are other types like compound and comminuted and …."

He had left the room and she mumbled something more about type of fractures and halted.

Damn! I should be more considerate. His mother ended up having a fracture and instead of being sympathetic I am telling him about the types of fractures.

After a few days of rest and recuperation in the hospital, Mummy ji was back at home with seething grudge against Rhea, implicating her for the fall. Whosoever was coming home to enquire about her health was fed with the different versions of information.

"Usne menu dhaka dita." (She pushed me)

"I was walking in front of her. And she said, "Oye Budhiya! And she kicked my butt, hurling a slipper at me."

"She was talking on the phone to someone giving my supari and then she said, no let me give it a try and she threw herself on me."

"She injected me with the horse medication. The needle was so thin that I did not feel anything but later on I got unconscious and fell down. She is a danger doctor."

"She deliberately wears heels so that she can use them as an excuse to fall on people. I came to know she did the same with a girl in her college."

Rhea was in the kitchen all the time and she could hear bits of the conversation.

What nonsense is all this? How can she keep on saying all this rubbish about me? It was a simple accident where I fell on her because I lost my balance. She has gone mad. I must talk to Abhi about her. The entire Pathankot will come to know I am a damn killer looking for victims. This lady is ruining my reputation in the city before I even get a chance to build it.

"Kimti, is she mad? What crap is she feeding the guests? And how can people believe all this?

He gestured her to keep quiet. "Let her say whatever she has to say. I know all this is rubbish, but she has been like this from the very beginning. She is a master story teller."

On Sunday morning, more ladies came to enquire about Mummy ji's health. This time, since Abhi was sitting besides her, the version got morphed into something else.

"We were going to the Mehta's. And I was walking and eating something. I did not even come to know when my feet got caught somewhere and I fell."

"But Rinku Bhenji was saying, you told her that your daughter-in-law pushed you."

Rhea was serving them tea and her hand dithered as the tea cups rattled in the tray. Mummy ji sensing the flaring of tempers immediately prompted a reply.

"Koi gal ni puttar ji. Let me get this. Arre, what nonsense are you saying Bhenji, my daughter-in-law is a qualified, intelligent girl. She is a doctor and so sweet and nice. Rinku Bhenji is like this only. She doesn't share good relations with her daughter-in-law, so she is trying to sabotage mine as well."

She smiled at Abhi who was engrossed in the football match running on the TV in the drawing room.

"Bol na Abhi!" (Say something Abhi!)

"Haan, Mama is right. She is very sweet and nice towards Rhea. Now please don't involve me in all this womanly talk."

"Rhea, is Kimti making pakodas with tea?" And, please ask him to serve us more tea. Your hands shake a lot" Mummy ji addressed other ladies and started again, "Waise she looks fine but sometimes people have this nervous disorder where their hands keep on shaking. No, I am not saying she is imbalanced or something. Nah ji nah! We always praise our daughter-in-law. Bas ik pota de de jaldi, te sadi sewa kare (I wish she bears us a grandson soon and takes care of us)."

"Bhenji, well said. She should have a kid in the first year. Oye Abhi, are you listening?" Auntyji ricocheted back and forth, wobbling on her gigantic tummy, trying to attract Abhi's attention.

He hardly reciprocated with his eyes fixed on the TV but finally he mumbled a reply.

"Should we get a ready-made one. It's been only a week since we got married and you are already baying for our blood. Is she a machine that you give her instructions and she pops a child on your lap? Chill ladies! Live and let live."

"This new generation is strange. I am telling you Bhenji that Rinku Bhenji's daughter-in-law said no kid for two years and now she is going to the doctors all the time because she is not able to conceive. Shame! shame! There must be some fault with her otherwise why would she not get pregnant? Tell me."

Rhea arrived with Kimti who was holding the tea tray this time. She sat along with Abhi while tea was being served to everyone. She chipped in the conversation.

"No, it's not like that. If you are not able to conceive it's not the fault of the lady only, sometimes the man could be responsible too. Less quantity and inferior quality of sperms produced in testis could be one of the reasons."

"Hehe, tuhadi daughter-in-law is very tej ji." (Your daughter-in-law is very sharp). Auntyji giggled.

Mummy ji smiled sheepishly. Her face turned red and she fixed her eyes on Rhea with an angry stare while she took a pakoda from the plate and layered it up with tomato ketchup before scrunching with her teeth

****

Over the coming days, the plethora of irritating visitors came to a halt. Rhea felt better but Mummy ji's taunts did not seem to abate despite her hubby taking her side in front of the ladies. She was peeved at her insensitivity at the baseless allegations but could do nothing about it. Mummy ji with the plaster on her foot would dictate instructions to her and Kimti and both of them would run helter-skelter, fulfilling the errands.

The fabric of love and care that Rhea has been ensconced into, at her parents' home was being demolished with a vengeance as Mummy ji hurled a volley of abuses at her all the time. Abhi left for work early morning and she was left at her altar like a sacrificial goat bleated in muffled tones at the doomed future. Papa always chose to be in the comfort of his room and never got embroiled in the dramatic happenings.

****

Abhi worked as an insurance agent in the LIC office. Every morning he used to dress up in formals taking extra care to be prim and proper, carefully preening himself in the mirror. After having a hurried breakfast, he used to run away. Abhi, for some weird reason would keep on shouting to be served the breakfast on time despite the assurances that he would be provided the same. He had been stressed with his work lately and they had no physical contact since the day they got married although they slept in the same room. He came late and woke up early morning to pester his wife. And even if some days he came home early he would prefer to sit and watch TV with his mother leaving his newly married wife alone in her room. She would spend those lonely evenings scrolling Facebook and when she would get bored she would pick up a book and read. He came in the room only to sleep and would start bothering her early morning.

"Rhea wake up, I would be late". He would jolt her.

"Abhi, it's just 5 am in the morning. You don't expect me to make breakfast so early. Let me sleep a little." she would reply lazily without trying to get up.

He detested the long and lazy mornings his wife indulged into. The very form of her lying comfily and sleeping without any worry in the world would make him jealous.

"You don't have a job. You don't realize the importance of work in life.''

"I had a job lest you forget Abhi and I was also working in collaboration with PETA. I was managing the dog pound all by myself. I have applied for a job. I will find it sooner or later."

Abhi would snigger at such explanations.

"I have deadlines to be met. So just get up and make me breakfast."

She would get fed up and reclaim the territory of the kitchen to avoid the temerity of being the one to win an argument. She would pick up her bearings and transport herself into the mundane world of culinary pursuits. She had undertaken a cooking course just a few days before the marriage and learnt to shell up a few delicacies. She had yet to showcase her talents before her in-laws and her husband but then she dreaded the day. Mummy ji was an expert at cooking and would make Pulao, Aloo Methi, Matar Paneer, Butter chicken, Dhokla and many more cuisines with such an ease that would make her feel ashamed of her culinary limitations. Yet, she tried and ended up making something or the other that lacked any visible splendour and taste which Abhi would gulp with no interest.

"Learn cooking from my mother!" He had remarked casually, yesterday when she made a half-baked chapati.

"Let me teach you. You roll it like this, making it as round as possible and when the tawa is hot enough then you place it gently on it."

And Abhi has made a very nice round and fluffy one while Mummy ji stood close to them with eyes wide at the shared proximity of husband and wife.

She could see that Abhi while making chapatis had stealthily touched Rhea's slender waist and slowly encircled her in a bear hug, getting too cozy, much to the chagrin of mummy ji.

"Haye, haye" she shrieked in horror. "No shame this boy has! Going gaga over his wife and teaching her how to make chapatis ,that too with all this romance shomance in the kitchen."

She plonked herself between them and shoved Rhea away from her darling son and took the dough and flattened it with her palm and started rolling it in deft motions and quickly made a roti.

"See, you make like this." She in the meantime produced few crisp chapatis and gave a self-satisfied smile and marvelled at her own productions in such a short span of time.

Abhi let go off Rhea and circled his arms around Mummy ji and kissed her and went out proclaiming that his mom was the best and he loved her so much.

Such public proclamations when came out of him greatly peeved Rhea for she could see the devotion that nestled in his heart which baffled her making her jealous.

Meanwhile, Abhi came in the kitchen and jolted Rhea out of her dreams.

"Where is the breakfast, sweetheart?" he was affectionate.

A demeanor that he assumes when Mummy ji was not around.

"Oh, I was just thinking something." she hurriedly procured two eggs from the fridge and cracked them open in a tumbler. Then with a dash of salt and pepper and diced up onions she started mixing them with an untamed vigour.

"Rhea, are you happy?" the words came out in a hurried manner but for her they were like the scent of water on a parched land. She looked momentarily at her husband. How handsome he looked! She fell in love with him at the first glance. He had the same Adonis looks that melted her heart. For some reason, she felt a guilt lurching inside her for interacting with her ex-flames on Facebook. She pursed her lips and contained her desire to disclose this little piece of information to Abhi.

No, she cannot tell him that she tried to get in touch with the past objects of her affection.

This will sabotage her marriage. She tried to hold back the embarrassment and her confusion. After all, it's been just a few weeks. And so much has happened.

He affectionately embraced her and nibbled at her ear as she moved away in a fake disapproval and yet propped herself close for some sweet nothings.

He brushed his lips against hers making the grip tighter. She felt relaxed and nestled herself in the closed confines of his chest. It felt like a dream. In the past few weeks life has cropped up with crazy happenings. Now he was finally warming up to her in a way she wanted him to. She wanted to be kissed and held and loved. Their relationship gave them the legitimacy and she wanted him right now.

Amidst the impromptu and unrestricted kisses, the tumbler holding the beaten eggs got upturned and came down from the shelf and plonk, there went the yellows forming a swamp pool of their own.

Abhi made her sit on the shelf and started kissing her with

a frenzy. He had unhooked her bra and with one hand under her top, he was pressing and squeezing her breast with his mouth fixated on her neck. She had caught a tuft of his hair and pulled him with a firm assertion down towards her breasts. Both of them did not notice when Mummy ji arrived and interrupted their amorous passion.

"Haye, haye besharmo! I have given you a room to do all this."

He rushed out of the kitchen, meanwhile Rhea kept sitting there, perched precariously on the shelf adjusting the bra strap and pulling her top to cover the necessary portions. She got down and hurriedly brought a rag and started cleaning the wishy-washy eggs.

Mummy ji stomped out of the kitchen raining profanities on the modern-day love that has sanctimoniously entered the domains of the kitchen.

"Chi chi, on the shelf too! Spare the kitchen for God's sake!"

Rhea after doing the mandatory cleaning ran into her room for some succor. She sat on the bed and the past ricocheted in front of her.

"They should spare the library", her own words boomeranged in her ears. Those times when she has witnessed all those odd couples making out in the libraries and the kind of offence she has taken at the libertine state of affairs.

She laughed at the sameness of the situation. All those people who used to scurry for proximity were provided a refuge by the fourth floor of the library.

And perhaps ten years down the line she was trying to salvage something with her husband in the confines of the kitchen.

Abhi emerged from the washroom all freshened up, with

the removal of all traces of tenderness and asked in his firm and authoritative voice, "Where is the breakfast?"

He saw Rhea giggling by herself and felt annoyed. "By the way, what are you so happy about? That was so embarrassing what we were doing out there in the kitchen."

She laughed and delicately adjusted a flicker away from her face.

"I think we are allowed to be intimate. We are married so nothing is off limits. Come home early today."

She winked at Abhi who was taken aback by the sudden boldness demonstrated by his wife.

That night they made passionate love. Their desperation so evident in their mannerism as they removed any tinge of shame and hesitation they had and finally consummated their marriage. Rhea's hopes and expectations soared after the multiple love making sessions that night. She wanted to be placed at some higher pedestal now, given more leverage and imagined a change in the hierarchies with this new-found status of a consummated bride.

And indeed, there was a change she noticed. Abhi's work load lessened dramatically. He started coming home a little early and his TV watching sessions with Mummy ji decreased drastically as he preferred spending more and more time in his room in the company of his charming wife. Mummy ji would fret and fume and try her best to monitor his moves and make him come around.

"Oye, Abhi puttar aa dekh WWE wrestling aa rahi hai TV te. Aaa ja dekhiye."

"Mama, I am watching DDLJ in my room. I will come later."

He would shoot back a reply cuddling his newly wed and bold bride in his arms.

The house had a weird architecture and both the master bed rooms were at an arms distance which made it easy for both the mother and son to communicate in loud voices sitting in the sanctum sanctorum of their rooms.

Mummy ji grew morose over the coming days, seeing the changed approach of his son.

"Pata nahi kalehni ne ki jadu tona karta, mere munde te!"

(I wonder if she has exorcised my son!).

Abhi, in the meanwhile was all love for his wife. The bodily pleasures had taken a hold over him and he kept on demanding more and more from her. She had not been shouted at for weeks neither by him nor by his mother which made her feel victorious. Sometimes at lunch beaks, he would come home demanding a quickie. She would be in the kitchen with Mummy ji when he would hurriedly come and ask her to come in the room for a while. Canoodling her, nuzzling her, he would remove her clothes swiftly to which she would resist a little.

"What would Mummy ji think, Abhi? Don't come in the lunch breaks. Did you eat your tiffin?"

"She would think, I am madly and crazily in love with you."

"She thinks I have done some jadu tona on you. That day I heard her talking to Kimti. She was saying all that nonsense about me. Please tell her to stop all this. It hurts me a lot."

"Jadu tona, haha! Yes, you have bewitched me with your soft skin, bountiful bosom and these long never-ending legs that make me move my fingers around them for an eternity. Love you Rhea! You look so better without clothes. And I think you should not wear them when I am around."

And he reached for the cord of her pyjamas giving it a tug, allowing it to fall down. Rhea caught hold of his reproving hand and looked at him intently.

"Listen Abhi, I want you to allow me to look for a job. I had a chat with Papa ji and he was thrilled to know that I want to work again. But he said I need your permission to go ahead with it. And moreover, it is difficult to spend the entire day with Mummy ji bossing around."

"Yes, why not. You were working before we got married. That's great news. But don't say anything about Mama. It is not fair on your part to garble unacceptable stuff about her. Arre, she keeps on appreciating you all the time in front of me. She is so happy that you are a part of the family."

"But she acts nasty with me. Try to see my viewpoint. She is obviously a very cunning lady. She appreciates me in front of you while snubbing me in front of others, ill-treating me all the time when it's only me and her at home. It is a ploy that she uses adroitly to create differences between us. For she knows that I am bound to discuss everything with you and we would be having two different versions of the story and end up fighting."

Abhi's affectionate demeanor changed immediately at the cold calculative words and he pushed Rhea who fell down with a thud on the bed.

"Damn it! What's your problem? Don't say one nasty word about my mother. You ruined the rest of my day."

He dashed out of the room in a fit of anger and collided with Mummy ji who was standing right outside their room eavesdropping.

"Oh, I am so sorry Mama. Why are you standing here?"

"Beta, I came to ask if you and Rhea would like to have some tea."

"I will get back to office and no need to ask her. Don't give her too much importance. She will make herself if she wants."

Mummy ji's eyes glowed and a blissful smile played on her lips.

"Waheguru, Waheguru. Rabba meher rakhin! (God bless us)."

Rhea got up from bed dejected, dispirited and propped herself in one corner. Tiny drops encircled her eyes and emotions surged inside as she made a huge effort to contain herself.

Over the coming days Abhi again became distant and unconcerned. Now most of the time was spent in his mother's abode while Rhea would flippantly change the channels cursing the inopportune timings and the impropriety of her remarks.

***

4

THE JOB HUNTING

Rhea had contacted many Veterinary clinics in the city to find out if they have a vacancy. Most of the clinics (though they were numbered) did not need any assistance since the work load was less. So, she ended up with lot of rejections and got disappointed with the state of affairs. Her job and contact with animals had provided her succor and the much-needed comfort. Devoid of it, she felt lost and wistful. At home front, things had not improved much. Abhi spent most of his time with Mummy ji, discussing the nuances of his job while she worked in the kitchen keeping an avid ear for all the happenings outside the kitchen. He never discussed work with her for he felt she was naïve and irresponsible. And Mummy ji kept on telling him all the time how badly she fared at the kitchen front. Continuous reinforcements led the young husband to believe that his wife was good for nothing and soon he lost interest in the bodily pleasures as well. Their steamy sex sessions came to a naught as Mummy ji created a wall of negativity between them that would not be easily breached without a conscious effort.

For Rhea, spending entire day under Mummy ji's tutelage was a horrible experience. The dominant and authoritative lady bogged down her mental peace with continuous insults heaped on her and her parents in a veiled form. She would never say anything to her directly, but kept on a steady stream of negative reinforcements directed towards her which deeply affected the poor girl for she did not know the ways to hit back. She felt stifled and sometimes she would feel as if Mummy ji was blocking the very oxygen that was needed for her survival. She would deliberately attempt jokes on her profession.

So, one day when everyone was sitting together, for after the dinner bonding, Mummy ji in her usual gusto took a pick on Rhea.

"So how do you see that the animal is sick?"

"We measure the temperature, Mummy ji."

"And how do you measure the temperature beta?" Mummy ji smiled her wicked smile. The same winsome smirk that reminded Rhea of Gracy, her classmate.

But she and Gracy have been on good terms. Gracy who was now a Professor at Montreal university had called up Rhea to congratulate her on her marriage. So, no ill feelings for her any longer. And they have moved with their lives

But the space that was left agape by Gracy seemed to be filling up with this new entrant in the guise of Mummy ji.

"I asked you something, Rhea! What are you thinking? You don't know how to do that?"

Mummy ji interjected Rhea's thoughts and demanded an answer immediately.

"Well, we insert the thermometer in the anus and measure it."

Mummy ji laughed with a loud guffaw. Her bulky frame ricocheted to and fro and she clapped her hands gleefully like a child who had been given a colorfully wrapped lollipop.

"The anus, OMG, haha!!!!"

"You people do that. Imagine if they did the same in humans, no one would have studied medicine."

Her eyes shone with excitement and she kept on laughing merrily and kept on mumbling the words in staccatos. "Anus,

OMG… you said that. The potty place… chee. That is one dirty job."

No one participated in the joke except Mummy ji herself.

Papa ji was oblivious to all the chatter going on, for he was mesmerized by the TV anchor who was making forceful entreaties to his viewpoint. The moment someone tried to gather the confidence to counter him he became more verbal and uncouth. And he was watching him fascinated by his ability to shut everyone up. His prowess at proving himself right at all fronts, at all costs greatly impressed him. If only he could acquire half of those skills life would be amazing. He had been listening to Mummy ji's diatribe against Rhea since the day she got married. But always under the shadow of a dominating wife had turned him timid and less vocal.

Rhea scowled and tried to garner attention of Papa ji who became conscious and left the room on the pretext of taking a pee.

I know, he knows that whatever is being said is wrong, it's unethical. But why he doesn't react and show some courage.

She looked at Abhi who was munching on peanuts and was oblivious to everything else. Their love making sessions resumed but were staid and boring and started late at night when he came after watching Animal Planet with Mummy ji. Gone were the affectionate kisses and sweet nothings. She no longer enjoyed the mechanical copulation. She felt a lack of gentleness in his mannerisms and it irked her that they didn't talk any more. He never told her anything about his job while he discussed each and everything with his mother whose advice was supreme to him. She had been reduced to a mere façade in the house. A wife in letter and spirit but not in meaning.

She wanted him to say something in her support the way he did few days ago but this time he chose not to. He sat in the same demeanor, relaxed, unhurried and carrying on as if nothing has happened.

She looked at Kimti who was a big time TV buff but then he did not care. He never had to pretend that he did not care because he actually did not care what the family talked about. He sat on the ground, looking determinedly with his eyes glued to the TV though Rhea knew he understood nothing, but he was one in the entire family who watched TV with such a steadfast resolve. As if this was the most important thing in the world, as if he was going to be personally thanked by the anchor for listening to his embittered discourse with such an ardent admiration. As if his association with the idiot box was sacred and nothing else mattered in this world.

He was the undisputed king of TV watching, for when he sat in front of it nothing could budge him and spoil his concentration. Neither the shrieking whistles of the cooker nor the blood- curdling words of Mummy ji to bring dhaniya from the market. He loved TV and the family knew it so his TV watching hours were usually not punctuated by demands from the household. So, when Kimti was besotted with his love affair with the telly, Rhea was the one running errands on his behalf.

She felt forlorn and misfit in a family where the members imitated the inmates of a prison, carrying on everything with a knowledge of a pre-determined fate and a kind of disenchantment.

Mummy ji, meanwhile got a call and took to her monologue where she kept on rambling about this and that giving a reprieve to Rhea.

She got up and escaped to her room and sat on the bed enervated and disillusioned. She flipped open her Motorola phone and decided to see if there was someone on Facebook she could chat with. Social media became her reprieve in a home crammed with people indifferent to her needs.

She fiddled with it for a while but then she started getting jealous scrolling down Facebook.

How can everyone be so happy while she sulked in the aloofness of her marriage? she wondered. Happy faces transcending joy and glamour in all those pictures and more of it spilling a feeling of contentment in their lives.

Were these people really as happy as they pretended to be? Or it's all part of a make-believe world. Were their lives filled with goodness all the time? The goodness of being healthy, happy, surrounded by loved ones and in turn loving the ones who love them. All that at the same time.

She thought of the Genetics professor and his sham marriage where people gauged the disgruntlement and the dissonance by the mood of the professor. But then he was not adroit enough to mask the state of affairs. But all these people on Facebook, how cleverly they hide the flaws and portray the perfection in their lives that might not be evident in reality.

She wondered at her own nascent marriage where the cracks were visible to her right from the beginning. How will she carry the veneer and hide the disappointments that were making way right at the beginning?

That feeling of rejection and not being part of the family. That feeling of being an outsider who is residing on their premises as if only under some kind of obligation.

"Things will be fine. Don't worry. Every girl goes through this. The mother-in-law gets insecure and launches a tirade against the new girl. It happened with me also and your mother as well. But slowly and slowly you will win their heart." Buaji had given her sound advice the other day when she lamented the behavior of her in-laws.

"But what about them winning my heart, Buaji? Who will figure out what I want?"

She remained mum and passed the phone to her mother who spoke in veiled tones of the necessity of a marriage and the compromises it involved.

Obliviously, winning her heart or her emotions did not matter in this arrangement. They were a family and they had each other for support. She was the new entrant who was supposed to get herself inculcated and included in the scheme of things.

Rhea had listened to her mother with a feigned indifference. Her mother has always been the one compromising on things she ought to have fought for. Perhaps she was creating a mould for her to fit in the same set of words and habits she resonated with.

Her eyes welled with tears as she gauged the sorry state of affairs. She was not good at adjusting. In the past few years with the company of canines day in and day out and with money of her own, she had ensconced herself in a world where everything appeared perfect.

Finally, Abhi came in the room as she was lying down with her mind full of recriminations. He switched off the light and moved towards his designated spot.

Rhea clenched and unclenched her fists and controlled any urge to say something. She closed her eyes and left the rough draft of her dreams gliding all the way to some unfathomed territories.

****

Next day she chose to brush the bitterness aside and again makes a fresh move. Everyday appeared to be a struggle but today a little positivity hovered around her heart.

Yesterday, she has received a positive response from a Veterinary clinic in the city. She was determined to make a sincere effort to get the coveted job. Abhi left her at the clinic which was not very far from her home. She calculated the distance and figured out that she could roughly cover the distance on a two-wheeler.

The owner was a retired Veterinary doctor from a Government department. After the exchange of pleasantries and a cup of coffee he entailed the details of the job. Since his only son was abroad and he was going for a long tour of the west he wanted the clinic to be operational. Rhea was happy to run it with an assurance that all the dealings would be transparent, and the expertise of her previous job would come in handy.

"So, when are you leaving, sir? Any particular date you have on mind?"

Rhea caught him staring at her boobs. She winced and self-consciously brought her dupatta a little low. There was nothing to show, no cleavage. She had carefully chosen this outfit that did not flatter her figure for she wanted to be taken as a serious contender for this job.

No, no not again. Look up! In my face, you dumbo. I will make this clinic a success. Please don't start all this rubbish of getting attracted to me.

"Did you say anything?" he looked at her suspiciously.

"No, I was just wondering that I have a good working hand. I am not exaggerating it, but I am good at practicals. Not the class practicals, obviously not. I was so lame at those. I mean to say, the professional stuff. I know my job and I can make this place swarm with pets."

"Okay, whatever! You are hired. Come at 9 am tomorrow and we will see what you are capable of." he smiled crookedly.

Rhea thanked him and made a dash outside.

Bloody tharki bhuddha!

Damn! why do I have to be servile like this? And how can he let himself be caught, staring at my boobs. Leching is an art where you have to see and not let the other person know when you are seeing or what you are seeing. And he definitely needs some lessons.

She chuckled as she reached the main road and took a

rickshaw back home. All smiling, she swayed down the road, sashaying like a winner who has been awarded the coveted trophy.

I would not let it go and what does it matter if he ogles at me. Who cares? Let him look wherever he wants to look. And moreover, he is leaving soon to meet his son. What was that ...Bahrain, Belgium??? Some place in Europe? Germany. Yes, he said he was going to Germany. Chalo jan do jithe janda, sanu ki (Let him go, wherever he wants to go, why should I bother?) He would not be in India for months and after he leaves the clinic, it's all mine. I will engage with people, create a devoted clientele. And when he comes back, whenever he does, I will move out of his clinic and coax Abhi to buy me a place to set my own private practice. And then we will see who the most successful Veterinary practitioner in the city is?

When Rhea reached home it was lunch time. Mummy ji was huffing and puffing in the kitchen along with Kimti, who was listening to her profanities as usual while running the errands. She could smell the aroma of grounded masalas, crushed pepper and kadhi pata. Mummy ji liked to make her own masalas by bringing the ingredients at home. She was wary of everything packed.

In fact, the other day when Rhea has added the MDH Rajma masala to the ethereal looking, kidney beans, Mummy ji came doodling in the kitchen for an inspection.

"What have you added?" she thundered at any discrepancies that might have crept in her absence.

"It's MDH Rajma masala." My mom uses this, and it makes them a lot tastier. I make the best rajmas in my home. And this is my secret recipe.

"From where did you get this packet."

"I brought it from home."

"You brought masalas from your home. I hate bazar ka masalas. Didn't you know that? You contaminated my kitchen by bringing outside stuff. Hai rabaa!"

And then Mummy ji did the inevitable. She took the MDH Rajma masala and emptied the contents in the dustbin and banged the empty packet on the shelf with such a thunderous jolt that startled Rhea.

"I do not like all these masalas and neither does my husband. How dare you defile my kitchen by using masalas without my permission?" She had marched on her lithe frame, towered on her in all her grandeur.

"Throw these Rajmas now."

"I am sorry Mummy ji. I will not use the masalas from next time. But why waste food. I am against wasting food. There are so many people in this country who don't get enough to eat, and you are telling me to throw a pressure cooker full of rajmas. This is treachery towards a nation that has more share of people who scrounge for one-time meals. Let's eat them and from next time I promise I would not bring anything alien in this house to disturb the sanctity of this sacred place.''

Mummy ji had been aghast at this little piece of information and recoiled in horror at the explicit words.

"You mean to say we are poor. We cannot afford meals. Look at the nerve of this girl."

"No, Mummy ji. I mean to say there are people who cannot afford even a single decent meal. We are fortunate that we are eating good food. It's all about not wasting food. Do not take it personally. Some things are meant to be understood in a bigger context. It's meaningless to get offended by my statements. Think about the nation in totality. Don't constraint yourself in your own selfish domain Mummy ji, think about the state, about the country, about the world, about the planet and yes, about the solar system, our Milky way. Socho Mummy ji socho."

"SELFISH!!!! You called me selfish. Let Abhi come, then we would see who is more selfish, you or me?"

She shook her head in disbelief and moved to her room and locked herself in.

Despite repeated entreaties by Rhea and Kimti, Mummy ji refused to come out. She would not open the door and when Abhi came home, it was well past the lunch time. Papa who was visiting his friend had also come home and was watching TV ignoring the drama that was being enacted in his own domain.

After Abhi's endearments, Mummy ji came out of room, her eyes full of copious tears.

"Your wife gave me a lecture on wastage of food. Does she think she has done PhD on food management? There is no respect for me in this house. And she called me selfish. Me!!! Who gave all her life for the betterment of this home, my kids and my family? I, who used to eat suki roti with namak when I was feasting my family on Gajar ka halwa and Sarson ka saag. I sacrificed my entire life for my family and this is what my educated daughter- in-law tells me. Hai rabba mein mar jaawan, menu chak le."

"When did you eat suki roti with namak? You were such a foodie, you used to eat my share of Gajar ka halwa also. Remember on the wedding night when my mother brought Gajar ka halwa in two bowls. I went for a bath and when I came out you had licked both the bowls clean." Papa ji winked at Rhea who stifled a laugh.

"Hai rabba, sharam karo. Liar!!! Abhi, look what your Papa is saying about me. He is insulting me."

"Papa, you stay out of this. Let me handle this. Did you call my mother selfish, Rhea? Tell me."

"Things were mentioned in a larger context. She is taking

them personally." Rhea squirmed and squeezed herself behind Papa ji to escape Abhi's ire.

"SHUT UP!!!! This is not the answer to my question. Did you call my mother 'selfish'?"

"Abhi, that's not the way to talk to your wife. Your mother is a melodrama, don't you know that?" Papa ji intervened.

"I will not take anyone's nonsense against my mother. If she has to stay in this house she has to respect my mother in every way or she cannot stay. Say sorry to Mama now or leave, Rhea. I will arrange a taxi and you can go back to that bloody Nurpur!"

Mummy ji smiled that same wicked smile where she knew that she had won. She was getting a high out of the look of horror pronounced so clearly on Rhea's face at the sudden and unexpected emotional outburst of her husband.

"Na Abhi! Don't say like this. We cannot send her back. She will live in this house and die in this house. Once you are married, it is forever. Rhea beta go to your room. You don't have to say sorry to me for anything. After all, you are a doctor and more qualified than me. I am only a twelfth pass lady. I am sorry for everything I said." Mummy ji spoke in a choked voice, breaking down after every few words.

Die in this house, what does she mean? Is she going to burn me with a gas stove or something? I should stay away from everything inflammable in this house. This lady is full of wicked ideas. She won't let me live in peace. If I did not outsmart her she would definitely make me crazy.

Abhi stared at Rhea. She flinched at the rancour in his voice as he vomited out his anger and rejections with a more pronounced effect. He thundered, taking a more vicious turn with every syllable that he spoke. "Learn how to behave with my mother, Rhea! From now on I would be watching you. One wrong move and you are out of this house."

That day no one ate rajmas but Rhea. She took food in her room and ate in absolute silence.

Mummy ji beamed at her success and decided to make Palak Paneer for the family. And yes, Kimti got his share.

The rest of the rajmas transferred to a bowl nestled in the fridge untouched, uncared waiting to be devoured by hungry mouths. Alas! there were no takers! Kimti had looked at them with a wishful glance and would have loved to partake of them but Mummy ji scared the day lights out of him.

"Kimti, don't look at them. You will die if you eat them. She has contaminated those rajmas by putting bazaar ka masala. You will get food poisoning." Mummy ji had warned him. "Arre you take this Palak Paneer nah. Don't you eat anything she cooks. She is a witch!"

"Nah Bibi ji, don't say like this about your bahu. She is innocent. She doesn't know the ways of this house. You teach her everything and she will be fine."

"Ohdi ma ne ta kujh sikhaya ni ohnu! (Her mother did not teach her anything!) She did not even tell her that when you are preparing food in your mother-in-law's kitchen you take permission from her. This is not her home, this is mine. I will teach her how to behave with her in-laws. You see Kimti, I will set this girl right."

Abhi did not come to the room that night. Rhea kept on waiting but he went in the guest room and slept. He did not talk to her for days. The breakfast duty was delegated to Mummy ji. So was lunch and dinner. Papa was the only one talking to her in whispers, but he was admonished again and again not to do the same.

"No one will talk to her." Mummy ji has passed the orders.

"But if you carried on like this she will tell everything to her parents and then they will gossip about you in the locality and everyone will know how you treat her." Papa ji eyed Mummy ji surreptitiously.

"Sachi! chlao you talk to her then but just a few words. I want her to be left alone."

"But why are you doing this to poor girl. Imagine if we had a daughter and her in-laws treated her like the way you are treating her? Think about it. Abhi is blinded by your love. He would only see and hear what you feed him. I would suggest, don't play these games and let them be in peace. Baki teri marzi (Rest it's your choice)" he picked up the newspaper and started reading the news.

"Ek bahu ne saas ko jalaya (A daughter- in- law burnt her mother- in- law)"

Last night a girl in Sapna colony, Pathankot poured kerosene over the sleeping frame of her mother-in-law and ignited her with a matchstick. Then she locked the door from outside and went to the market to buy a packet of chips. The neighbors rescued the victim who has been identified as Mahinder Kaur, 64. She has been admitted to the hospital with third degree burns. The daughter-in-law Amrit Kaur, 25 is absconding. The neighbors testified that the victim used to taunt her daughter-in-law who was unable to take this savagery anymore and tried to burn her tormentor.

Mummy ji gasped in horror, "What kind of news you keep on reading these days. Your retirement has made you crazy! Chalo go to market and buy some paneer."

"Kida da zamana aa gya aaj kal. Oye Kimti, do we have kerosene in house. Check the kitchen. We don't need matchstick as well. Take them away. Give it to Bhalla bhenji. Tell him this is a gift from my side. The kerosene and matchsticks."

Rhea who was standing in the corridor caught bits and pieces of the conversation. She smiled at Papa ji who winked at her.

"Kerosene...He he. This is too much Papa ji. You are fabricating news these days. What if she reads the paper and found out that you made it up?" Rhea giggled.

"We will see if she does that! We are a team, you and me. If they have theirs, we have ours."

And with this Papa ji and Rhea had shook their hands and sealed a silent bond.

But that was last week, and things were better now. Mummy ji had mellowed a bit and was acting a little less nasty. She sighed!

****

"Rhea, you have been standing at the door for a long time. Do you want to stand there for the rest of your life?'' Mummy ji's voice boomed breaking Rhea's reverie.

"Hai rabba! this girl dreams a lot. By the way, where were you all this time?''

"Mummy ji, I got a job in a local private clinic. The Doctor is going abroad to meet his son, leaving it at my disposal. I have to join tomorrow.''

"What job? Arre who will take care of the kids then?''

"Whose kids?"

"Yours beta! Your kids! The little chunnu munnu ones that you will give me to play nah!"

Rhea narrowed her eyes trying to gauge the meaning and then widening them in disbelief once she grasped the essence. She opened her mouth to start her charade of being a woman and not a baby popping machine but remembering the rajma episode and the verbal drubbing she got from Abhi, she kept quiet.

"Mummy ji, we don't have any plans to raise kids yet. And it will take time for any eventuality to happen.''

"Haye, haye that day toh you people were so desperate. No sharam at all. Papiyan japhian on the kitchen shelf. And now you are telling me it will take time."

"You don't have kids popping out of you, all the time you have sex. It's Biology. There are days when you have sex and the egg is there all ready to be impregnated. If you can have kids just by having sex, our country would burst with population explosion."

Mummy ji gasped and placed her hand over her mouth to muzzle the shrill cry that let itself out anyway.

Rhea knew she crossed the line again this time. She morphed the words quickly to contain the damage.

"No, Mummy ji, I mean to say that we are young, and we have time. Yes, I will give you chunnu munnus my dearest Mummy ji. No offence. Did anyone tell you that you make the best Matar Paneer in the whole world? And it tastes so yummy that I wonder why you are here in this crummy city of Pathankot. You should go out and enthrall this world with your culinary skills. Start a chain of restaurants. 'Mummy ji & Co'. or something like 'Mummy ji da tadka'or 'Punjab di favourite Mummy da laziz khanna'.

Mummy ji gurgled with pleasure at such effusive praise. She looked at Rhea with a pleasant expression.

"I have always been very good at cooking. I helped my mom with kitchen all the time. She taught me the tricks to make good recipes. I was not like you at all. You toh always keeping yourself locked in a room reading pata ni ki ki all the time. If you want Abhi to listen to you, learn to make good food. It is very important for your relationship to grow. Serve your husband good breakfast, lunch and dinner and make him nice yummy dishes all the time. He would love you a lot and never ever shout at you."

"But from where to get the skill of manipulating your loved ones. Even if I learnt good cooking I will still be bereft of that special skill. You should teach me that also."

Mummy ji rolled up her eyes and raised a brow questioningly, "Ki matlab aa tera? (What do you mean?)

Damn! I can't get her all worked up. She will infuriate my husband again. It's so humiliating to be shouted at!

"Mummy ji, forget that! I mean to say you are not forgetful, not at all. I mean forget what I said." Rhea laid specific emphasis on "I" to avoid any confusion later on. For she knew the old lady was too good with the contortion of words and had an iron grip over the mind of her boy who has elevated his mother to a super human status.

Mummy ji rolled up her eyes at Rhea, looked at her a little unconvincingly, stared at her for a long time before nodding her head in approval. Finally, she smiled and beamed with supreme confidence.

"Families are all about fighting and making up. My mother-in-law was so nasty towards me all the time. Despite that I loved her and always touched her feet in the morning." She looked down at her feet, wriggling her toes.

Rhea looked at her with annoyance.

How can she even expect that I would perfunctorily do, as she desires? And what does it matter if I touch her feet or not. She needs to create that space in my heart where I respect her, and the actions will follow. When you really respect someone from the bottom of your heart, the hands inadvertently follow, and you bow down to touch a fragment of that greatness you want to imbibe in yourself. Is she trying to submerge me into some kind of subservience? In which era is she existing?

Rhea quickly averted her gaze and tried to find ways to wriggle out of this situation where she does not have to stoop low on her own ideals.

Mummy ji waited for a few minutes, with hands crossed around her arms, waiting for the ceremonious display of unabated, undiluted affection. Rhea stood there, desolate and in despair wondering at the stupidity of the situation.

Kimti stood outside the kitchen, waiting for them to thaw this cold war that had turned the house into a battlefield.

"Bibi ji, why don't you teach choti bibiiji how to make fresh masala by grinding all the ingredients."

"Okay! Come in the kitchen and learn something. Seems your mother didn't teach you anything at all."

Damn! Why can't she keep quiet? Can I just poison her with something? Like some rat poison or inject her with over dose of Gentamycin. I must calculate the dose in humans. For that I need to buy some books on human medicine. Perhaps I can give her something that makes her lose her power of speech.

She opened her mouth to ricochet an appropriate reply but desisted from doing the same. Kimti folded his hands beneath Mummy ji's back imploring Rhea to keep quiet.

"Chalo, let's teach the bahurani how to make homemade masalas. Kimti, bring all the ingredients."

Kimti immediately placed all the plastic pouches, packed with various kinds of spices on the shelf

"But from where did you bring the ingredients in the first place, Mummy ji?"

"Arre bhai, from the market, where else." Mummy ji, blabbered.

"Then if you get everything from the market and grind it and MDH people are doing the same thing. Then how can you say your masala is better than them." Rhea questioned in all her earnestness.

She was looking every bit of an able pupil ready to encapsulate the essence of knowledge that would come tumbling out of Mummy ji any second.

"Here is the difference beta ji. These big company wallas add chalk and saw dust to increase the volume."

"But Mummy ji, how can you be so sure? Where is the proof? Do you know if they come to know that you are spreading rumours about their masalas, MDH can sue you?" Rhea shot a salvo.

In fact, I am planning to write a letter to MDH people to file a criminal case against this lady who makes a mockery of their esteemed product. This lady, who did not let anyone eat the yummy rajmas made by me, not even Kimti who had yearned for them and smacked his lips every time he saw them in the last compartment of the refrigerator. I have been eating them for the past one week to finish them off. And still a huge quantity is lying in the fridge. I should throw them perhaps. Damn! I can't throw away food.

"Why will they sue me?" Mummy ji raised an eyebrow and looked at Rhea in complete horror.

"Hai rabba! You don't know. You cannot speak ill against any product unless you have a proof. Indians are contracting this western habit these days of suing people all the time. A friend of mind got sued by the Zandu balm people recently because she posted on Facebook that it is a fake product and exaggerates the pains with no healing effect. And you know Mummy ji what happened? Just imagine."

"What happened?"

"A post from Jalandhar reached Mumbai in no time and Zandu balm people slapped a case on her and filed a defamation suit for bad mouthing their project. And now I have come to know all this big brand people have sleuths in all small cities. So that the small city people do not create rumors for they feel the problem lies with the midget mentality of small town folks who harbour a grudge against the big industry people in big cities."

"What nonsense is this?"

"Be careful Mummy ji, I am telling you. Watch out! Defamation suits eat up lots of money. Perhaps someone from MDH masala might have heard you also and relayed the information to Delhi and Mumbai. And perhaps they have already initiated action against you. But then Delhi and Mumbai are too far, it will take some time to know if they do something."

Mummy ji's pontification of homemade masala came to a halt and she murmured something about being unaware of any such implications as she moved to her room to get some rest.

"Rhea, we will make masala some other time. I am little tired. You also get some rest."

Rhea smiled and felt appeased at her success in cornering Mummy ji.

Yes, I scored a Brownie. I will beat her at her own game.

She shelved out the forlorn Rajmas from the fridge and helped herself with some spoonfuls placing them in the microwave for reheating.

"Bibi ji, it's been a week, you have been eating them. They don't smell good now. Maybe you should throw them."

"No, they are fine."

"Then give me my share also.

"Kimti, they have the contaminated masala. You don't eat them. You will get sick."

"Then why are you eating them."

"Me...Oh! I have sentimental value attached with them. Let me be sick and suffer for the sake of these beautiful kidney shaped beans. Let me sacrifice my life for the love of this culinary ecstasy that has always given me succour and hope. Those dreary lectures that I would not have endured without the support and encouragement of my proteinaceous protectors who filled up my tummy to the brim. And led me to snooze so deep that I did not hear a word said by the Professor unless I was woken up by a chalk. They are my saviors, my protectors, my energy givers. How can I turn my back on them and throw them in garbage just because someone thinks they have the contaminated masala imbued in their soul?"

Kimti took a spoon and helped himself.

He looked at the bright red kidney beans swimming in the thick inviting gravy with a desire and a sparkle in his eyes.

"You won't tell Mummy ji that I ate rajma."

"Kimti, are you crazy? We are best buddies. Not fuck buddies but real buddies. Like save your ass, buddies."

"What do you mean by that?"

"Nothing, forget it! I would not tell anyone. Here take this bowl and savor in the goodness of rajmas."

He looked at her with a difficult to fathom expression and happily accepted the bowl and ran to his room.

"If Mummy ji asks tell her I have gone to attend nature's call."

Rhea giggled.

"No tell her I am going to the market to bring lahsun(garlic).That sounds far better."

He came back again, " No, tell her I have gone to bring adrak(ginger). There is so much of lahsun in the house already."

Rhea smiled and yes, that was brownie number two!

If she has to beat Mummy ji, she needs Kimti on her side.

After having his lunch, Kimti came running towards the house with the empty bowl.

"Bahut sawad si rajma! (Rajma were very tasty!) Can you get me some packets of this masala, so I send them to my wife in the village? She makes very bad sabzi bhaji."

Rhea smiled and now she and Kimti had a secret to share and they were accomplices in the big rajma mystery. The rajmas shunned by all but devoured by Rhea and Kimti.

****

In the evening Abhi greeted the news of Rhea's job with elan. He hugged and kissed her and this time she was intelligent enough not to discuss Mummy ji. He had managed to get the policies of some eminent people in the city and was in a happy mood.

"I wish you had lot of people coming to you for policies as I can see, it makes you so happy."

"My job is very stressful, and it keeps me on tenterhooks all the time. Somedays when I am home after spending a hectic day at office I am so pissed off. It's really terrible running after people all the time." Abhi wiped the sweat off his brow.

"We should make some kind of rule - don't bring home, office stress. It's kind of important or we will end up bickering over trifle issues and over things that don't have any value."

Abhi smiled and moved his hand lightly over her cheek.

"My beautiful and intelligent wife!"

"Am I? Than why don't you say that more often."

"It's been so many days. Come here!"

He pulled Rhea closer and encircled his arm lovingly around her waist. Placing soft kisses on her face, cheeks and neck he moved downwards.

Rhea bit her lips in anticipation and sunk her head in his chest thinking about a night full of promises. She fiddled with the buttons of his shirt, opening them deftly while he found his hands inside her kameez. She removed his shirt and moved her hand over his bare chest. It gave her goosebumps and a heady excitement.

Abhi pulled up her kameez and she raised her hands so that he could do it with an ease. He rolled it and with a swift motion flung it on the nearby chair.

"Don't throw it like that. What if Mummy ji comes in the middle of our love making session? We need to keep our clothes handy."

"My mother is one intelligent woman. She would never come and barge into our room."

"Yeah, like the way she did last time or in the kitchen that day."

"Shhh… Let's not talk about that. I have locked the room today, so no one can disturb us."

"Wow!! That's great Abhi. You have become so smart."

He kissed her bare shoulders and his hands moved towards the roundness of her breasts. With the other hand, he tried unhooking her bra.

"Damn! Open this for me. The hooks are so weird."

"You only need practice and a sleight of hand to open them."

Rhea smiled as she opened the hooks of her bra for him.

"Wait, did you buy the condoms? I don't want any chunnu munnus for the time being."

Abhi laughed and nodded his head in affirmation and pulled her on the bed. He took a mouthful of her breast and sucked the nipples gently as she closed her eyes. The rest of the night passed in a blur. This was one beautiful night she would dream of again and again. And she counted it as brownie no.3.

* * *

5

THE FIRST DAY AT JOB

The next day, Rhea was all ready for the new job. She chose a pink salwar kameez, matching danglers, neither too big nor too small, just the appropriate size, and applied a jet-black eyeliner. Eyeing herself happily she lingered on for a while prancing in front of the mirror to look at herself a little while longer.

Abhi was having his breakfast and was oblivious to the charms of his wife. He was munching on a toast and kept on reading newspaper. She eyed him lasciviously to elicit any response, but he did not pay her any attention. After prattling for a while in front of him, picking up solitary objects she gave up and clutched the newspaper from his hands.

"What are you doing?" his voice boomed.

"You didn't notice me."

"Ya, you look fine! Now let me read."

He bore no resemblance to the soft and gentle Abhi who kept on kissing her last night at every conceivable place. He appeared like a stranger to her now, so distant and weird.

"Husbands!" she threw her hands in exasperation and composed herself.

Today was her first day at job and she cannot allow herself to get jittery. She has to be all calm and composed and well prepared for the rigours of the new job.

Mummy ji sat on the dining table which doubled up as the kitchen table top for cutting up of sundry veggies. She wielded the knife in Rhea's direction and then turned it to slice up a carrot. With a deft motion and a practiced ease, she kept on with the job at hand without throwing a second glance in her direction. Her eyes widened with disbelief and then narrowed when she saw Rhea with the perpetual glow on her face that did not dim by her presence.

"The girl is trying to fly high" she mumbled to herself. She pursed her lips to construct some more profanities when Abhi came in with the newspaper stuffed under his arm.

"Okay, Mama see you in the evening."

"Bye, beta see you. Where is Rhea going? "she faked innocence and masked the impression of perfect ignorance the way only she could do in front of the mollycoddled son.

"Mama, she got a job. Didn't she tell you? Rhea come here. Weren't you supposed to tell Mama the good news."

"What, who says I am pregnant? You should not have given last night's details to Mummy ji. Oh! it's so embarrassing." She blushed and hid her face in the dupatta.

Mummy ji cringed, thinking about the last night and the pleasure-soaked face of her daughter-in-law.

'What rubbish! Sex is not supposed to be enjoyable. Just make the kids and raise them.' She muttered to herself.

"Mummy ji, did you just say sex!!!!"

"No, beta ji I was just wondering you should sleep early and finish whatever you are trying to engage in. Abhi has a tough job. You should not unnecessarily trouble him with your demands. You are getting my point Rhea beta! Are you?

Rhea laughed and whispered shyly, "Oh! Mummy ji! how do you know how much your son is capable of?

Mummy ji picked up the neatly sliced veggies and off she went plonking her feet wedged in Bata sandals.

"Jao ji jao! Do wherever you want to go? Come home soon, both of you. I am making Aloo Gajar ki sabzi."

Rhea smiled. Brownie no. 4 !!!

She started laughing heartily, oblivious to Abhi's presence next to her.

"Why are you so happy? You should listen to Mama. See how nicely she cooks and takes care of everything. And always tell her everything."

"I did tell her yesterday. She might have forgotten. You know how sharpness of senses wanes with time."

But Abhi had moved on and was now inspecting the car by lifting up the bonnet and checking for any fuel leakages.

Rhea flipped open her phone to find a message from Ranbir on Facebook. She flinched and clicked on it, making sure Abhi did not notice and was busy in his work.

It was a simple 'Hi' nothing so grand. She flitted for a while then pressed on the reply button and wrote a Hi and sent back.

'A Hi is not indicative of anything' she reasoned and a 'Hi' back also does not count much. Moreover, he and Ranbir were lab partners. She is bound to reply. They did so many dissections together which made it mandatory for Rhea to answer the perfunctory Hi.

"Oh! the hi' s and bye' s. They don't mean much. The usual pleasantries." She pushed the Motorola phone back in her purse pushing it further down into the recesses. Putting her notepad and hand towel on it. Putting her sun glasses and lip balm over it. She needed more stuff to hide the phone in the ruckus so that she forgets, it even exists.

Abhi was still inspecting the engine, all bent over as if

canoodling with the esoteric machinery of the car.

She kept on fidgeting and looking at him in the hope to make a start. But he won't even budge.

"What are you doing? I was supposed to reach at 9 am. That buddha might change his mind. What if he tells me he doesn't need me any more because I am late on the first day of the job."

Though she knew the chances of a happening of this kind were negligible as he looked smitten and she unknowingly has worked her charm over the retired Doctor.

"Come on! Just a few more minutes. I want to check some things in the car. What if it stops midway?"

She was getting impatient. She adjusted her chudda, placed her finger on it and kept on moving hither and thither till she was bored by the activity. She instinctively reached for her phone. She made a desperate effort to connect with the virtual world by switching on the mobile data once again. The beep of the Facebook messenger let her know there was a message. She dreaded the fact that it could be Ranbir. She waited for a second and with one admonished finger clicked on the app and there sprung a world of possibilities.

"How are you?"

"I am fine. What about you?"

She immediately replied.

'Harmless messaging' she countered. The kind of things people write when they meet after a long time. Asking about the heath, general well-being and family.

Abhi was back in the driver's seat and she smiled and relegated the phone to the unreachable domains of her purse.

He dropped her at her work place with loads of good wishes and made way to his office. Rhea took out a pocket mirror and checked her reflection to find everything prim and proper. She moved with an alacrity and propelled herself towards the clinic.

There were some cases and the Doctor along with his attendant was putting the intra venous on one of the recumbent dogs. He saw Rhea, but he chose to ignore her and kept on with his work.

She kept on waiting, trying to make herself useful by interacting with one of the owners and taking history of a sick dog. She took the prescription pad and noted the vitals and after the Doctor was done with administering the intra venous, presented him the details of the case.

"You should learn to come on time. It's 9.30 am and my patients start coming at 9 am. How will you take care of my place when I am not here?"

She unceremoniously adjusted her dupatta and it got lifted up a notch higher giving him a glimpse of her young, succulent breasts in perfect shape and size. He was fascinated by the spectacle. He coughed a little and corrected his words.

"Well, it's okay. Today was your first day. So, you are excused dear."

He needed water to ease the heightened anxiety with a sudden need to pee. The enlarged prostrate presented problems of itself.

She heaved a sigh of relief, checked the color of her nail polish, brought the dupatta at the original place and smiled at the attendant who got embarrassed at the sudden attention.

'You are very beautiful madam! You should try modelling."

Rhea smiled, "Oh yes, I am trying. I have a contract which I am reviewing but they are paying me less so not at all happy. By the way they also want a male model. If you don't mind we can suggest your name."

"Hehe, madam you are funny. You are joking, right!"

Rhea smiled, took her rubber band and pulled her hair back, tying them to a knot.

"By the way, we were not introduced. I am Dr Rhea and I would be working in this clinic. And you are...?

"Das, Call me Das. Though my full name is Dagshman Bandhu, but I prefer Das. I am Das, the servile, the humble one."

"Das, that's nice. You don't look like you are from Punjab."

She took a careful look scanning him up and down. He was young, seemed to be in his teens, scrawny and a little unkempt. And he kept on looking affectionately at her.

"Yes, I am not from Punjab. I am from Samastipur in Bihar but Punjab is my home now."

"Tell me more. What about your family? Are you married?"

"My parents live in my native village. I live with my sister whose husband works in the sugar mill. I am not married! Looking for a smart, beautiful, funny Punjabi girl." He smiled coquettishly and started playing with his phone.

"Hmmm. That's quite an ambition. But don't run after girls looking for the special one. She will come in your life at the right moment. Find a suitable ambition. Marriage toh ho jayegi anyway. Think about something else you want to achieve."

Das looked at her wistfully and murmured, "Yes, she has come into my life at the right moment. She is smart, beautiful, funny and she is a doctor. Lethal combo! She only has to get divorced and marry me now and I would take her to Samastipur and then never let her come back."

Rhea meanwhile was looking at the patient charts lying on the table.

"Did you say something?"

"No ji! Nothing madam."

"Don't call me madam. Call me Rhea or Rhea di is perfect."

"Why I have to call you di? How old are you?"

"Well, it doesn't matter but I am your senior in age as well as position so call me Rhea di. We will make a great team Das and we will make this place a success."

"This place is already a success. We keep on getting cases throughout the day and sometimes even at night."

"Ambition, Das! Strive for more! This is lacking in you. Don't worry I would create a hunger for success in you."

Das encircled his fingers, turning them into a fist and swayed his arm in an upward direction.

"Inquilab Zindabad! Inquilab Zindabad!"

"Okay! Calm down. You definitely have some revolutionary blood brimming inside you. When I say ambition, I mean to say, you keep on pursuing something doggedly."

"Doggedly! Like a doggy!"

"Yes, exactly you chase your dreams like a doggy. You think of something and never let it go and keep on chasing it for the rest of your life with a zeal, forgetting everything else."

Das looked at her mesmerized, besotted, "Determination, chase. I am so glad Rhea didi you came to my life. No one ever told me about determination and ambition the way you are telling me. Be a doggy and chase."

She felt elated in securing an able pupil in Das.

"I skipped my breakfast today. You have some doggy biscuits here. And give me your number. Here save my number and my hubby's number as well in case of an emergency if my phone is not reachable." She retrieved a prescription pad from her purse and wrote down the numbers.

"You are funny, didi. Let me get samosas from the nearby shop. My treat to you on the first day." And he ran out of the clinic with gusto and a new-found doggy determination.

****

Rhea falls into a routine. With a job in hand she got busy and came home only in the evenings. The days that were spent under the watchful gaze of Mummy ji were forgotten and a new determination took hold inside her. The few weeks that looked threatening and teetered close to destroying her marriage were forgotten with an ease.

Life looked beautiful and held new promises and she was determined to fulfil every day with new hopes and dreams. She dreamt of having a clinic of her own someday or a chain of hospitals. But then Pathankot was such a small suburb with a sparse canine population, so it would not be feasible to maintain a big chain when the patients were scarce. But her dreams were grandiose, and she began nurturing them with same efficiency, she did at university.

The retired Doctor was very much involved with the daily affairs of the clinic though he gave Rhea a free hand. He flitted on and off, trying to chat up with her, giving her unsolicited yet useful advice. He was obviously an experienced man in his sixties and no matter Rhea abhorred his constant intrusions, she knew he had the wisdom on his side. And the number of surgeries that he had done gave him an added advantage and though she knew a lot, there was so much to learn from him yet.

"Didi, can I click your picture?" asked Das who was helping her administer an intravenous, one day.

"Hmmm!!! What did you say? Which picture? And for what? Please don't distract. This animal is anemic, and I am finding it difficult to locate the vein."

The smug owner who owned a local silk store and was famous among the NRI clientele that he catered to, did not indulge in any talk. He smiled at the sudden demand of the attendant. "Lagda affair chal reya dona da" (It seems they are having an affair) he murmured.

"Did you say something Sardar ji?" Rhea caught the word affair.

"Nah ji nah. I didn't say anything Bhenji."

"What Bhenji? I am not Bhenji. I am a Doctor. You said something!"

"I did not say anything Madam. He wants to take your picture. Lao ji lao, take mine also. But Madam should put on some nice silk suit, so she would appear prettier. Only yesterday I have received high quality silk that is especially for my customers in Amerika and Kaneda. Sade lokan nu kadar nahi ji (Our people do not care at all). The ladies who come to me all the way from sat samundar par (from far away) are the ones who know about quality."

"Bhaji, I also wanted to get silk suit stitched for my mom. And I want to gift one to Rhea di. When should I come to your shop?"

"Das buy some good clothes for yourself instead of getting me silk. And please hold the IV bottle properly. Let me take your picture and then you can tell your friends you are kind of a Veterinary Doctor." Rhea giggled at the imagined, amused expression of his friends when they will see him holding the intra venous bottle.

Das persisted, "Didi one picture lene do. I told my friends that didi is a very good Doctor. And she is my friend." He smiled sheepishly.

"You did not tell your friends nah that I am your girlfriend. See this chudda. I am a much-married woman." Rhea grew suspicious of his motives.

"No, Didi. Ram, Ram. What say! Only friend. Doctor friend."

The owner pitched in and said "Koi gal hi nai ji. Madam ,let the boy take a photo. Include me in the frame also. And if my dog gets well, a silk suit pakka for you Madam ji."

"Sardar ji, the dog is having Parvo infection. Just look at it. It's oblivious to everything and no movement at all. The chances of it getting well are bleak. You are busy with your work and you did not even care to get the poor fellow vaccinated."

"Time ni hega ji. (There is no time). Tell me who will sit at the shop if I will run after the dog."

"Then don't keep a dog. Who is telling you to have a dog at home when you cannot take care of it?"

"For safety ji."

"And what about it's safety. Do you have any idea how deadly this disease is? The chances of recovery are negligible."

"You are a Doctor so that's your problem. See if someone comes with a problem in my stock we get it rafu or we replace it, but we never fight with our customers like this."

"I am not some silk selling bania. I am a Doctor. Stop degrading my profession by making a mockery of it."

No sooner had the words escaped her lips she dreaded them.

"No, no I didn't mean like that uncle. Your profession is noble just like mine."

Sardar ji pursed his lips and narrowed his eyes.

"I have been in this business and in this city for the past thirty years and I am the most respected man in this town."

Rhea knew she crossed the line. She was not supposed to get emotional about the treatment part. She tried to assuage the feelings of the owner by being mild and even adjusted her dupatta a few notches higher. The dupatta hung around her neck and her boobs literally spilled out of the tight fitted shirt she wore. But the owner did not even look, he would not relent. His anger compounded, and he was all uncouth and unruly.

Rhea was trying her best to calm him down, apologizing for every single word.

"This is how you talk to owners, disrespecting them. Is it my fault that my dog is sick?"

"No, uncle I am not disrespecting you. I am sorry for my words" Rhea pleaded.

The dog moved a little bit and the scalp vein came out. Rhea got herself busy putting it again. As she leaned down her dupatta kept on falling. She got irritated and removed it, hanging it on the nearby chair and bent down to find the vein of the emaciated and anemic dog. Das got a clear view of her sexy cleavage. He sensed the perfect opportunity and clicked some pictures. He zoomed the camera on her boobs and took a few exclusive boob pics and smiled at the success. He definitely had something to boast about. He has told his friends that the new Doctor is damn sexy and has the most beautiful, perfectly round boobs and now he has the proof and he can forward the pictures to the needy ones. They have always harassed and made fun of him by calling him a wastrel. Finally, he would get some special attention and the applause of the gang.

"Band karo treatment. You people disrespect the owners. I will tell the local press about this insult and it will be in the newspapers. I will tarnish the reputation of this clinic." Sardar ji glowered.

Rhea was teary eyed and full of remorse. She could not fathom the suddenness of the events.

Just now he was talking about gifting me a silk suit and now he is all out there baying for my blood.

"Uncle, I love animals. I really love them. I am sorry, I got emotional. I feel so bad when owners don't take care of their pets."

"Who is uncle here? Are you talking to me?"

"Sardar ji, please calm down. This is my new job. See I am newly married. Look at my chudda. I am new in this town. I did not know you at all."

"You called me a bania."

"Did I? Must be a slip of tongue. I am so sorry Sardar ji."

Rhea gently patted the dog. "I will do everything I can, so that it recovers. I can also take it to my home if you don't want it."

"Why will I allow you to take my dog? You are again insulting me by telling me that the best shopkeeper in the whole town cannot take care of his dog. You insulted me twice. I am calling a press conference tomorrow. And I will make sure your clinic gets a bad press coverage and no one comes here for treatment."

Rhea looked at Das who was busy punching numbers on his phone.

"Das, leave the damn phone! Talk to him. Salvage his pride somehow. The Doctor will kick me out of the clinic if Sardar ji called a press conference. Do something?"

"Sardar ji, didi meant no harm. She is so innocent and beautiful and hard working. Just look at her with my eyes. How pretty she is? If she comes to Samastipur someday we would crown her …The Queen of Samastipur."

"Das, what nonsense are you saying? Calm him down."

"Sardar ji, please don't get agitated. I would be your charnon ka das forever. Please forgive us. Didi is a very good Doctor, trust me."

The dog who was oblivious to all the chaos that had erupted around him, opened its eyes, looked around in a daze and lolled his head to another side.

"Uth gaya oye. Moti uth gaya. He has not opened eyes

since yesterday. And he is looking at me right now." the owner clapped his hands in excitement.

"Give him more DNS, give him more. Mera bacha uth gaya."

Rhea sensed the change of mood and got a fresh lease of life.

"Yes, it might survive. We should continue the treatment. We cannot give more DNS but seems the medications are working fine. Das get some samosas."

Das made a dash for the samosa shop.

"Tu pher aa gaya, samose lene (You have come again, to get the samosas).

"Hanji. There is a pissed-out client. Give me three plate samosas with channa."

"Pehle paise do! (First give the money)

"Arre what money? You have a hisab with the Doctor saab. Put in his account."

"But he has told us, not to put your samosas in his account."

"What nonsense! A samosa is a samosa. You are trying to create confusion between a Doctor and an attendant. Sharam karo (Shame on you). I know you sell stale samosas to all the people. You make them a week before and keep on frying the same things again and again."

The samosa seller mellowed down, "Arre, what are you saying? Did I tell you I also belong to Bihar? Your Bhauji (sister –in- law) is from Samastipur only."

"Sachi! When are we going to meet the Bhauji then? I will come home someday. Does she make better samosas than you?" Das winked as he took the brown paper bag and made his way back enthusiastically.

"Saala, muftkhor, harami (The son of a bastard, freeloader).

Oye agli bar aayaga na, toh julab mila dena samoson ki chatni mein (If he comes the next time, mix laxative in the ketchup.)

The dog after giving them some hope by giving that fleeting nod of his head, again slumped into a stupor. It has placed his head on his forelimbs and for a while it appeared to Rhea that there was a hint of a serene smile. The face so calm and tranquil like a monk, lost in meditation oblivious to all the ruckus outside.

The owner accepted the chair willy-nilly but turned his head away from Rhea to give her the impression that he was still under the shadow of offence.

Das, meanwhile appeared with three plates of steaming samosas and placed one in front of the owner.

"Pehalwan de samose. Wah ji wah!! It has been days I didn't taste them. Thanks."

Rhea smiled meekly and decided to control her flow of words and took a plate and started munching. She stood next to the dog and kept on looking at it to elicit any response.

Everyone went quiet, lost in the gastronomic delight, happily devouring the samosas.

Sardar ji had stopped grumbling and hungrily devoured the samosas. Rhea tired by the verbal tirade stood next to the dog who was sleeping peacefully. Das stood at a little distance and was busy sending Rhea's pictures to his group of friends.

He texted the pic to all his friends on WhatsApp with the tagline 'Beautiful Vet doc with hot boobs in our clinic.'

What he did not realize was that Rhea had given him Abhi's number as well which he had saved in the contact list.

Das unknowingly had texted Rhea's picture along with the catchy tagline to the husband who was caught up in files and work precisely at that time.

Poor Rhea, munching on samosas, accused herself for speaking out her mind, oblivious to the calamity that was yet to unfold.

The owner after devouring Pehlawan's samosas looked upbeat and praised her lavishly.

"Hanji, kinne paise dewan for the treatment?" (How much should I pay for the treatment?)

"Aree, nahi Uncle ji. Sorry Sardar ji. We won't take money from you. You are the most respected person in this town.

He smiled at her.

"We will call a press conference. I will tell the press, your clinic is the best in city."

"That's so nice of you. But can we just leave the press out of it. You can spread the good word by speaking well about us."

"You are new in this town. You don't know my impact on press. I can make and damage reputations. I have the power ji. I am machoman, superman" Sardar ji flexed his muscles and posed for Das.

"Khich photo kake." (Click my picture, boy!)

"Khich laan, pucca?" (Are you sure, I should click?) Das pulled out his phone from his pocket.

"Aaho ji. Send me on WhatsApp. Okay ji. Tata bye bye. Rab rakha. See you soon Madam ji and Das ji."

Sardar ji picked up Moti from the table and moved out of the clinic. Rhea flopped on the chair and heaved a sigh of relief.

"Owners like him suck my energy! I would not be able to sustain myself at this pace. Pathankot is full of crazy people!!! And why he keeps on mentioning press all the time. Is he that influential?"

"Hanji, he was a former peon at the press club in Pathankot. So, he knows all the journalists. Later on, he opened his own cloth shop."

Both of them broke into an impromptu laughter.

"Haha. Now I know the source of his press connections."

"Rhea di, who will pay for medicines?"

"I will." She fished out some crisp notes and gave it to Das who took them hurriedly and moved it towards the money counter.

"The Doctor is very particular about the money. But you should have taken money from that rich fellow. Ate a plate of samosas and did not even pay for that."

"It's okay, Das. You are such a sweetheart. I am sorry I said no for the picture. This is a small city and you should not click my pictures and save them in your phone. What if someone sees them or forwards them without your permission? It is a dangerous world out there, full of creeps. I am not talking about you. It's the other people I am talking about."

Das tinkered with his phone and hid it in his trouser pockets. The constant pings of received messages on WhatsApp kept on interjecting their talk.

"You surely have lot of friends. You are getting lots of messages. Did you forward something interesting? Send me also."

"Rhea di, I am sorry." He dashed out of the clinic, sweating profusely, his hands shaking, his body shivering. He spat on the road and kicked a mongrel. "Damn! How can I be such a bastard? She is so nice to me and I have done the damage."

Rhea wondered at his weird behavior.

He acts strange some time.

****

Rhea wrapped up the day's work. Quite an eventful day it turned out to be. She picked up her purse and waited for Abhi but when he did not come at the designated time she called him up. The phone kept on ringing for a while before she muffled its cries by clicking on the red button.

He seems to be busy. I should take a rickshaw.

He waved to a rickshaw puller who careened his way towards her.

"Bhaiya, Model town. How much?"

"10 rupaiye"

She sat on the rickshaw and smiled at herself.

How beautiful has life turned out to be! A few months ago, I felt so forlorn and embittered but nothing really mattered now. The only thing that matters is that I have a job in hand and I would be in touch with animals. Finally, in connect with my profession.

She was lost in her own thoughts when she finally spotted the turn.

"Yahaan se left (Take a left from here) This is it. You can stop here."

As the rickshaw came to a screeching halt she hopped out of it and smiled graciously at the rickshaw puller.

"Ten rupees are very less you should take twenty at least." She smiled and handed two 10 rupees notes in his frail hands as he watched with an amused expression.

"I have got a job and I am so happy about it. You know how important it is to have a job for a girl. It makes her financially independent and emotionally secure and so much more. I would tell you more if we meet again." She blabbered as the rickshaw wallah nodded his head and smiled, giving her a toothless grin.

Another winsome smile and with a flourish in her steps she moved towards home.

The moment she entered the main door she saw Abhi's car parked inside.

How come he is home before me? Wasn't he supposed to pick me up?

She checked her watch. It was around 5.30 pm and Abhi was never home before 6 pm. She entered the main door that led to a hall and into the living room that was adjacent to the kitchen. The dining table was propped in front of the kitchen and it occupied lot of space. If anyone is sitting in the living room, he could clearly be a witness to the happenings in the kitchen due to the peculiar architecture of the house.

But today the mood in the house was somber and she witnessed three clay models sitting on the chairs without making any movement. Abhi was having a dead pan expression, his face devoid of any color, looked pale, as if he had witnessed some tragic happening. Mummy ji was having his phone in her hand and was fiddling with it contorting her face in different ways. Papa ji was watching BBC today and it was running in mute tones.

For the past few days he had been enamoured with a particular news anchor who was gorgeous with wavy blonde hair and has charmed him with her perfect smile. And he assumed she was there only for him while she was the heartthrob of a million people who watched her enraptured, every day, same time. So, he only watched BBC and nothing else. He got a much-needed reprieve from his favourite angry anchor whom he tried to emulate for years but finally gave up for he realized he was no match for his theatrics. His current heartthrob elucidated all the qualities he had and in turn bore a semblance to his own self. Soft, calm, gentle and so womanly, all that he missed in his wife.

The moment Rhea entered, three faces looked at her with lot of interest. Abhi kept on staring at her, Mummy ji gasped in horror and then rechecked the phone and murmured, "Same suit. Beta, she is wearing the same suit. It is today's pic. Che, che the girl has no shame!".

"What happened Abhi?" Rhea sat on the dining table without having any inclination of what had transpired.

"Rhea, you tell me what happened? You are getting intimate pictures of your body parts clicked and circulating them online. Is that your idea of becoming famous?" Abhi banged his fist with anger, the crystal glass lying on the table rattled, threatening to spill the contents.

Rhea was perplexed at his sudden bust of anger. "But tell me what happened , which pictures are your talking about and why will I try to be famous?"

Abhi snatched the phone from Mummy ji's hands and thrust in front of her eyes but she could not see anything from such a close distance. She held the phone a little away from her eyes and carefully scanned the boob pics with the tagline. For a split second, she could not believe that it was her picture. She scanned the suit she was wearing and checked the picture again to make doubly sure that it was hers and no one else and on a closer scrutiny she could see the edge of the scalp vein she held in her hands.

"Who clicked this picture? OMG! it looks damn sexy though and it looks somewhat morphed also. It has to be Das. Abhi, it's Das, that attendant. I would kill that bastard. We should report him to the police."

"No, do nothing of that sort. You will neither go to the police nor confront, whosoever, clicked these pictures. She should leave this job. Delete all these dirty pictures and the matter stands resolved here. Women should not be given more than their fair share of freedom. They are bound to misuse it." Mummy ji rolled up her eyes and looked at Rhea with hatred.

Das! OMG!!! He clicked the picture while I was treating the damn dog.

She remembered that she was bending on the table

administering the IV and she placed the dupatta on a chair.

Damn! I should start wearing an apron. It would have provided some cover.

It's so hot in the clinic with only a rickety fan so despite carrying an apron that day she did not wear it.

I will kill Das. That son of a bitch! So, this was the forwarded message that was receiving lot of pings.

Rhea recoiled in horror thinking about the views this picture must have received.

Tears clouded her eyes as she left the phone on the table and ran towards her room mortified at the chain of events. Such an awful day it has turned out to be and she had such a terrible fight with the owner and Das has clicked some boob revealing pics and circulated in the city. How will her husband and in-laws let her continue at this job after all this hullabaloo?

She tried calling Das from her phone, demanding an explanation, but his phone was switched off. She tried calling her employer and he picked up at the second ring.

"Yes, Das is here sitting beside my feet begging forgiveness. He says he is sorry." The old Doctor tried to placate her and after disconnecting the call kept on seeing the pictures with a salacious glee.

"Oye Das, tu ta kamal kar dita! (Das, you did a good job!). Such perfect shots. Why you did not forward me these pics? I am proud of you. Now everyone in the city will bring their sick animals to our clinic. This will become the famous clinic of Pathankot with the sexy Vet."

But Das went on crying. "I broke her trust. She will never talk to me. I am in love with Rhea di. I want to marry her".

The Doctor smacked his head lightly.

'Bhenchod, she is already married. Haven't you seen that

bloody big chudda she is wearing. And saale sister fucker you are in love with someone you call your sister. "Rhea Didi haan. Enna pyar pe gya tera ohde naal! (You are so much in love with her!)."

Das sobered up and answered in all fairness.

"I call her didi because I respect her. Otherwise, I don't have any sisterly feelings for her. I will die if she doesn't marry me. I am in love with her like crazy."

"Oye Das, you are a bhola panchhi! It's not love, it's called lust. You should lay your hands on some college girl. You are not in love with her, it's her boobs, you are in love with. Don't say that again. Sala lover, get lost and find a girl appropriate for your age to flirt!" The Doctor kicked Das and busied himself in household chores.

Next day, Rhea did not report for work. The situation in the house was tense. Abhi had left for work and they were not talking to each other. Mummy ji was pestering her with comments that bled her heart and she cried more. Papa ji did not look her in the eye. He averted his gaze the moment she came in front of him.

That day Papa ji was watching BBC with a sickly expression. Rhea gauged the situation and realized that he was missing the specific blonde anchor who read the evening news.

"Papa ji, she will come at 5 pm" and she winked at him. "By the way, I also find her very pretty!"

He smiled and winked back and gave her thumbs up. Mummy ji came in the living room and he immediately morphed the thumbs up and started scratching his bald head.

Rhea engrossed herself in the imaginary dusting she was doing so assiduously. She dare not look at Mummy ji and shot out of the living room to escape her ire. Papa ji, meanwhile kept on scratching his head and looked helplessly at the clock. It was still 4 pm and he would have to wait for an hour for that beautiful anchor.

The Doctor called Rhea as he was not able to manage the work load since morning. People were bringing their perfectly healthy animals claiming them to be sick. After checking the temperature and prescribing multivitamins he was sending them back.

Most of the people who came to the clinic that day enquired about a young lady Vet working there. They reasoned that their friends have told them about her good working hand. They were disappointed to see the sexagenarian when all they wanted was to have a look at Rhea.

She did not pick up the calls by her employer. She did not know what to say. Her future rested undecided and Abhi was yet to take any decision on her job prospects which was heavily influenced by Mummy ji's take on decision making and would sway any side his mother lent weight to. So, she was keeping her fingers crossed and was determined not to broach any fight with her. She had stopped counting the brownies as Mummy ji had scored a direct hit with this uncalled controversy and was now, way ahead of her.

Kimti was confused at the strange animosity that has percolated in the house. No one seemed happy any more. The newlyweds were enveloped in sadness and they were not talking to each other at all. He missed the shy glances they used to exchange with each other in Mummy ji's presence. Abhi was silent and left for his job earlier than usual, Rhea was not reporting for her work anymore and Mummy ji kept on saying 'haye, haye' all the time.

He questioned Rhea, "Bibi ji why you are not going to work?You were so happy with it. Did they kick you out?"

Rhea, whose eyes appeared puffy all the time, started sobbing.

"Kimti, something terrible happened at the job and now I don't know if Abhi will let me work again. He is not even talking to me anymore. We are living in one room like strangers. Unintentionally, but it all got messed up. Life is tough, and things don't happen the way we want them to be. How happy I was to get this job? And now it has been taken away from me, Kimti."

"Don't worry chhoti bibi. Life has a way of teaching you all. It will all settle down. All you need is time and patience. And just keep calm and remain steady and keep on praying. Prayer has the power to move even the toughest of mountains."

6

DAS APOLOGIZES

Rhea started doing path, making it a ritual. The more she thought about Das the more agitated she got, so forgiveness was the only way she could calm her heart. The moment she closed her eyes, his bony frame wafted in front of his mind.

He looked so innocent, yet he acted in such a devilish manner. And I thought we would make a good buddy team. How difficult it is to gauge the intentions of people?

It had been a week and she did not report for work. Things between her and Abhi were not hunk-dory either. She had apologized a million times for a crime someone else committed on her, but he had not relented. He replied in monosyllables and did not care for any explanations she had to offer. No matter how much she explained that if some crazy guy magnifies her boobs and posts obscene pictures for his friends how could she be held culprit. No matter how much she tried to thaw the bitterness, things did not ease out.

Abhi did not budge and he nursed the grudge day in and out. She grew miserable and no matter how much she tried to find solace in cooking and gardening, she did not feel elevated.

Her profession was her calling, she was missing handling the furry creatures, injecting them, healing them. No matter how much she tried to amuse herself with other pursuits, she felt trapped and stuck in a household that did not care about her reasons to be happy.

The retired Doctor meanwhile had booked tickets to Germany to meet his son and daughter-in-law and was getting restless at Rhea's absence.

"Bhenchod Das! you fucked up. You and your amorous desires fucked up my clinic."

"But Doctor saab, the clientele is increasing by the day. There are more people coming in with sick and needy dogs."

"They come here looking for Rhea and once they know that she is not working here they will stop coming. Yesterday the guy brought the perfect healthy labrador and asked me to put it on a drip. He wanted the best doctor in the clinic. When I told him, I am the best doctor he murmured 'Nahi ji oh kudi jisdi photo dekhi aa' (That girl whose picture I saw). Bhenchod! sister fuckers!!!! Haven't they seen tits of their mothers and sisters? I don't understand what is happening to the people these days. The people of Pathankot have gone crazy over her. The poor girl must be having a hard time."

"People keep on asking for her number all the time. Most of the people think she doubles up as a... ...a...Chalo rehn do (Let it go). I can't even say that word."

"Sharm kar, Das. She is a good soul who came to help me run the clinic. Her husband might divorce her. Don't you dare give her number to anyone, making a hell out of her life."

"You think, she might get divorced, she might!" Das closed his eyes and smiled generously. "There are chances that she might, you know, consider my proposal."

"I will call the police and get you arrested if you try to sabotage her life any more. She is a damn good clinician and you created all this stupid controversy by circulating her pics. Paap laguga Das tenu. (You will be punished for this) Mark my words. Waheguru is watching, what you did to her? You will rot in hell. I would be leaving very soon, and I would shut the clinic. You saala illiterate! How will you handle everything? You would kill the dogs the way you killed the bright future of a promising girl."

Das started weeping, "That day you were saying it was good that I clicked her boob pictures. And now you are accusing me and telling me to rot in hell. Is this dignified?"

"Oh yes! Clicking pictures of a doctor's cleavage when she was trying with all her might to save a life is dignified! Is it? Justify yourself, Das! Mein ta awein kehta khadi piti ch. (I said it because I was drunk) I did not wish bad for her. And stop crying. Be a man, Das and correct your folly. We must save her honour. Write an apology and send it to all your friends. We can also get it published in newspapers."

Das went quiet and felt forlorn. He has not eaten properly since the day, Rhea left. He was desperate to see her and ask for forgiveness.

And he had been boasting to his friends that she deliberately pushed the shirt down and removed her dupatta to let him have a clear view and pestered him to get the shots. He knew it was all made up. He knew he acted like a dog. That day, the poor girl was literally in tears and on the verge of a collapse, the way that owner was treating her. And how much she trusted him and depended on him. And he, of all the people betrayed her and did something that jeopardized her whole existence.

Das hung his head in shame and rued the fact that he was capable of so much destruction. He needed to correct his folly.

"Dactar saab, do you know where Rhea didi's husband works?"

"Kamla aa tu! The husband will kill you. And moreover, you sent him the pictures. We must make a visit to her home and meet the elders and they might relent. I know she wanted this job desperately. She would come back but perhaps the family is not allowing her."

So, next day the Doctor got packed a big fruit basket and took Das in the tow and off they marched towards Rhea's home on the trusted Bajaj Pulsar.

"Doctor saab, drive slow! Are we chasing someone? The fruit basket will fall off my hands if you drive at this speed."

"Das, bhenchod! I will kill you if this basket falls and I will not pay you this month's salary."

He held on to the basket more firmly adding his weight to it and squeezing the fruits, pushing the Doctor way ahead of his seat

"Das, saale get back! I have slid off the seat. Do you want me to sit on the engine?"

"Dactar sahib, can you please talk decently? You use too many expletives while talking to me. This is not acceptable. I am a decent guy so don't use this kind of language with me. You keep on humiliating me. I am not some ganwaar that you keep on insulting me. I have self-respect and I am a proud man."

"Aho Das, sale, bhenchod! we have witnessed your decency. So, shut up and hold on to the basket."

Das mumbled something about Punjabis being uncouth and heartless but the same thing did not apply to Rhea.

Oh! she is the most beautiful and sexy Punjaban I have seen as he swooned and imagined Rhea running towards him in a pale chiffon sari. All wet and soaked. Her boobs throbbing like a jelly trying to break away from the constraints of the tight blouse. And she was whispering in his ear, "Das, mere Das, open the choli and let my babies be free! Only you can do this. Come Das, do the honour. I am waiting."

And Das comes running from somewhere far away and kept on chanting.

"Meri Rhea, meri pyaari Rhea, mein aa raahan hun."

And Das went on mumbling,

"Rhea, I am coming to set you free. I am coming."

The motorcycle was parked in front of Rhea's house now and the Doctor was looking at Das with abject horror and he gasped at the sound of her name.

And Das in all this dreamy state kissed the fruit basket with such a passion that he nibbled on the end of the shiny cover and chewed it.

"Das!!!" Doctor glowered.

"I will kill you if you say her name once more! Bhenchod, she is married!!! Kaka, try to understand. You don't harbor crushes for a married woman. Tomorrow she will have a kid and that kid will call you uncle. How will you feel then?

"Is she pregnant? No, dactar sahib I did not do anything to her. I swear. I did not even touch her."

"Her husband might have impregnated her. Who is talking about you? But I am impressed Das! High hopes! Now listen to me seriously. You are immature and young while she is mature and married and would end up having kids in a year or so. Don't chase the things you cannot get mere bacche. It will hurt and hurt so much that you will be left with nothing but emptiness. Why you want a deflowered woman when you can get a rose bud which you can turn into a flower?"

"Wait, wait."

Das fished a pocket dictionary from the folds of his trousers and looked for the meaning "de.. flowered"

"You own a dictionary."

"Yes, I bought one. My English tutor is teaching me how to read a dictionary. I am taking IELTS classes."

"Haha!! How can you do that? You don't know anything

about this language. Earn money and go back to your village in Samastipur and marry a nice Bihari girl.

"I knew it. Ultimately, it's about the great Punjabi -Bihari divide. You Punjabis always think we are inferior."

"It's not about divide. It's about common sense. Now stop this drama and pick up the basket."

The Doctor moved his head to and fro in irritation, lamenting the state of affairs and the improbable logic of Das.

"You seriously need to sort your mind."

As the bell rang, Kimti ushered them in the living room with exchange of pleasantries.

"So, you are Rhea bibi's boss? Did you say anything to her? She was so happy with the new job. What happened? Why she is not going anymore?"

The Doctor tried to evade the difficult question and demanded water while Das sat there shuffling his feet feeling uncomfortable under his glare.

Kimti started the monologue again after serving them water.

"She is new in the family and the city. And this job is very important for her to find her footing. I have seen her crying day in and out since the day she has been married. Please don't do anything that will hurt her."

And Kimti stood with folded hands, tears flooding his eyes.

Then he looked at Das. "You look one amongst us. You can understand the pain of being in a place where you are not required and abused all the time. Same is the state of Rhea Bibi ji. Don't let her lose this job."

Das, now a pale shadow of himself, his face devoid of any colour, hung his head in shame.

He could understand the pain very well. His extended family was left in Bihar. His father, ailing, afflicted with cancer bade him farewell with numb eyes. His mother who did not have the energy and vigor to take care of a large brood sent him to Punjab to his sister's home. It's been years and he has not gone home. His own people appeared so distant to him now. They appeared like tiny fragments embedded in his mind belonging to some bygone era. He was forgetting their faces. He tried to visualize but he could not remember what they looked like. His head swirled, and he felt giddy while his entire body convoluted in an unfamiliar rhythm.

"Das, are you okay!" The Doctor placed a firm hand on his shoulder trying to reassure him.

Meanwhile, Mummy ji entered the living room in her Bata slippers and landed on the sofa with a thud.

"Hanji, dasso. Who are you people?"

Das got up and plonked himself on the floor, next to Mummy ji's feet.

"Mata ji, forgive me. I am sorry. It was all my fault. You can kick me, beat me but I am the culprit."

And he held on to Mummy ji's feet with such a firmness that scared her and she got all jittery, started fumbling around his fingers to loosen the grasp.

"Let me go, let me go."

Das moved a notch higher from her feet towards her legs and encircled them with such a vigour that crippled her for a while.

"Bachao, bachao!!! Kimti, Rhea!!!" She shrieked.

The Doctor was trying with all her might to move Das out of his current location where he sat resolutely holding on to Mummy ji's legs with the might of a wrestler.

Kimti and Rhea came running in the living room to see the spectacle of Mummy ji being clutched in the strong grip of Das.

"Das, what are you doing? Let go off Mummy ji. You are scaring her." Rhea held on to one of his arms while the Doctor pulled the other one, but he would not relent. He held on to Mummy ji's legs and swivelled his body and moved his bony frame encircling her legs.

"Call the police! Call the ambulance! He will kill me."

"Das, let go. She will get a heart attack. Are you crazy? Doing all this tamasha in my home."

"Rhea di, forgive me or I will keep on holding to her for an eternity."

"Is this your way to ask for forgiveness, you scoundrel? Leave her or I will call the police."

Mummy ji, in midst of all the drama was getting nervous.

"Rhea, forgive kar de kudiye. My BP is rising. I am fainting! I am dying!!!"

Rhea pursed her lips and gauging the state of pandemonium mumbled to Das, "Okay! Forgiven. Leave her legs now".

"Haye rabba. Meri blood supply ruk gaye. I cannot feel my legs. Rhea puttar call a Doctor."

Mummy ji tried getting up but fell back on the sofa.

"It's okay, Mummy ji. You would be fine. Let me get you a glass of water."

"I am sorry, Aunty ji. Maafi de do" Das folded his hands and sat in front of her with half crouched legs.

"Move away from me. Sit back and talk to me."

Kimti could not stop giggling and exchanged a glance with Das. He nodded in affirmation and gave thumbs up to him before rushing to the kitchen.

"Das, shut up and let me talk. Dekho Mata ji, I mean Madam ji, I am running this clinic for the past five years. I retired from government job. I am a respectable man in the city. Whatever happened on my premises was indeed shameful! I have brought the culprit with me. You can do whatever you want to do with him. If you say we can hand him to the police for trying to outrage the modesty of a married woman."

"What is the meaning of 'outraging the modesty' please explain Dactar sahib." Das mumbled.

"No need of that. What's there in that shining tokri, you have brought?" Mummy ji looked at the goodies surreptiously.

"These are fruits for the beautiful lady. We have plucked the chosen and the most delicious ones for you so that you can enjoy their taste and wholesome goodness. Please accept this tuchh bhaint. (token of gratitude).

Mummy ji, perked up at the mention of the fruits. She smiled warmly and graciously and accepted the tokri of fruits.

"That is way too heavy. How much did you bring? So, kind of you!"

She looked at Das viciously. "You are a good man, Sardar ji. You understand our predicament. Such a small town, Pathankot is! I can ask my son to let Rhea work, but he has to say yes. But you must kick this guy out. What if tomorrow he raped her? What will we do? Our honor will be spoiled, we would be devastated. Waise bhi people are saying so many things behind my back. Because of these gandi photos, I had to miss my kitty also. Pata nahi what those Mehtas might be thinking?

"Mata ji, don't do this to me." Das made a desperate attempt to grab her feet again but Mummy ji gauged his mood and quickly shuffled her feet up on the sofa to thwart any pre-empted strike. "Get away from my feet. Take this stupid person away, Doctor sahib."

Sardar ji growled, "Das, behave yourself! Khabardar you tried to grab Madam ji' s legs again. You are disgusting. Piece of shit! Madam ji, he is very poor. His family has no means to sustain themselves. He sends money to his parents in Bihar every month. He does not even own a house. If I kick him out of job, his sister would not allow him to live with her anymore. Very poor people."

"If he is that poor, how come he is having an android phone."

Das tried to hide his new Samsung phone but to no avail. Mummy ji has already seen it and noted the discrepancies in what was being said and what she observed.

The Doctor was obviously not lying. But Das manipulated the owners to give him tips when the Doctor was not around and some days he would oblige the owners by administering injections, going all the way to their homes. He made a paltry sum out of it which he had been saving to buy himself a new phone.

"Show me your phone. Have you been stealing again?"

"When did I steal? It's my hard work and my money that bought me the phone. Don't accuse me!"

"Haan, haan I know which hard work. You go to their homes and give the shots so that they don't bring animals to the clinic. You eat into my clientele, you snake."

"Dactar sahib, mind your language. Do not call me a snake. It's disrespectable. Call me something else. If you had a Punjabi helper, you would have never used such derogatory language. It's because I am from Bihar that you insult me. You consider me your bandhuya mazdur (bonded labor) I know that."

"Confiscate his phone and give it to police." Mummy ji ordered.

"No, it's my phone. I would not give it to anyone." Das

started weeping. His tears would not stop, and he threw himself on the floor, curling his body. The tears that had not flooded his eyes for the past many years found an outlet and would not stop gushing out. His muffled cries turned into howls which scared Mummy ji.

"Chup karao isnu (Tell him to keep quiet) What will the neighbors say? They might come here any moment."

"Das, baas kar, all this drama or I will pack you off to your village on the very first train." Doctor scolded him for creating a ruckus.

Das got encouraged by all the attention and intensified his howls which scaled new heights bringing Papa ji out of his room.

"Who are you people? And why is this guy crying? Tell him to stop it. Our neighbors are very nosy. They might come here any moment."

"Das, calm down. They might call the police. They don't like noise and you are giving them enough reasons to do the same." Rhea placed a hand on his shoulder.

Her presence had a calming effect on him and hearing the word police, he went quiet. He got up and sat cross legged on the floor now.

"You can sit on the sofa please, Das." Rhea pursed her lips.

"I cannot bear to sit on the sofa in your august presence. I am the perpetrator of the crime. I am the sinner. O Lord, take me in thy fold and punish me."

"He was sitting on the sofa before you came. And don't be impressed. He is taking IELTS classes. He is stealing my clients and using the money to buy new phones and sponsoring his phoren dreams." Doctor said everything in one go.

Mummy ji nodded her head.

Meanwhile, Rhea briefed Papa ji about the situation.

The bell rang. Mummy ji flinched. It must be the neighbors. They must have heard all this howling. Kimti came running from the kitchen.

"Should I open the door?"

"Yes, but do not let anyone come in. Tell them we bought a new dog and it's feeling home sick." Mummy ji blabbered, without looking at Das.

"Yes, I am a dog now. This is a part of a conspiracy. A big one. Of alienating us, Biharis, turning us into dogs and making an animal out of us. When your people do not want to work, it's people like us who come and work for you. When your men are running away, chasing their phoren dreams, it's us, who plough your lands. We, who leave our families behind us, to serve you people only to be called dogs and Biharis. Shame on you and your culture if you can't respect the people who come into your state to earn a decent living. I don't want to live amongst people who call me a dog. Enough, I quit Dactar Sahib! I quit right now! I will work as a daily wager."

"Das, I did not know you had such a good vocabulary. Bravo!" Rhea mocked him, and he lapped up the false praise and looked at her, exuding a shy smile. He looked nervously at Mummy ji, who did not care for any speeches and Doctor sahib who looked askance and was busy making calculations of his own.

"Rhea, listen to me! They want you to continue with the job. Are you fine with it? To work in a place where a 'rapist in making' is working. And by the way, how much salary they are paying you?"

"Mummy ji, salary is not an issue. And even this boy is not an issue. It's Abhi. He is not even talking to me, since all this has happened?"

"I will handle my son. Are you ready to work? What if

tomorrow, he does something to you?"

"I want to work Mummy ji. Yes, I want to work so much. I am blessed to have you as my mother-in-law. You are acting like some goddess, Mummy ji. No in fact you are one. The one and only, my Mummy ji, my goddess."

Mummy ji beamed with pride. She looked at Doctor sahib who reciprocated her smile by nodding his head. She looked at Das who was standing still with downcast eyes mumbling incoherently to himself.

She called Doctor sahib to one side and spoke in a hushed manner, "He looks deranged to me. Are you sure you want him as an attendant? Hire a new one."

"He is perfectly fine. He is a little emotional and stupid. Don't worry. He means no harm. I know this kid for the past few years. He has been under my tutelage. He will never do anything to your daughter-in-law. You have my word on that."

*****

Next day, Rhea was back to work. She wore jeans, a long-sleeved kurta and covered herself with a stole. She had tied her hair in a bun and chose not to do any make up.

Mummy ji convinced Abhi that it's important for Rhea to work and earn her own money. Somewhere, the antics of Das really moved her as she realized how sorry the young Bihari lad was. After Doctor and Das left, the diligently decorated fruit basket cheered up Mummy ji. The colorful paper and the muslin cloth made it look wondrous and she was in awe of the packed goodness.

"This is the best gift to present to anyone these days instead of sweets. Your employer is a very thoughtful man. He knows I love fruits, you must have told him, hain na!"

And Rhea had bobbed her head up and down mechanically, a tad satisfied that the situation was improving, and things looked positive.

"Money is so important these days. Abhi's salary is not sufficient to cover the home expenses and your Papa ji has lost so much money in the share market. We need a working hand and you have to make sure that you contribute a part of your salary to the home expenditure."

Rhea had assured her that she will help in every way.

"Make sure, you are not making empty promises, or you know the ways I can make the tide swing." She had grated her teeth and it scared Rhea and she had acquiesced and acknowledged the secret pact. It was obvious the conditions should not be discussed with Abhi. For as Mummy ji said the menfolk should not be involved in womanly affairs. This was heart to heart talk between mother-in-law and daughter-in-law and she should not take offence at something so fundamental. All bahus contribute to the home expenses and she should follow the path of an ideal daughter-in-law.

The thought of parting with half of her salary made Rhea gloomy. The despair in her voice next morning was not because of the doings of Das anymore, it was more or less out of the concern over the meagre amount of money she would get to spend on herself.

The salary was already not sufficient and if she donated half to Mummy ji she would be left with nothing much to cheer about. But then she was happy, she was allowed to move out.

Life under the watchful gaze of her ever-attentive mother-in-law was unbearable. She used to question her every move and then nag her for the same as if nagging was her second nature.

Meanwhile, Das had noticed Rhea standing in front of the clinic and rushed to fetch the bouquet of flowers he had bought early morning. She had called up the Doctor last night to let them know that her family has given her the requisite permission to join the job again.

This has been the cause of immense happiness and Doctor and Das celebrated the success with 'The black label' that was procured from the nearby liquor vend. The joy was so palpable in their spirits that Doctor commanded Das to fetch some fish pakoras with the chutney and some Aloo cutlets.

"Bhenchod! tell them to make fresh. Don't bring stale fish like last time."

And Das for once did not mind the cuss words. He had sprinted his way, frolicking in the market like a cherubic girl. The object of his affection was coming back to his fold and he would be more careful this time.

"She is mine! All mine! From head to toe." Das gurgled with pleasure and swooned at the close proximity he would enjoy. He loved the little touch of fingers while handling the medication or a little brush of bodies here and there, moving in the small cubicles for the sick dogs. He would hover around her like a bumble bee, watching her all the time for her presence was reassuring.

The late-night revelry that led the Doctor and Das to drink, carried on till wee hours.

"Mere bache, Das. I am all set to go. Bhenchod! don't ever try to do hanky panky with the girl. "

"Dactar Sahib, can you speak properly. German police will deport you when they hear the way you talk." he erupted in peals of laughter thinking about the imagined scenario.

"Dactar Sahib, will you talk to the goris there? Can you get me hooked with one decent girl?" he said with a twinkle.

"Hehe, Das have you ever seen yourself in the mirror? You won't even get a decent girl in Bihar, leave alone a gori. And we are Punjabis. We are not scared of anyone. By the way, my own daughter-in-law is a gori. I don't feel like going. My son wanted me to sell everything, the clinic as well but I do not want to do the same. The six months visa looks like an eternity to me."

He grew quiet, his mind lost in thoughts about the repercussions and the changes that will entail moving to a different country, a different continent.

Das gauged the somber mood and moved his hand up and down his back murmuring.

"Nah, nah, Dactar Sahib don't get serious. Keep up the banter. Everything would turn out fine."

****

Rhea coughed a little, making Das aware of her presence who seemed to be lost somewhere trying to reconnect the dots with a bouquet in his hands while she stood in front of him.

Doctor sensed the unease and hurriedly plucked the bouquet from his hands and placed the same on Rhea's arms and ushered her inside.

"Chalo, chalo ho gaya welcome. Das move out of the way and make yourself useful."

The clinic was without any hubbub for the time being.

"Rhea beta, do you need tea?" the Doctor was at his best behavior. She rolled up her eyes and nodded her head.

"Make it coffee. I don't drink tea anymore. Strong coffee."

"What are you doing? Standing and staring. Go upstairs in my kitchen and make coffee." Doctor saab ordered Das who rushed upstairs in his living quarters.

Rhea flipped her Motorola phone, opened What's app, pretended to do something important. The Doctor flitted around her, trying to start a talk, but she ignored him. She scrolled Facebook, Instagram and then retweeted something inconsequential and kept a steady gaze on the phone.

Das brought her coffee and biscuits and now both of them

stood obsequiously in front of her.

Why don't you grab chairs? Stop staring at me."

Doctor smacked Das, "Stop staring at Rhea beta! I will gouge out your eyes if you even dared look at her breasts. I mean any part of her body."

"I am not staring at her. Dactar Sahib you are staring at her!"

"Don't create a scene, both of you. Let me enjoy my coffee in peace. Finally, there is some solace."

After what seemed like an eternity Rhea thawed the muteness by standing up and making a speech.

"Das, will have to go. I cannot work in a place where people click my pictures without my permission and that too gandi wali. You will have to choose between me and Das." she looked at the Doctor with a firm assertion of her words.

"But I think the matter was settled in your home but if you insist I choose you. Das, you can go back to Samastipur. And I will give you the salary today."

"Hor bolo, Rhea beta. Any other demand. I am going to Germany, Berlin precisely, next week and the clinic is all yours. I will come after six months. Oh, and yes, I will give you my account number where you can deposit the monthly emoluments. And I will be depositing your salary in your account." he smiled and went upstairs indicating Das to talk to her.

"Rhea di, please don't do this! What will my sister say? She will kick me out of her home." Das begged and prostrated himself on the ground.

"Das, get up. You can't work out this 'holding the legs' magic on me. And if you touch me, even the legs I will file a police complaint that you tried to molest me."

Das recoiled in horror and immediately stood up and moved far away from her.

"But how can you file a complaint, I tried to rape you. I have to actually attempt it and then you can say the same.''

"Das, mind your language! How dare you say that?"

"No, but you only said that nah, Rhea di. Why make baseless allegations against anyone? Let it be something substantial for police to act upon.''

She realized her folly and tried to deviate the discussion.

"Okay Das, you have to mend your ways. We have to act like a team if we have to run this place smoothly. This in-fighting will be bad for the clinic. It might lose the clientele.''

He nodded and folded his hands prostrated himself on the floor once more.

A lady entered with a giant Saint Bernard. She looked at Das with a certain amusement who was lying on the floor with hands folded and his lithe frame outstretched.

"He is doing Surya Namaskar." Rhea smiled. "Please come in. Das, ho gya! Get up and check the temperature of the dog."

He got up and shoved the thermometer up the rectum of the burly dog while she started taking history from the owner.

The Doctor came downstairs to see both of them busy and heaved a sigh of relief. He went back to do the rest of the packing. The days were numbered and there was so much to do. And with Rhea coming back to clinic he was relieved to concentrate on more pertinent tasks.

* * *

PART 2

THE DOCTOR'S STORY

7

REMINISCING THE PAST

For the past few days, the Doctor had been feeling uneasy. Going to Berlin to meet his only son and staying there for six months really peeved him.

His retirement from the government job prompted him to set up his clinic which he nurtured like a child. After working hard for twenty-five years, running a Veterinary clinic was easy for him and it got him good money. He was comfortable, living a life of solitude. His wife had left for heavenly abode when his son was young and after the boy left for Germany for higher studies he lived alone in the house.

The ground floor was converted into clinic and he lived in a room upstairs that had a kitchen and an attached washroom. It was nothing grand but enough to meet his meagre needs. His profession provided him the ultimate solace and succour as he wove his life around cases and treatments.

Leaving Pathankot was such a difficult decision. His son wanted him to come and settle with him but on the contrary, he wanted to be in this city and nowhere else.

He sat down on the bed all messed up with sundry stuff and thought about Jagsir, his only son and the good old times. How the little boy would run up to him and make a mad scramble for his turban placing it on his head as the Doctor affectionately used to call him 'the little turbanator'. But everything has changed with time. The day Jagsir landed in Berlin he shorned off his hair, his beard and uploaded pictures on Facebook. The Doctor had cried bitterly and moaned about the loss of his Sikh identity for days.

"We are Sikhs. The hair and the beard were your identities and by getting rid of them, you have excommunicated yourself from the religion." he hurled abuses, on and on.

Jagsir had disconnected the phone and did not call up for days altogether that mellowed the heart of the father and he ended up apologizing for his behavior. The motherless son had been raised by the Doctor with great care and affection on his part. The overbearing relatives and friends had pestered him for a second marriage, but he never let their clouded vision envelope his mind. They brought pictures and information of prospective brides. The girls who looked young and fair, had supple bodies and pliant minds but appeared diffident.

And when Doctor rejected every single one of them, citing the reasons that the girls in the pictures appeared too naïve they brought proposals of more mature and much married women. Those who lost their spouses or those who willfully chose to unshackle themselves of the constraints of a marriage. He would reason, "Why they got divorced in the first place? What are the chances they will treat my son with empathy? What if they do not give him the love and comfort he so much deserves?"

"You are young, you have desires. You need a woman, or you will end up fucking up your mind. And the boy needs a mother. Chose any one of them. They will make good wives. Listen to us. Trust us."

"What if she insists to have a kid of her own? Women are very territorial in that matter." The Doctor had his fears.

"So, have another kid. What's the harm? You are young and Jagsir will get some company."

"No, I do not want more kids. I don't have the time and

energy to take care of a new life. I have one son and he is enough for me and all I need in my life."

He could not trust anyone. He never did. He never took a second chance and never got married again. He always had his own intuitive mind at work and he had taken decisions throwing the weight of his ideals behind him. He chose not to get married and dedicate all his time towards his son and carried on with his professional obligations with devotion.

But he wanted to get away from his village, where the overbearing relatives kept on pestering him to get married. The move to the city provided a physical distance from the preening relatives and also a certain equanimity and soon the father and son fell into a rhythm of life.

He always had high hopes from Jagsir. Sending him abroad for higher qualification was his dream that he yearned to turn into reality by working day in and out. He used to work hard, treat sick animals at all times of the day, haggling over the cost of his services which came at a higher price depending on the time of the day and the distance from his place.

His Vespa scooter served as a reservoir of medicines. With injections of all kinds stuffed in his medicine bag, bottles of Calcium, DNS and Rintose perched precariously on the scooter, his stock of medicine kept on increasing every day. His phone kept on ringing incessantly even at odd times and he would attend each and every call. And some days he would rush away, leave the dinner half eaten to attend to an emergency case. But those days he used to charge a lot.

The little boy would look at his father with a yearning. There was so much to tell him that happened at school but only if the Doctor could listen. He reconciled to a life where his father did everything for him, except giving him his valuable time.

Soon, a household help was employed who doubled up as an attendant in emergency cases. Jagsir, was dumbstruck at the glacial attitude of his father.

The happy man who had a zest for life became a money minting machine. He would go for treatments early in the morning while the little boy was still sleeping. He would come back home, dress him up, take him to school and report for his job. He would pick him up, eat a hurried lunch and leave once again, to do the rest of the cases and come back late in the night. The cases never stopped coming, the calls never ceased for the animals never remained healthy throughout the year.

There was always a harried farmer, expecting a sudden recovery with a fervent plea to be acknowledged immediately. And the Doctor could not hold himself back. He found peace in work and yes, the money that came along was an added bonus. Work helped him suffice his grief and kept the emotions in check that otherwise took the better of him and made him morose and sulk all the more.

The growing distance between the father and son spoke volumes and a shrouded silence enveloped them day and night. The lack of love and attention had a devastating effect on the boy who suffered silently the loss of his mother and the nonexistent presence of his father.

Jagsir turned out to be a mediocre student, with no special aptitude for Sciences and Mathematics and not even for languages. Much to Doctor's dismay, he did not excel at anything. No matter how many extra tuitions he was enrolled into, with all the extra money that he got from the cases, but to no avail.

Despite his protests, he made him go for the IELTS test and got him admitted to a University in Berlin after paying a fortune. The fortune that he had amassed at the cost of alienating the loving nurturing relationship with his son. The money came handy and Jagsir fuming and fretting, boarded the flight to Doha from where he would change flights and then off to Berlin.

The father and son did not exchange a single word at the

Amritsar airport. And when the time had come to say goodbye, he hurriedly moved his trolley with a perfunctory "Bye, Daddy ji".

And the Doctor kept on looking, tracing his tiny form till it turned hazy, submerged in the crowd as he kept on standing, till he could see him no more.

He had come home and cried bitterly for the son who meant the world to him, for the son he had spent his entire youth caring for, for the son that was his very reason to survive. Jagsir never called him up until he took the initiative. Despite the lack of conversation between them he kept on sending him the money like a dutiful father. And the Doctor wondered where he went wrong! Was earning money for his only son a crime in itself? Was loving him so much an illusion? Did he not see the kind of sacrifices he made for him?

With an emptiness inside, he had returned to work and the very next month when he retired from the government service, he started his own clinic and it turned out to be a huge success.

After years of bitterness, things had improved. The father and son got on talking terms. The Doctor has accepted the changed equations and the entry of a gori daughter-in-law. He was in no state to complain. He merely complied with him and his life.

He removed his spectacles to wipe his moist eyes and began packing with a fervent zeal. After checking and rechecking items on his list he was left with a small packet. It weighed a little and looked very strange to the Doctor. The packet was given by one of Jagsir's friends. It came all the way from New Delhi, to be taken to Berlin.

The Doctor had called Jagsir to know the contents of the packet to which the boy gave evasive replies.

"Just pack it nicely in the bag. Inside the clothes. And

don't open it at all."

"But puttar, what is it? It's heavy and you know I am carrying lot of stuff with me."

But the son won't relent. The Doctor unpacked the Besan ladoos and the Aam ka achar and placed it on the kitchen shelf. How much Jagsir drooled over Besan ladoos?' the Doctor reminisced. Every time he missed functions at his school, he would come home bringing a box of Besan ladoos from his favourite shop to cheer him up.

And the boy would forget everything and happily gorge on the ladoos.

The Doctor thought of Rhea and Das and took the dabba and moved downstairs towards the clinic.

"Rhea beta, have ladoos. I brought for my son but there are weight issues. I cannot take them along. "

She smiled and picked up one.

"Das, you also have."

He grabbed two and stuffed in his mouth. They laughed seeing his fluffed cheeks engorged with ladoos which he was finding difficult to swallow.

"Dactar Sahib, didn't you want to take them all the way to Berlin?"

The Doctor smiled, "They have everything available there. But then these ladoos are special because they are from his favorite shop. There is an additional packet, the one you received, that had been heaped on me at the last moment. So, I have to take some of the things out because of weight restrictions."

"Oh yes! I remember. A strange looking guy delivered it to me."

"Rhea, keep smiling bacha! And I hope to see you back, the way you are now, all radiant and smiling. And never let people get the better of you or bog you down." He threw a sarcastic look at Das.

"Why are you looking at me like this?" Das felt victimized.

"Like what?"

"Like this, rolling your eyes in a bad way. Do you think I am a criminal?"

"Well, in your heart of hearts, you know what you are? We all know, what we have been doing? Isn't it? We all face the judgement day? Do I need to tell you that, Das? You are being watched all the time."

"Who is watching me? You have put the CCTV cameras in the clinic. I knew you would be watching the footage all the way in Berlin. I knew you would do something like this, Dactar sahib? U always treated me like a petty thief. And today you called me a criminal. Watch your words. Sometimes tables get turned. What if you end up being victimized someday? Being mistaken as a criminal."

"We all commit everyday acts of folly, although not crimes. I committed the folly of sending my son to a distant land."

He smiled at Das and patted him affectionately. "No one is calling you criminal. Stop assuming and taking everything in life so seriously. You need to give yourself some breathing space. And don't act foolish in my absence. Act mature. You are the man, in charge of this place."

"I am the man, yes I am the man!!" Das bloated with pride.

He looked around menacingly, territorially, displaying a certain candour, taking a round of the clinic, looking at the syringes, IV cannulas and the patient records with élan, like a lion marking its territory. But his enthusiasm soon fizzled out when he noticed that Rhea and Doctor got busy in the discussion of a case. And they took no notice of his new-found machoism.

"Das, where are the Rintose bottles we ordered from the

chemist shop?"

"It's with me. I am getting it Dactar Sahib." He shook his head, a tad disappointed and started opening the cartons.

"At the end of the day, I am just a worker bee. And he is the mother bee and Rhea is the queen bee" he smiled.

****

The next day, taxi came at the designated time and was parked in front of the clinic. The flight was at midnight so there was sufficient time as the Doctor checked all his bags before loading them in the car. Rhea and Das helped him and he hugged both of them and looked at the clinic board wistfully.

"So, here we are, at that juncture in life where I bid a temporary farewell to you guys. See you after six months. Make lot of money but do the right treatment and do not fleece the poor ones. And Das please desist any attempt to click pictures of anything living or non-living."

"You mean to say, I cannot even click pictures of the mange infested dogs to study the cases"

"We know the extent of your knowledge. Stop pretending! Rhea, you should take his phone at 9 am and give only at 5 pm so that he is not clicking unwanted pictures."

"This is a bias. If I am not using my phone for eight hours, Rhea di should also not use her phone at the same time."

"Arre, why? I am a Doctor, you are an attendant. And I don't click gandi pics of people and circulate on social media," she shot back.

"But I feel you are going to take revenge very soon. You will click a dirty picture of mine and put on social media. I had this dream last night where a picture of me, only in my VIP underwear was circulating on WhatsApp groups. But I don't mind, even if it comes true. In fact, I would love it. I have the physique of a model" he flicked his eyelids and shot a hand through his hair.

"Shut up, Das. Rhea, lock his phone, the first thing in the morning and give only when you have to leave."

"And what if I get important calls. People will feel bad if I don't answer their calls."

"No one ever calls you. You are always busy chatting with that vehla lot of your friends on WhatsApp."

Das started grumbling at this tightening of the noose around his neck.

"No, you cannot do this!"

"I can do everything. I am the owner of this clinic and you work for me. When I say, 'no phone allowed' I mean it."

"Why make separate rules for everyone. She should also not use the phone. This is the great Punjabi Bihari divide. This is a bias and I am going to call a press conference and I will make sure everyone knows what is being done to me. The Doctor is a Punjabi, so she can fiddle with her phone while she is working but the poor, helpless soul who is a Bihari is being denied the phone pleasure."

"What's phone pleasure?" Rhea guffawed.

"I cannot tell you that. It's a guy thing. I seek pleasure and solace out of my phone."

The driver got impatient and honked the car, "Are you going to Amritsar or should I leave without you?"

"Let me say bye to my family. Why are you getting so impatient?" Doctor shot back.

"We are family" Das spoke teary eyed.

"Yes, both of you are family now. In fact, the only people who really care about me."

They kept on waving till the taxi was out of sight.

"I can't believe he has gone for six months. I will miss Dactar Sahib." Das turned gloomy and sat on one of the tables meant for treatment of patients.

"Don't sit on that. It's already rickety. Your weight will do it no good." Rhea admonished him.

He sheepishly lifted himself up and started scrubbing the table clean.

His mind wafted down the memory lane, reminiscing the past. It's been seven years. He must be around eleven when he first came to Punjab to live with his sister who was working as a household help in the city. She introduced him to the Doctor. He needed an attendant to help him administer injections and Das fitted the bill. "How much the Doctor taught him?' From taking temperatures to putting injections he became an expert in his own eyes and a big help.

When the Doctor retired, Das started working in the clinic. He dreamt of having a home of his own and he has been saving money for the same. But no matter how much he saved it was not enough. And yet he carried on with a dogged determination to be independent enough to make a move out of his sister's home.

And how much the old man loved him? How he won't talk to him without attaching Bhenchod with his name. And somedays Das wondered if the word was a prefix to his name and he called himself 'Bhenchod Das'.

He started giggling, mumbling again and again 'Bhenchod Das! Bhenchod Das!

Rhea who was reading a book shot him an angry look, displeased at his ramblings and kept on reading.

The boy had been affected by Doctor's absence.

She stared hard at him and saw his bony frame and childish demeanor. Apart from the swanky phone that he owned there was nothing swanky about him.

She wished she could put him in school once again.

"Das you must be around sixteen! You should be in 10th class. I feel you are lagging behind."

"I am not sixteen any more. I am not going to disclose my real age to you beacause I want to be struck with sweet sixteen. And I took my 10th exams last year and I have passed also. I was enrolled in an open school. I am taking English classes now for IELTS exam and I am on my way to become a Doctor, Rhea di.I will go abroad and study."

"That sounds wonderful. But you cannot become a Doctor by working as an attendant in the Veterinary clinic. You need a degree from a recognized professional college to do that. I think you will make a great Doctor if you really make a sincere effort."

"Can I really become a Doctor some day, like you? Can I?" Das said the words slowly, soaking in the essence, taking pleasure out of the context of words.

She got up and picked up the Besan ladoos and handed them to him.

"Yes, we can be anything what we want to be. All we need is a focus, little sacrifices and lots of hard work. And if you are ready to do that you can achieve a lot. And these are for you. Chalo, time is up. I am leaving. You lock the clinic and go home."

She looked at her watch.

"I think he must have reached Amritsar. Should we call him up?

Das picked up a Besan ladoo and stuffed in his mouth as he nodded his head.

Rhea flipped open her phone and dialled doctors number.

* * *

8

THE RICKSHAW FIGHT

The Doctor picked up the phone instantaneously as if he was expecting this call.

"Hanji Rhea beta, I have reached. I am waiting in the lounge. Lot of time at my disposal."

"Wish you all the best for the journey. And don't worry about Das. I will handle him. I will confiscate his phone during the working hours so that he can play no hanky panky," she giggled.

After weeks of miserable existence, she could finally laugh it away. Life looked picture perfect with a job in hand and home front being tamed. With the Doctor being away she would be in charge of the clinic.

Her thoughts were interjected by the Doctor who started coughing.

"Doctor saab, are you not feeling well?"

"Rhea, there is something I wanted to talk to you about. I am worried. I feel uneasy. There is something not right."

"Everything is fine Doctor saab. You are undertaking international travel for the first time. And since you are meeting your son after a long time you are a little nervous. It will be fine. Take it easy."

"No Rhea, it's something else. I have a feeling that something very wrong is going to happen."

"Come on! Nothing wrong will come out of it. Stop worrying now. Chalo, I have to go home! Tc. Bye."

"Rhea, listen puttar. Something..."

But she had disconnected the call and moved towards the main street with a swing in her step. She felt good to be back in the clinic.

"Rickshaw, hello" she shouted but the diligent rickshaw wallah didn't look her way and moved on with a determination away from her.

She expressed disbelief at being ignored and lamented the state of affairs.

He didn't even look at me. I am pretty sure he heard me. The problem with this country is that people don't want to work at all. And no one was sitting in that rickshaw, still he chose not to stop by.

She shrugged and started walking towards the bazaar looking for a ride.

She tried calling Abhi, but as usual the phone was out of coverage area. She moved around leisurely partaking various aromas of the bazaar.

The clinic was located amidst the busy bazaar. A hub of movement at all times, it cheered her up to see the constant flurry of activity near her premises of work. The samosa wallah, the one who catered to them on regular basis asked her while frying the latest lot.

"Didi, samosa lelo. You didn't get your regular quota today."

Rhea waved her hand absentmindedly "Tomorrow bhaiya. I will take two plates" and she moved on.

She checked the time to realize that it had been twenty minutes, and she hadn't found a ride yet.

She wondered how time lost its essence with happiness

and precisely when you are doing something you really love. The days glided effortlessly while she was working, treating animals and injecting them with the required medicines. The same time that made her morose and sulk at home did not even make its presence felt when she was working in the clinic.

Life is all about learning to find your own happiness. I found mine in my work. And I feel so lucky I am able to do what I love the most in my life.

Her thoughts veered around the Doctor. She wondered why he was so anxious. He was trying to tell her something, but she had disconnected the call for she did not want to talk to him all the more.

The positive role the Doctor has played in the whole fiasco had thawed the difficult situation and she was getting more inclined towards him. She has started caring for him in a fatherly way and they have chatted so much in the past few days. She had helped him with the packing and shopping. She brought bangles, Punjabi juttis and suits for the gori daughter-in-law. She had developed a liking for her owner and felt loved and protected under his watchful gaze.

But on the other hand, she derided all these emotions. She didn't want to get overtly emotional about anything.

He is not my father. Not even close to him. He is just my employer and I need to maintain the requisite distance. I cannot get entangled in his life. That will take the focus away from my life.

She knew the Doctor was having a strained relationship with his son and was in constant search of solace. But for some reason she did not want to occupy the same position in his life as that of a daughter.

Let it be Das. He can make Das the object of his fatherly affections. Not me!

Her eyes welled up with tears thinking about the pitiable

state of the Doctor where he was missing his son day in and out rummaging through the old toys, torn books and all kinds of paraphernalia. She shook her head in disbelief.

I cannot do this to myself. Why am I getting sucked up into someone else's life? I cannot be pulled down by all this emotional mumbo jumbo.

But now, with the Doctor placed away, with the reduced physical proximity she can forget everything and concentrate on her life.

And finally, after an interminable wait she spotted another rickshaw devoid of any passengers. She gestured him to stop and asked for the fares.

"Model town jaana hai. How much?"

"Fifty rupaiyya."

"OMG! It's only twenty other guys take, and you are saying fifty. I am a daily traveller. Look at your nerve! You people see young, beautiful girls and you want to cheat them."

The rickshaw moved forward but she held onto the handle and stood resolutely in front of the tyre.

"Where are you going? You cannot go without dropping me home," she gritted her teeth in anticipation of a full-blown fight.

"Get aside. I will take fifty. And if you don't have the money, let me look for someone else."

"Okay! Thirty! Please maan jao!" she pleaded.

"Forty and that's it!" The bony framed rickshaw-puller lowered his count but would not relent sensing her desperation.

"You know I have to give half of the salary to my mother-in-law after all this drama. And if I will give half of the salary in paying the rickshaw fares where will I go? Tell me."

The man looked at his shabby clothes and then removed a small sachet from his shirt pocket. He poured some of the contents on his hand and looked at the girl in front of him who was looking immaculate in her bright orange salwar kurta and silver earrings.

After rubbing the powder on his hand for a long time, he deposited the same in his jowl and spoke in an incoherent manner.

"You have all the money in the world to buy flashy clothes, but you would not give ten rupees extra to a rickshaw wallah."

She felt embarrassed and fished out a fifty rupee note from her purse and handed it to him.

"Happy, now let's go."

He smiled, his teeth lined in a zig zag fashion which she found a little disconcerting as she looked away.

"Ruko, ruko. Let me clean the seat." He wriggled a sodden cloth from a corner of the rickshaw and cleaned it, clearing it of the invisible specks of dust yet making it wet in this process.

"Arre, it's all wet now. How will I sit?"

She looked at the watch. It was 6.30. Damn!!! She was getting impatient.

"It's okay. I can sit on the wet seat. Let's go."

"No, let me dry it. You cannot sit like this."

"I want to go home. I am getting late. It is fine. No issues."

"No, wait." He shrieked and ran away to a nearby shop to find a dry cloth to clean the seat.

"Take care of my rickshaw, Bhenji. I am coming." and off he ran away while she stood dumbfounded in charge of his precious commodity.

Bhenji, he called me Bhenji! Fool! I am not going to sit on this stupid rickshaw. But I gave him the money and if I leave and someone stole this thing what will the poor man do!!

So, she stood there waiting for the owner, fiddling with

her watch all the time growing more restless every moment.

She tried calling Abhi, but the phone would not connect.

Shit! Where is he? He could have picked me up or I could have walked home and reached by this time.

Her helplessness bordering despair was making her uneasy and it was difficult for her to contain herself at one place now. She kept on looking evasively in all directions hopping to catch a glimpse of the rickshaw owner but he was nowhere in sight.

Another hopeful contender of the ride came and stood beside her.

"Bhindi Bazar jaana. How much?"

"What the fuck!!!! Do I look like a rickshaw puller?

"You are standing next to it, sorry. But where is the guy? And by the way, girls can do everything these days. In the south, there are ladies driving rickshaws and autos ji."

"Whatever! I don't care, and this rickshaw is booked. Move now."

"How can you say this is booked? Is your name inscribed on it?" and the young lad got on the rickshaw and sat on it and smiled mischievously.

"Now, it's booked."

"Get down. This is my rickshaw." Rhea tied her dupatta on one side and took hold of one of his arm and started pulling him down.

"Why are you pulling me, girl? Leave my arm, look at the way you are behaving. You don't even look educated. Oye! Dekho logo, she is crazy. See, I am telling you for the last time to let go off my arm. If I did something and it touches here and there, you will say I tried to molest you."

"We will see what happens. First you get down, bhenchod! Get down. I booked that rickshaw."

"You don't even know how to talk with men. And don't you say all these cuss words. Didn't your parents teach you anything?"

By now a sizeable crowd had collected around the fighting parties.

People were giggling and getting entertained as Rhea kept on mouthing profanities pulling the guy but he steadfastly sat glued to the rickshaw defending the choicest of abuses.

The confused rickshaw puller shoved the melee of crowd and reached the venue unable to fathom the cause of fight.

"This is my rickshaw" Rhea was shouting.

"It's mine." the guy mouthed back in equal intensity matching her tenor.

"Shut up! It's mine. And you Bhajji get down. And you Bhenji take your money. My girlfriend planned an impromptu date, so I have to go and meet her. She called me up and is waiting for me. Sorry! Love comes first."

"You drop me at Bhindi bazaar first. ''

"You drop me at Model town''.

"You walk to Bhindi Bazaar and you walk to Model town because I am going to meet my sweetheart. Tata!"

And he peddled away in all his glory singing a filmy song, with moon eyes, without a care in the world.

"What the fuck!!!! He has a girlfriend. Of all the people in the world, he has a girlfriend. Unbelievable!'' Rhea blabbered.

"Hahaha…. He is a man and he can pleasure them, so he has the right to love any woman.''

"Did you say that? How rude. A decent lady… I mean a girl is standing in front of you and you are talking like an illiterate. No class.''

"Yeah! Look who is teaching me class. You, who says bhenchod with such grace that it warms the cockles of my heart. Wah! Wah! Girl power!!!!"

And the guy left her rooted in the spot wondering how come she was using the same cuss words used by the Doctor.

No, it can't be. Did I say that to him? OMG! It's the influence of the Doctor.

She buried her face in her hands when she heard the familiar voice of Das.

"Rhea di, Panga pe gya. I just got a call from Dactar sahib. He has been arrested at Amritsar International Airport on charges of drug smuggling.

"FUCK!!!!"

Rhea was flabbergasted at this new revelation.

"He did drugs. Damn!!! Why we never came to know he was a drug addict?"

"No, he did not. He only drank whiskey and some days Vodka, on special occasions. He would never do that." Das voiced his opinion.

"Then how can he be arrested for smuggling?" Rhea chewed her fingernails in exasperation. Damn! Das that packet. You know he was all jittery about the contents and he would not open it also."

"Yes, he removed Besan ladoos and Aam ka achhar to accommodate it."

"Das, that packet had drugs. OMG! Doctor was a carrier and he did not even know this."

"That packet was harmless. I don't believe it."

"How do you know, Das? Did you open it?" Rhea looked at him intently.

"No, not at all, I have this feeling… the gut feeling that packet was harmless." Das tried avoiding any eye contact as he said that.

"Whatever! How did you know he got arrested in the first place?

"He called me up and told me the same. He was crying, Rhea di. He is a strong man and he would never ever break down no matter how immense the strain is. And he was crying!"

Saying this Das started sobbing. She placed her hand on his head and tried comforting him.

"It's okay, Das. Things will be fine. Don't worry."

His sobs turned into wails and he sat on the ground, covering his face in his hands.

"Das, you cannot go on like this. Control yourself. We can talk to his son or we can talk to his relatives. They can hire a lawyer to bail him out."

But he would not relent. He would not keep on the charade anymore. He wailed and rolled on the ground and did weird serpentine motions all the while babbling, "Dactar Sahib come back. Someone bring my old man back."

Some people gathered around him to watch his antics.

"I will kill myself if something happens to him. Bring my annadaata back. I will never look at any girl with gandi nazar if he comes back. It's a promise, pakka wala."

The bazaar was in full swing with people out with their families relishing gol gappas, chat papri and various other delicacies. The shops were all decked up with the ill assortment of goods, the colorful paraphernalia displayed on the pavements made encroachments on the bylanes. A group of ruffians who were out their following a gaggle of girls now turned their attention towards Das.

Rhea stood embarrassed next to him, mortified by all the unwanted attention, she coaxed him to get up.

"If you want to cry, fine, but stop acting crazy. Do you want to summon the entire bazaar to tarnish Doctor's reputation? If people come to know that he is arrested on charges of drug smuggling no one will come to the clinic anymore."

He assimilated the poignant words and finally sat down, cowering his legs around him.

After being implored to come in the clinic he stood up and with weary steps moved inside the clinic.

"Das, I have to go home. It's late. You call up his family. Someone should go and look into this matter."

But he would not speak. He sat motionless in the chair like a zombie.

"Das, say something! Are you okay? I am going. I hope, you will be fine."

"I am going to Amritsar. I am catching a bus right now and I would rescue him."

"Don't worry, things would be sorted out. Once he explains that the package does not belong to him they would let him go, so stop acting crazy. Don't go, as they might arrest you for being an accomplice. And then someone will save the Doctor, but you will be in jail for the rest of your life."

"Rhea di, Let's go to Amritsar. Let's save him. The poor man is helpless out there. I tried calling his son, but he would not pick, and his relatives only have eyes on his property."

"Das, are you nuts! I cannot go to Amritsar. He has relatives in a village somewhere and they are family. They would help. Look at the time. It's 7 pm. I have to be home. Can you drop me home? We will think of something tomorrow morning."

He bit his lower lip and moved away from her. He looked

away frigidly and sat on the patient bed. And then he curled his legs and lied down submerged in thoughts of his own.

He had not seen his father for so many years. His father, who is dying a slow and painful, cancerous death and who, he knows is not going to survive. And then a vision of Doctor alights and glides before him. He is wearing white and he looks angelic as he beckons him to come and hold his hand.

"Noooooooo!!" Das shrieked.

"What happened?" Rhea who was still in a fix whether to leave him alone in the clinic, jolted and freaked out.

"The Doctor is dead. I just saw his soul. He was dressed in white and he beckoned me to hold his hand."

"They killed him to hush up the case. I saw his soul."

"No one gets killed in custody. People... well people don't die but sometimes... well sometimes I have read... somethings."

And she halted, morphing her own words to lessen the impact of the calamity that has fallen on the Doctor.

She looked at Das and they sealed an abstract pact, albeit, in glances only.

"Das, we cannot let him die out there! Can you hire a taxi? Let's go right now."

He jumped and fell on her feet clutching them with the same madness and anxiety he elicited at her home.

"You are a goddess, Rhea di!"

"Das, get up. What is with you? Why you have to prostrate yourself all the time to exhibit all those uncontrollable emotions?"

He got up, grinned and sprinted outside to get a taxi.

✳✳✳

9

MISSION TO SAVE THE DISILLUSIONED

Within fifteen minutes a Tata Nano stood at the door of the clinic.

As Rhea looked at the compact car with wonder and Das locked the clinic gate, she remarked at his promptness and his choice of vehicle.

"How come you did not get any other car?"

"This was the only one available at taxi stand."

"It looks battered. You think it will be safe to go in this." She took a few steps and inched closer to look at the skirmishes that pockmarked the beauty of the car entailing a tail of caution and courage.

The owner, a brusque, middle-aged Sardar alighted from the car and shot an accusing look at Rhea.

"Don't say anything about my Nano. This is a gift from Tata sahib."

"You mean he gifted it to you and you didn't buy it."

"Hehe, bholi Madam! Why will he gift me ji? I mean it's cheap. The cheapest in the market. Though personally I do not like this word. And the moment this car came in the market, I just bought it as there was no requirement of any loan from bank. My Nano, my pride."

"Whatever! Let's go. Why are we wasting time?"

"Nah ji nah! First tell me why you people are going to Amritsar. I want to know the reason. Is he your husband?" he looked at Das who blushed and started giggling.

"What the fuck, Sardar ji! You are the driver and we are paying you. Now fucking take us to Amritsar or I will take another taxi?"

"You are wearing chudda so it's an indication you are newly married. And he told me he is unmarried so definitely not your husband. Elopement!!! Che che! You are doing all this very bad Madam ji, very bad."

"You get lost. Das, find another taxi."

"I am calling the police right now. You shameless, immoral people, you are running to guru ki nagri and you want to defile the place with your dirty acts. I won't let you go to Amritsar Sahib. Let me call the police."

Rhea snatched his phone and pleaded.

"Sardar ji, it's a matter of life and death. The old Doctor is in custody and they will kill him if we did not go. I work in this clinic. Can you see the board? The Pet well clinic."

Later on, Das narrated the tale of sorrow and misfortune and Sardar ji got emotional and started whimpering.

"The son of a bitch made his own father a carrier. Shame! Shame! That father who gave him everything. Provided bread and butter and mayonnaise to the son who made his own father a carrier." He wiped his tears on his sleeve and now Das and the driver both weepy- eyed looked so much like perfect companions with shared insolence for the son and grief for the Doctor.

"If you have shared the sorrow, can we make a move? I have to come back also. My husband will kill me when he comes to know what I am doing."

"Chalo, chalo let's save the Doctor and let's name it

"Mission to save the dying Doctor." Sardar ji's eyes brightened up at the proclamation of the mission.

"Wait! First of all, this is no mission. You are the driver and you drop us and come back. Rest we will figure out."

Sardar ji turned glum and somber at this indignant refusal.

"Are you sure you don't need my help? I have contacts in Amritsar. I can help you bail him out." Sardar ji pleaded Rhea to make him a companion in this great life saving mission.

"I have never done anything worthwhile in my life. I have done everything wrong.I have cheated people in every business I ever started and now when I go to Gurudwara I am ashamed to be there. And when I started this taxi, I decided that I would take genuine fares from people but again my evil desire to fleece people got hold of me and I started charging exorbitant rates. I want to do something worthwhile, so my Guru can be proud of me. Please ji! Man jao!"

"Das, did you talk about how much money he is going to take from us?"

"He said he would take genuine rate only. And moreover, we are friends now." Das smiled and placed his arm warmly around Sardar ji giving his shoulders a tight squeeze.

"Haha!!!! You just went and called a taxi and you are friends with the cabby. You don't make friends instantaneously. Moreover, it's a temporary kind of arrangement. After we are back from Amritsar with the Doctor amongst us and pay him the money, you would forget him."

Sardar ji looked crossly at Das.

"You would forget me, Das! Really, but in your eyes, I see a long-lost friend. A friend for a life time. You cannot do this to me. We would be friends for the rest of our lives and forever and ever and we would bridge the great Punjabi Bihari divide you were talking about."

Sardar ji hugged Das and they got lost in the tight embrace while Rhea looked baffled at the new-found affection.

Das looked at her with imploring eyes but she would not budge.

"You are a driver. Don't take excesses and stick to your job. We don't need your help."

"I am a human first and then a driver. I am going to help a fellow Punjabi who has landed himself in soup for no fault of his. And if you have any problem go find another taxi, I am going."

Das prostrated himself on the ground and held on to his feet with all his might.

"No, you cannot go. You are part of the Mission to save the dying Doctor."

Sardar ji smiled and picked up the petite frame of Das from the ground and hugged him.

"No, you do not have to do this. Up my boy! If she does not want to make me a part of this mission, it's completely fine. At the end of the day it's all about the educated and uneducated divide. She is a Doctor, more intelligent than me, who did not even complete his schooling."

"Wow! Now you talk like Das. Super awesome! He sprinkled some of his essence on you. Yes, the great divide talk. I can see where it comes from."

"Arre, I did not do anything. Do not look at me like this! I did not say anything to him. These are his original words." Das shot back.

Sardar ji, hung his head low and covered his eyes with his hands looking all the more sombre and disconcerted.

"Well it's okay Das, I am going. Chal meri Nano, let's go home. To a place where people understand us. Where you are not just valued as a mere driver, but your worth is judged more as a friend. Where people do not value you only for the degrees you hold but actually see your worth as a person. By the way, I wanted to tell you that though I look younger, I am much married and have two kids. A girl and a boy. I call them Chunnu and Munnu affectionately. I am a respected and a much-married man and satisfied with my wife. So, you don't have to be afraid of me, Madam ji."

Rhea nodded her head in disapproval and murmured something about people in Pathankot being so dramatic.

"You are generous, Sardar ji. But some people who are standing here have their hearts turned into stone. So, don't bother." Das gazed at Rhea, albeit mournfully.

"Wait" Rhea shrieked as she saw Sardar ji trying to get into his Nano while Das, with his lithe frame making every attempt to obstruct his way.

Now both Das and driver looked at her with a curious look.

"Fine, you can chip in, Sardar ji but we should change the name of the mission. It should be "Mission to save the disillusioned."

"What is the meaning of disillusioned?" Das inquired

"Das, you need to complete your education, or you will keep on hugging people's feet for the rest of your lives."

He grumbled about life not being fair and the educated restricting the knowledge to themselves.

"So, we are all set to go. Driver, you have to tell me how much you are going to charge us. I do not like to be fleeced by taxi drivers."

"Kindly call me Sardar ji. And do not call me a taxi driver. I might overcharge people at my whims and fancies, but I never harbour any ill will for them. That is why people call me by the name of 'Sardar with the golden heart'."

"Can you please stop revelling in self-praise and tell me how much you are going to charge? At the end of the day you are a cab driver. And by the way, earlier you said you have never done a single good deed and now you are all going gaga about yourself."

"I don't like to tell people about my good deeds, so I let them think that I am not doing anything for society at all. And when I actually tell them all that I have done they are shell-shocked to hear my good deeds. So, they know how self-effacing I am."

"Well, yes that's interesting. Being modest and having no qualms about contradicting self."

"Isn't it a good idea? You should try the same way. The kind of look they have in their eyes when they see you doing amazing stuff. It's priceless!"

Das who went back to clinic emerged out with a sling bag and sat next to Rhea.

"Das, you cannot sit with me, noooo!!!" Rhea fumed.

"Come in the front, Das." Sardar ji promptly tried to settle the conflict.

"No, I want to sit with Rhea di."

"No, I don't want this scoundrel sitting with me, touching and feeling me up."

"If you want this mission to progress please settle down." Sardar ji affirmed.

"Mission to save the disillusioned." Rhea proudly proclaimed.

"Das, mere bache. Let madam ji be comfy. You come in the front."

"I don't want to sit in front. I get scared of moving things."

"What moving things? My foot! This car will start moving in a short while. You are disgusting, Das. Sit here. I will sit in the front seat, Sardar ji."

Sardar ji smiled as he felt pleased at this new development.

"Aa jao, aa jao. I love it when intelligent people sit besides me.

"And you toh ji are a Doctor. So, intelligent. No lady sat on the front seat ever, except for my wife and my girlfriend."

Sardar ji beamed with pride at Rhea occupying a place of pride in his car.

"You have a girlfriend and a wife. You surely are a man with a big heart. I mean golden heart and your sheen is blinding my eyes. Too much of gold dust falling in chunks here and there." Rhea chuckled.

"How did you manage both? Isn't it tough?" Das looked bewildered.

"It is double the pleasure and doubles the fun." Sardar ji winked at Das who snickered.

"Sardar ji, please! More driving and less talking. And you can later discuss with Das about your wife and your love interest. And since, you are not telling me how much money you will take I would pay you what I feel is right."

Rhea fidgeted with her phone. She checked the incoming calls to see if Abhi called up. And she wondered if she should call him up and tell her the impromptu plan that erupted in her mind.

What impact this journey will have on her marriage, she was yet to fathom?

"Madam ji, I think you should call" Sardar ji prompted unsolicited advice when he saw her toying with the phone.

"Uncle, drive the car and please stop looking at me every

other minute. You are making me conscious."

Sardar ji recoiled in horror at bluntness of her words. He flinched, "I am calling you Madam ji and you are calling me uncle. Lo ji, I will call you aunty. How does that sound now?"

Das rolled over the back seat in laughter and gave a loud applause, "Wah! wah! sardar ji. That's what they call, paying back in the same coin."

Rhea looked at him angrily and snarled, "You look very happy, Das. Where's the empathy gone? Try to find out where they have taken doctor saab? We need to meet him first."

Das sobered himself up and immediately dialled Doctor's number.

Meanwhile, Sardar ji again motivated Rhea to call, "You make that call. Lot many times when we don't let those words tumble out of the recesses of our minds, a gap is left. Don't do that to your marriage. I know you are thinking about your husband. Tell him where you are going, or it will create a wedge and you won't be able to fill it up with explanations because it would be too late."

She mustered up the courage and called up Abhi and explained him the entire situation. Though she could hear him shout and roar at the other end of the phone she disconnected the call telling him she will be home as soon as possible. Only she herself did not know how soon will be soon.

"Das, did you connect that call?"

"It's switched off, Rhea di. "

"Damn! We need to find the whereabouts. We have to tell him, we are there for him. He looked so uneasy in the morning as if he had the premonition that something bad was going to happen."

She closed her eyes, her mind a whirlpool of emotions.

What am I getting into? This is not me. How come I am getting entangled into all this?

"We should go to the airport and find out the exact story. And we can come to know where they took him to. We need to be strong in front of him. We need to tell him to stick to the point that he knew nothing about the contents. The police might make him confess but he is just a carrier. He should not become the sacrificial lamb." Sardar ji spoke in a cool and calm tone.

"Sardar ji, that's clarity of mind. You are quite intuitive."

"Thanks! Sardar ji is better. Please don't call me uncle. It feels kind of odd when people call you uncle. It gives me a feeling, I am getting old when I am very young at heart. Even my girlfriend calls me uncle sometimes. I don't like it at all."

She looked at him intently but then she smiled and nodded. "Okay, done. By the way how old are you uncle, I mean Sardar ji? How do you manage to stay so agile and fit? You must share your secret with me.

"Yes, definitely. I can share all my secrets with you, if you plan to take on a handsome and caring boy friend, someone like me!"

"Well, I am just married. So, I think I would let it go. Perhaps later when I am bored of my marriage, you can give me ideas."

"Sure, anytime." He grinned, and Rhea reciprocated it with smile.

He is not that bad, anyway. Deep down he is kind and gentle. I hope he turns out to be a good help in finding the Doctor.

Meanwhile, oblivious to everything Das sprawled on the back seat and snoozed off.

"He wanted the back seat because he wanted to sleep. Such a drama he is! What can you expect from him? He is so young and immature. Sardar ji, would you come back after dropping us at the airport?"

Rhea sounded worried at the prospects of the impending ordeal of tracing the Doctor. She wondered if with Das in her tow she would be able to manage anything concrete.

"Who says that? I won't. I will be with you till I bring you back safely to Pathankot. After all you are our daughter- in-law. How can I leave you alone there? This Bihari kid doesn't even know what to do and you are banking on him. Look how peacefully he is sleeping without any worry in the world."

"Thanks. I am sorry for being curt. I was just so confused and worried but now it makes sense. We have to get the Doctor out."

By the time, they reached airport it was almost midnight. Rhea was exhausted but there was no time to rest.

"Das, wake up you idiot!!! We have reached the airport."

But he won't budge and seemed to be in a deep slumber, smiling as he transcended into those beautiful dreams holding Rhea close to him.

"Rhea di, I love you!" He was mumbling incoherently and passionately.

"Rhea, meri Rhea!"

She took a water bottle and sloshed some water on the sleeping figure of Das with a sense of exasperation uncalled for.

"What happened? Tsunami! Tsunami!"

"Das we are at the airport. Pick yourself up and let's make a move. We are here on a mission. Seems you forgot all that."

He got up rubbing his eyes and looked around amazed.

"I am at the airport. I have never been to an airport. I want to see the aeroplane, Rhea di."

"Shut up! We are not here to see the aeroplanes. We have

to find the whereabouts of the Doctor."

"By the way, Das, you were mentioning Madam ji's name again and again. What were you saying? I ……Rhea. What was that?" Sardar ji winked at him and poked him gently in his chest.

"Nothing, Sardar ji. He is crazy. Chalo, chalo, let's go.''

"Nahi I heard it with my own ears ji. Tell me Das what you were saying. I …. Rhea. I hate Rhea di nah. I know you don't like her at all." And he held on to his wobbling tummy and started giggling.

"This is no time for jokes, Sardar ji. Please let's go." Rhea fumed.

"One more thing, why are you calling me Sardar ji again and again."

"You only said, don't call me uncle. Call me Sardar ji."

That's right. But call me something else."

"Driver bhajji sounds fine. Is it okay?"

"Aree, what bhajji. I would like to be called, Tony. That's my nick name. My girlfriend calls me Tony. Though you are more beautiful than my girlfriend but alas not my girlfriend, you can still call me Tony." Sardar ji smiled giddily at her.

"Hold your tongue, Sardar ji. You cannot take a girl that is already taken. She has a suitor who is here to do anything for her. So, mind your language." Das fished out a pocket knife from the deep recesses of his worn-out jeans.

He brandished the measly looking knife towards the tall and muscular Sardar who immediately retaliated by getting a hockey stick from the car.

"Aa gal aa. Theek aa pher!"

"Yehi baat hai Sardar ji. Aao dekh lete hain kisme kitna hai dum. Today a Punjabi brother stabbed a Bihari lad by casting an evil eye on his love. I am even ashamed to call you my friend.

166

When I was sleeping peacefully at the back seat you were doing ishqbaazi with my would-be wife. The love of my life. Shame on you, Tony Singh!"

"And no shame on you, Bihari. You, who is hellbent on destroying marriage of a beautiful girl. Though I agree, she is more charming than my girlfriend, I do not have ill feelings for her like you have. I toh have two, two ji. You don't even have one. Look who's talking!"

"Are you sure, you don't have any feelings for Rhea di."

"Nah ji nah. She is a pious soul. She is roaming with two strange men in a city she knows nothing about, at a time when no decent girl would come out of the house. It definitely requires a lot of courage and stupidity to do such daring. And even her husband was shouting at her."

"He was!!!! REALLY. That's awesome! Sardar ji, that's great news."

"What the fuck!!!!! Shut up both of you. What shameless, amorous creatures you both are? I am going on my own, inside the airport and you both keep on debating this wife and girlfriend issue. I am married and you both are idiots!" Rhea stomped away

"Ruko ji, Madam ji. You can call me Tony Singh or simple Tony, or you can only call me T." Sardar ji blurted out.

"T like a tea pot, or T like a tube light or T for tatti, chhee chhee." Das guffawed.

"My girlfriend calls me T someday. Those days when I roam in her house only in my T-shirt. Those days when she hides my trousers and my panties."

"Well, Tony Singh you call them undies. It's the girls who wear panties."

"Aho ji, same to same. Ki fark penda hai."

Sardar ji hugged Das as both of them laughed out loud.

"Punjabi, Bihari bhai bhai. No fight now. It is worthless. Whom are we fighting for? A girl who is much married and not even a virgin anymore."

"She is a virgin. I know that. I know she has not slept with her husband yet. I have proof.'' Das whispered.

"I think we should not get into details here. We will keep this topic open for discussion after we get back to Pathankot. Right now, we have to help the Doctor. We have to get the girl home. Look at the trust she reposed in us by coming all the way with two strange men. Not many have the courage to do what she is doing. Let us respect her conviction and not sully her by talking nonsense about her."

Das nodded his head.

"Okay, I agree. Not fair on our part. Let's focus on the Doctor."

"Now that's like a man."

"I am a man, Tony Sardar. You want proof!"

****

As they entered the edifice of the airport, Das was wonderstruck. He looked at the huge infrastructure and was gobsmacked. Sardar ji had to literally drag him away from kissing a wall that looked so esoteric to Das with the life size murals.

"Where are you going? Show me the tickets." The guard stopped them at the entrance.

"I want to go to 'Kanneda' but I don't have a ticket. Can you smuggle me somehow? I have a cousin who will look after me. Just put me inside with the luggage." Sardar ji blurted out and started laughing but the joke was not taken in a lighter vein.

"Show me the tickets." He repeated angrily this time.

"No, we are not going anywhere. There was an arrest at the airport few hours ago. We need to know more about it." Rhea hurriedly explained the scenario.

"Yes, there was! Lot of commotion but I don't know much. You have to see the head and now please back off. I have to let the passengers in. Please go away. It's rush hour. Give space to other people. You are blocking the way."

"Sir, this is his son. He is mentally challenged. We don't know what he will do if we don't come to know about the whereabouts of his father." Rhea winked at Das.

"What do you mean by mentally challenged? And where is Doctor's son? Where?" Das looked here and there and wondered what gibberish she was babbling.

Rhea looked at Das and winked again and again. He smiled shyly and giggled.

"She is giving me signals. I knew she is in love with me."

"Das, Das the feet. Go, damn! Do that thing you idiot!" She whispered.

And finally, what seemed to Rhea like an eternity Das got the clue.

He prostrated himself on the ground and held on to guard's feet all the while clutching and wailing.

"My dada, dada. He has been arrested. Bring him back or I will die."

"Arre take him away. Leave my feet." The guard non-plussed at the suddenness of his actions.

"See I told you he is mentally challenged. Last night he held on to my feet and threw me on the ground and tried stuffing chilies in my mouth. He has the power of ten elephants." Sardar ji chimed in.

"Let me go. Okay, I will let you in! You can meet the

manager on duty." The guard tried to shove a reluctant Das away.

This was a clue and Rhea winked at Das to let him go.

But he mistook the gesture and held onto his feet tighter and the poor guard went wobbly and fell on the ground. And he kept on perfecting the grip wailing all the more.

"Das, you are overdoing it. Stop now! "Rhea hissed in his ears imploring him to let go off guard's feet.

But he won't listen. He kept on with his grip and made it firm and started shouting at the pitch of his voice.

"Bring back my dada!!!! My dada."

No matter how much Rhea and Sardar ji tried, Das won't relent. He kept on mouthing invectives and held on to the security personal as if he was under a spell and acted like a possessed man.

Several men in uniform appeared and pulled him away.

Now there was no need to escape as they were rounded up and ushered to the office of the airport manager.

There is something wrong with Das. I realized, the first day I met him. If he is asked to act he gets under the skin of the character and does it very well. In fact, extraordinarily well. No, he gets absorbed in the character and forgets who he really is! Here we are rounded up like petty thieves, people are looking at us as if we are criminals but he is grinning from ear to ear. Stupid Das!!!! Can I kill him right now? I want to poison him. No, I want to asphyxiate him to a slow death.

"What is all this? Who are you people and why are you creating a ruckus at the airport? You can be arrested for creating a nuisance. It is an offence and you can be in jail for a few months. Do you know that?" Thundered the manager.

"We wanted to meet you, sir." Rhea mumbled.

"This is the way to meet! You molested our person on

duty. I will charge this nincompoop for roughing him up. "

Das moves closer to Rhea nudging her, "What's nincompoop?"

"An idiot! Das. They are saying, you are an idiot." She smiled with a maniacal gleam in her eyes.

Yes, it's proved. Das is indeed an idiot. I knew, I was right somewhere. He has more brawns and less of brains. Infact he has bovine brain in human cranium.

Das looked at her suspiciously, "Why are you smiling? You are definitely getting some happiness out of this word… Nik poop."

"Poop is potty. He is calling you something similar to that."

Das ignored her. Recovered from his mad frenzy, he sat with his eyes closed with perfunctory calm hovering on his head. His hair in a dishevelled state, his clothes torn by the subsequent push and pull, he balanced himself on the chair with legs folded, looking like the perfect caricature of a baba.

"Madam ji, he looks like a saint. Saint Das." Sardar ji guffawed. But realizing that no one laughed, he controlled his emotions sensing the complexity of the situation.

"Sir, I am a Veterinary Doctor. A few hours back a fellow Vet was arrested on charges of drug smuggling. He is innocent. We are here to get more information about him. Please tell me, where is he? It's a matter of life and death. Please tell us and we would leave."

All of them looked at the in-charge with sorrowful eyes to elicit a favourable response.

"Look Doctor, your friend was carrying heroin in a packet that was hidden cleverly in his bag. But we have sniffer dogs who can trace it very efficiently. The government is in full swing these days to arrest the drug peddlers. I know he was just a carrier, but he will not get bail."

"No, don't say that. We will save him." Rhea fumbled.

"What is there to save missy? You cannot save him now. It is too late."

"Noooooo. He is not a drug trafficker. He did not even know what was in the packet." Rhea waved her hands frantically.

"Damn it! He is innocent."

"Madam ji, calm down. We will find a way out."

"No, Sardar ji. This is a big white lie. Someone hatched this plan with pure perfection and instigated the old man to carry it and he became a pawn in all this. They will kill him." Rhea was struggling to breathe. Her head was a vortex of emotions as she pictured the Doctor behind bars for the rest of his life.

"Bring water for her." The manager issued the instructions.

"Sit down and listen to me. I think there is only one way to save him, though I am not sure. If the person who gave him the packet testifies that he gave it to him while the receiver was unaware of the contents, he might escape. But I don't think this is possible. Don't get your hands dirty in all this shoddy business. You will all be wrapped up as well."

"You have to tell us where he is! We want to see him once." Rhea folded her hands as her eyes welled up with tears.

"He is in custody of Narcotics department. They have an office in central Amritsar. But it's too late now. Go in the morning. I hope they let you meet him once."

"We need an address."

After making several phone calls, he wrote an address on a paper. "

"They have holed him up at this unusual place for one night for he was not well, and they did not want anything to happen to him on their premises. I have been told that they will be taking him to Delhi in a day or two. A lot of drug smugglers have consumed poison in their custody so this time they are taking precautions and they have put him in a place away from media spotlight. There is meagre security and no police paraphernalia guarding him. Try your luck. All the best and just leave."

"Well, can I see an aeroplane up, close and personal? From inside also. I have only seen tiny ones in the sky." Das was unable to control the flurry of excitement in his voice. He looked mesmerized at the glass encased office from where he could see the airplanes parked in a line. He stood transfixed for a while and placed both his hands on the glasss and touched the bridge of his nose and then closed his eyes and touched his cheek to the cool surface.

"Do you have a boarding pass?"

"What's a boarding pass?"

"Son, you need a boarding pass to get on the flight. This is not a fucking toy shop where you can run and scurry for entertainment. We run an airport and it's serious business and now get lost and don't bother us with all your dramatics."

"How mean! I am never coming to this damn airport again without a ticket in hand." Das felt a surge of determination run through him.

They came out of the airport around 2 am.

"We need to rest and eat something." Said Sardar ji but no one was listening.

"Rhea di, how big is an aeroplane from inside?"

A flight departed and Das clapped his hands in glee and ricocheted up and down in excitement.

"Aeroplane! Aeroplane!! Look up, up in the sky."

"See Rhea di, plane. Sardar ji, plane. Wo dekho it's so big.

How majestic! Someday, I will sit in this same plane and go all the way to Samastipur."

"You need an airport for the flight to land. First build an airport in Samastipur and then you can fly planes" Sardar ji bantered.

And Das stood there watching in awe and wonder as the plane ascended to heights and off it went as it eloped somewhere into distant destinations.

Sardar ji procured some packets of biscuits which all of them devoured hungrily. Then all three of them dozed off in the car for a few hours.

They woke up bleary-eyed, exhausted and tried to find the given address.

They located the place, which was in one of the posh localities of Amritsar. A solitary guard resting on a rickety stool was slurping his early morning tea. He saw them alight from the car with an uninterested glance.

"Hanji, bolo whom do you want to meet?"

"We want to meet a Veterinary Doctor who was arrested last night from the airport on charges of drug smuggling?"

"Are you family? Who gave you the address?"

"Yes, we are family. I am his niece, and he is the mentally challenged son, and he is the personal butler. Your senior gave us the address. We have direct links with the SSP. Here, talk to him on phone." Rhea controlled her nervous demeanor and tried to appear nonchalant.

Sardar ji performed a little curtsy and smiled cherubically all the while.

"What's mentally challenged? Why are you making me mentally challenged again and again? Say I am mentally intelligent." Das sounded hurt at being relegated to something that sounded inferior. Yes, I do like challenges, but I want something appropriate for me."

"Das, that's just for sympathy sake. And when I say mentally challenged it means that you are actually very intelligent from inside, but you act little funny from outside."

He perked up at Rhea's explanation.

"Intelligent inside and funny outside. So, you have to act really funny to show them our desperation."

The guard sensed something fishy and went close to the troika trying to listen to their talks in a hush hush manner.

"Ahem...well nothing, we are just discussing."

"I have also come to hear what you are discussing." The guard grinned to reveal a missing tooth and stood resolutely in their midst disrupting their intimate discussion.

"Yes, they brought him last night. He has been howling all night. The guard on night duty told me about him. You want to see him one last time before they take him away to Delhi. Do you? Do you have any heroin or cocaine or anything substantial? I am ready to let you meet him if you give me a little fix." And he winked at Rhea with an expectant sigh.

"We are not drug dealers. I am a Doctor. How can you even think about that?"

"Oh yes! They all say that. No one wants to deal in drugs. But the lure of money is such that you get hooked to it. The easy money and you are ready to transport the small packet anywhere for you don't know the consequences that will follow. And nowadays they are choosing people like doctors and engineers to do their dirty stuff. Where has our country landed!"

"So, you have no drugs. Not even this much." He brought his fingers closer and formed them into an arc, squeezing them further together.

"No, not even this much."

"Well, I don't accept money. I have my own standards. You look well-endowed though." He looked at Rhea with a wistful glance, moving his eyes up and down.

"Can we have an hour in my make shift room? Then you can meet your uncle for 15 minutes. What say? And he smiled the same toothy grin.

Before Rhea could make out anything, Sardar ji grabbed him by collar and started shaking him vigorously.

"You want to meet our girl in the room, bastard! Meet me in the room and tell me."

"Arre Sardar ji! Maybe he wants to talk something in private. So, what! I am a brave girl. I will go to his room and listen to what he has to say."

" She is ready. Leave me now." The guard tried extricating himself from the firm grip of Sardar ji.

"Oh! Madam ji, you are not understanding. Going into the room is not talking. It's that! Are you understanding what I am trying to say?"

"What... that? Sardar ji you think too much. He will let us meet! I will go and come, like this. Chill karo!" Rhea snapped her fingers to prove the agility of her actions.

"Hai rabba! Madam ji, you are bholi very much. He is taking you into his room!!"

Sardar ji let the guard go and clasped his head in both hands.

Das started sobbing, "Rhea di, you are ready to go to his room. Then what is wrong with me. Tell me! Bias bias. Punjabis always do this with Biharis. I knew that."

"Shut up! You both are idiots. I will go to his room and listen to what he has to say. Maybe it's something he doesn't want to tell you guys. I don't understand what is the problem with you guys?"

The guard was all set with the proposition being sealed.

"Chalo, let's go. I have a lot to tell you." And he winked at Sardar ji and Das who stood defeated at their inability to deflect Rhea who was oblivious to the ulterior motives of the guard.

"He wants to do ...that with you."

"Explain that or I am going."

"No, I can't say. I feel ashamed to say that in front of you. Das you say what 'that' is?"

Rhea looked at Das, who now shifted from one foot to another uncomfortably.

"No, I don't want to spoil my equation with Rhea di. I am not saying anything. Otherwise she will say I am the dirty one."

"Das, we don't have any equation. We never had in the first place. Now if you don't speak up, I am going."

"Jaldi karo, I am dying waiting while you talk nonsense. India is a democracy and when she is ready to do 'that' so what's the problem. It's twenty first century and look how intelligent, smart and bold girls we have who make their own choices. I am proud of you."

Rhea smiled and bowed her head "Yes, very true. Girls over- think and over analyze. I mean I actually don't waste my time thinking too much over these things. I believe in the act. Our actions should speak for ourselves and that is what matters."

"Okay enough! Listen Madam ji. He wants to do hanky panky with you. Do you get it now?"

"What hanky panky? What you want to do with me?" she narrowed her eyes and looked at the guard with amused interest now.

Sardar ji tip toed close to Rhea and finally broke the ice,

"He wants to do sex with you Madam ji. That's why he is taking you into his room."

"What the fuck! You son of a bitch, you want to fuck me!!!"

The guard squirmed at seeing Rhea transform into Jhansi Ki Rani now.

"It's okay, if you don't want to do the full thing. You just lift your shirt and let me fondle the breasts and a little sucking here and there. That will do. I am a simple man and I am happy with little pleasures of life." He smiled in all his earnestness.

"Saale ruk jaa!" Rhea removed one of her slippers and held it upright in her hand. "You wait there! I am coming to get you."

The guard sensed a change of heart and tried making a hasty retreat.

"Arre, I was just joking. You took it seriously. You should not think much about what other people say. I was just playing with the words. You don't have to do anything at all."

"Das, Sardaji hold him. Don't let him go away."

They shook away their melancholies and got into action at her prompt instructions. They caught the guard, one from each arm and held on to him firmly.

She swooped on to the culprit and started raining blows. She was tired and hungry and yet she sourced out that last drop of energy to avenge her intact honor. What made her so angry and agitated that she started punching and kicking the guard with ferocity that both the men trembled in horror?

"Rhea di, don't kill him now. He is apologizing. We don't want to share the prison with Doctor for the rest of our lives."

To Das, she looked like a Devi in all her glory trying to assuage the pride by killing the perpetrator.

Sardar ji came to guard's rescue as well.

"Let it go, Madam ji. He had enough of his share. He won't

even look at a girl now."

But she won't slow down. She continued punching and kicking him with all her might. And when her arms and legs started aching she finally mellowed down.

Exasperated by the whole scenario, she moved away from the men and plonked herself on the nearby lawn.

Das and Sardar ji came running after her.

"Are you okay, Rhea di? That was sound beating you gave him. What happened? I have never seen you so angry."

"Why it all trickles down to something so basic? Why he wanted to get physical with me for letting us meet the Doctor. Why at the end of the day you are just reduced to a mere female form to be exploited? Why he did not see that I was a qualified Doctor? All he saw were my physical traits. What's the whole point of being a woman when you will always be booed and jeered by people, becoming a victim of their unassuaged physical desires?"

"Don't get emotional and worked up. You will find people like him everywhere. Be discernible yet be the way you want to be. You are one intelligent girl and remember we have a mission." Sardar ji tried to close the sensitive topic in a hurry.

"Mission to save the innocent." Das blurted.

"You are also one of the lot! Exploiter of womanhood."

"What did I do now? I apologized for the pictures. And how can you compare me with him? He wanted to take you in his room and you never gave me a similar chance. Bias, bias!"

"Shut up Das! Madam ji let's go and forget all this. He is taking us to meet the Doctor."

"Das, you don't walk besides me. You walk behind me." She gave him a little shove.

"Why should I walk behind you? I want to walk in front."

"No, you go back to Samastipur. You are an exploiter. I hate exploiters."

Sardar ji jumped in the fray and placed himself between them.

"Madam ji, in front, myself in centre and Das at the back. That way the exploited and the exploiter don't see each other."

Now let's go and meet the Doctor.

"Why should I walk behind both of you? You both are Punjabis and I am a Bihari. Odd one out. You gang up against me and make me walk at the end. At the bottom of the line. Bias bias! How wrong this is?

"Are we running a race where the winner will get a gold medal? Don't lose the essence of this mission. The Doctor is languishing in a room and they are taking him to Delhi very soon. And then he will be gone forever. Quick, we have just fifteen minutes."

10

MEETING THE DOCTOR

"We have to be strong in front of the Doctor. Das, you cannot cry and crib in front of him. We have to uplift his morale despite the gravity of the charges." Rhea instructed them and went away leaving them at the entrance.

"Where are you going?" Das called out.

"Wait for me here. Do not move an inch. I will be back soon. I want to meet him first. Later on, I will call you guys." Rhea instructed.

"For that you need to say, Statue!" Das tattled.

"What? Neither you are a kid, nor are we playing some kind of game!"

"Then I am moving here and there." Das started hopping on one leg.

"Damn! statue!" She pointed a finger at him and he stood still for that particular moment.

He appeared frozen with his one hand pointing towards Sardar ji and other hanging limpidly on one side. He wobbled his eyes and stood like a mannequin affixed at a place waiting to be placed on a pedestal for some public viewing.

Sardar ji looked at him with an amused expression and poked a finger in his chest.

"What are you doing? It hurts."

"You cannot complain. You are a statue. I can touch a statue anywhere."

"No, you cannot. Just because they stand still and don't choose to hit back doesn't mean they are less human then you and me. They stand the test of time and are witness to the fate and only if they could talk, they could narrate stories of an era gone by with such an élan. Yes, they have feelings, but they choose not to elicit them. They hide their true color and assemble in whatever color and attire we choose to dress them up in. Statues have feelings. It's only that you and I cannot see through the inner recesses of their heart."

Sardar ji smiled and sat down on an empty chair.

"How thoughtful and insightful! You should be a literature student. What are you doing here, injecting animals all the time? You should put your mind elsewhere. In writing and poetry. We can hire someone who can do the part with the pen. You just have to narrate, and he will write it down.

"Please say 'statue' again so I can move."

"Statue" Sardar ji clapped his hands as Das did an impromptu dance.

"You are full entertainment, Das.

He smiled" I am glad you like my company, Tony Singh. We will be friends forever. You and me, Bihari and Punjabi and we will become a lethal combo. And people will envy our friendship.

"Amen!"

"Why can't we kidnap Doctor from this place before they leave for Delhi?"

"No, we cannot do that."

"Yes, we can. Rhea di has beaten the guard so badly that he can hardly walk. Look, he is limping. We can tie him with a rope and escape with the Doctor and no one will know."

"I don't want to live the rest of my life like a fugitive. So please don't make me part of this wild plan. You can go ahead if Madam ji says yes." Sardar ji got a little away from Das in measured steps so as to put some physical distance between them as if his thoughts were infectious.

"Or we can kill the guard and put the body in the back seat of Nano and dump it in some river, likewise no one will know anything happened."

Sardar ji repulsed and looked at Das in horror, "You have a criminal bent of mind. Did anyone tell you that? And by the way you cannot defile my Nano, no way. You take the body in a bus, anywhere you like."

"Lol, Sardar ji, you are funny. You think I will take the body in a bus and won't be caught? No, they always take bodies in the boot of cars."

"They wrap them nicely and tie them with a rope and then two people take the car in wilderness or near a water body and plop. Off goes the body."

"Das you are actually mentally incompetent. Madam ji is right. Things do not happen in the sane world like this. Grow up. Those are movies. In real life if you kill people you will end up spending the rest of life in jail or being chased if you are not caught. So, come out of your wild fantasies."

Rhea emerged from a long corridor and came running to them.

"The Doctor is fine, and he wants to see you, Das. Come hurry up."

Das followed Rhea while Sardar ji kept on standing at the same spot lost in his thoughts. She came back to fetch him.

"What is wrong with you, Tony ji? You came all the way from Pathankot to help him. Isn't it? Now you don't even care to meet him."

"I am comfortable here. He does not know me. I am little scared to meet strangers." Sardar ji was still under shock of being an accomplice to an imaginative crime perfectly caricatured by Das.

"OMG! Since when have you become such an introvert? You have to come. I told him about you. He wants to see you also."

"I had a change of heart. I realized it's uncomfortable meeting new people."

"Unfortunately, the realization has come too late. You are into this along with us. Don't act so coy. We are not marrying you off to him. He is feeling very low. You are the mature one amongst us, so go and talk to him. Just say a few nice lines and he will feel good about the same."

Sardar ji relented and followed Rhea through a mish mash of rooms and reached the end of the corridor where Das was lost in embracing the Doctor and crying petulantly.

"Das, I told you, no hysterics. What are you doing? Stop it, you are making him too emotional."

Rhea tried to get Das away from Doctor but no matter how much she pulled, he spooled his bony frame adroitly around him.

"Das, leave me. I cannot breathe." The Doctor implored but he clutched on to him with a firmness and a grasp that kept on growing tighter.

"Das, let me go you idiot! If they don't kill me, you will definitely, by suffocating me. Rhea, do something. Get him away from me."

"Let him go. It's okay, yes, we know he is your dada, your annadata. But you are squeezing him a little too hard."

Das wailed his inability to rescue the Doctor.

The guard came running.

"What are you doing? Don't create ruckus. My job is at stake and I am not even charging any remuneration."

He looked wistfully at Rhea who raised her fists immediately as he hid behind Sardar ji not wanting to be punched again.

Das meanwhile all charged up, lifted the Doctor like a baby as he tried getting out of the room.

"Das, bhenchod! Put me down. Rhea, where is he taking me to?"

"Stop that. Put him down. We will hire a lawyer, we will do anything and fight this case. But please don't take law in your hands." she pleaded.

"This is not law. This is Doctor sahib and I am kidnapping him."

Sardar ji and the guard stood resolutely in front of the door.

"Put him down. You cannot kidnap him like this. I am calling police if you don't put him down right now." guard thundered.

"You are the police. Tell him, I am the police." Sardar ji whispered into his ear.

"Oh, yes! I am the police. Put him down now. And I am going out to see if my colleague has come. My duty is going to end soon. Five more minutes and all of you leave. I have risked my job allowing you this meeting."

Das cornered on all sides finally relented and put the Doctor down. He got punched in his belly by him no sooner had the old man's foot touched the ground.

"When will you start behaving properly? Why you have

to be so dramatic all the time?"

Rhea placed herself between the raining blows of the Doctor and the overzealous Das, now crouched behind her for saving him from the repercussions.

"It's fine. Calm down. He was just trying to save you. That is his way of interpreting situations and deducing calculations." she held on to Doctor's shoulders nimbly who slouched in the nearby chair and then off to the ground with a loud thud.

"Doctor saab, are you all right. Get up!" But the Doctor seemed to have wafted to a deep slumber and no amount of vigorous shaking could wake him up. "Doctor saab, wake up.This is not the time to sleep." Rhea jolted him slightly and then more vigorously.

"He is dead. Poor old man. We need a vehicle to take his dead body all the way to Pathankot. I have a nephew who works in a mortuary. Though I am not on good terms with him but I will call him." Sardar ji promptly premeditated the conclusions and began his preemptive actions.

"Sardar ji, have you always been like this? Damn!!!Hypothesizing, planning and looking for opportunities to be in charge." Rhea glared at him.

"Hanji, Madam ji. Always! I am the eldest sibling in the family. And I have a way to deal with all the oddities and the inopportune circumstances. And you know, even in the mohalla everyone takes my advice. People love me for that." He beamed with pride.

"Now since he is dead let me be in charge of all the ceremonies. He doesn't have a family here. I will assure him a decent burial with proper customs and traditions. I am calling my nephew to get a mortuary van. And don't worry about the money, both of you, I am here. The 'Sardar with the golden heart' is here, so please, I will take care of the expenses." he dialled his nephew's number and stood there calculating the expenses in an abstract manner moving his fingers up and down.

"Stop this nonsense! He is not dead. And that was an intended pun and you didn't even get it."

"You see Madam ji, all dead bodies were alive at some point. And most of the time loved ones hallucinate that the dead body will get up but that doesn't happen. I have seen many cases where they took the family members to mental hospitals for saying all this insane stuff. He is clearly dead."

"No, he is not. He is very much alive. He is physically and emotionally wrecked. He is just unconscious. We need a Doctor."

"You are a Doctor. I am also a Doctor. We can treat him." Das recovering from the bout of raining blows, finally found his mojo back.

"Das we are Vets. We cannot treat him. And I can still be called a Doctor, but you are no way near it. You are an attendant who has been trained by the Doctor. You are actually a quack. Quake and crack Das. Hahahahaaa."

Rhea clapped her hands gleeful at this new-found discovery.

"I know you hate me, Rhea di. I knew this from the very beginning. You hate me because I am not a Punjabi. You hate me because I come from a land that is far away from yours. My country where people are not as beautiful and as rich as you are. People who have no land holdings and who are dependent at the mercy of others. But things are changing. I read in the paper that these days our boys are reaching places. They are in IITs and IIM s and someday I will also be there."

"Where do you want to be Das?" she eyed him curiously at the sudden revelations.

"In IIM. I know that's a college and if you get degree from there you get lots of money. They even take you abroad and give you all comforts. Even women?" he winked at Sardar ji and blushed.

"Oh teri! Which college is that? Let me type the name." He stared fiddling with the phone.

"STOP!!! All you think about is women and their boobs. You first complete education quack Das and IIM is a far-fetched dream for you right now." Sitting next to the unconscious Doctor, she crossed her arms and shook her head in disbelief.

I can't believe he has an inherent desire to get into a prestigious institute.

When Rhea wrote prescriptions and Das sometimes explained it to the owners she used to tip toe closely to listen to his weird version of explanations in his own dialect.

"Why you moved your head like this?" Das saw the familiar side tilt when Rhea looked displeased with things and bent her neck a little to register her disgust.

"What?"

"You abused me in your thoughts. You think I am incapable of doing anything in life."

"Did I say that? I just thought that you need to complete your basic education first before aiming high."

"No, you said more than that in your head. You do that all the time in your head. I am from Bihar and I am from a village, so you do that to me. You are biased." Das covered his face in his hands and started sobbing.

"Fuck off Das! You are just a drama attired in human skin sent to exorcise innocent people. You are... you are..."

The guard came in the room once again "Leave all of you. Your time is up."

When his instructions elicited no favorable response, his eyes careened from one face to another. And he gasped to see the Doctor lying on the ground, unconscious and recumbent. He shouted at them.

"Is he dead? You people came here to kill him, you bloody drug peddlers!"

"He is comatose. You need to get a Doctor or we can take him to hospital." Rhea placed her hand on his chest to reaffirm his living status "Yes, the heart is beating. It is!"

"But why he needs a Doctor when he himself is a Doctor." Guard glared at her.

"Dactar saab, please get up and treat yourself. Unfortunately, he is not listening." Sardar ji laughed out loud.

"Shame on you! Tony Singh. He is dying a slow death and you are making fun of him. Say anything to me but not even a word about my annadata." Das glared at him.

"Hmmmm... slow death. So, should I call the mortuary van? You decide first whether he is alive or dead."

"Damn, you are obsessed with the rituals. I am saying for the last time, if you pronounce him dead one more time, I would kill you." Rhea grated her teeth as Sardar ji recoiled in horror and flinched back.

"Lao ji, I am keeping quiet now. I have also put a finger on my mouth. And I am not going to give any free advice because I have realized there are no takers."

"But how can he get unconscious, isn't he a Doctor himself?" the guard shook his body and tried moving his hand.

"I want to correct you. He is a Veterinary Doctor and not a human Doctor." Sardar ji chimed in.

"Does that even make a difference? He is an unconscious man right now who needs a Doctor. I am surrounded by fools." Rhea was teary eyed by now.

"Well, he looks like a dead body to me. I am pretty

sure he is dead. You better let me call my nephew. I will pay for everything. We will do a rasam pagri also and Das can be formally declared his heir." Sardar ji flitted his eyes from the Doctor to Rhea and finally transfixed them on Das.

"Me.... the Doctor's heir. Really????" Das closed his eyes and folded his hands and imagined himself to be the renowned Veterinary Doctor, Dr Dagshman Bandhu aka Das Bihari. He envisages a vision of doing a complicated surgery on a dog and Rhea, a becoming assistant handing him scissors and forceps, wearing only a white apron. And when he looks down, he sees her shapely legs, bereft of any clothing. He looks at her with an amorous desire as he muses to her, "I want you on the operation table after this dog. I want to dissect all the love that is hidden somewhere in your heart. And then we can stich it together with a catgut. Your love, my love would be sutured with my strong and able hands and I would never let those sutures dissolve. Sutures of love. Meri Rhea, pyari Rhea."

Rhea sat on the floor, cross-legged caressing Doctor's hand and shaking him after a few minutes. The guard sat beside her, moving the unconscious figure of Doctor gently and stealing looks at her to gauge her mood.

He brings his face closer to the unconscious man's nostrils.

"What are you doing? Are you smelling him?" She questions him when she sees him sniffing like a dog.

"I am checking if he is alive? Perhaps your Sardar ji is right, we do need a mortuary van. If he dies right now, I won't have to go to Delhi all the way to accompany him. It's a nuisance, all this travelling."

"He is dead. And finally, I can take over his hospital. I love you Tony Singh." Das threw his arms around Sardar ji and they get lost in an embrace when Rhea breaks the reverie.

"Das, few minutes back, you were trying to kidnap him,

he was your anndata and know you too want him dead. Just because someone told you that you can be his heir. This is disgusting. Shameless, selfish people! Proclaiming him dead when he is very much alive. Shame on all of you! Perhaps he should die right now. He doesn't need people like you around him. Get lost, all of you!"

Sardar ji averted his eyes. Das mumbled something and guard sat down next to Rhea holding Doctor's hand nimbly as if giving him some solace.

"Put your fingers here and feel his pulse. Here, like this."

She took guard's hand and placed it on the wrist. He squirmed at her touch and started giggling.

"You are soft like silk ji."

She yanked his hand away and propped herself a little away from him.

Sardar ji glanced at her direction and looked intently at the guard who had placed his ear near the wrist of the recumbent man.

"You have to place your head on his chest, not on his wrist, you idiot! You feel the pulse and you hear the heartbeat."

"Now it's my turn to hear the heart." Das immediately jumped out of his somber mood and placed himself next to guard nudging him away for some space.

"Why are you doing this? I want to hear the heart beat first. I first asked her to show me if he is alive."

"No, you are touching her. I saw that. You are one khooni darinda who wants to take advantage of Rhea di." Das elbowed him more vigorously.

"And you keep on eyeing her lewdly and looking at her boobs all the time. You also want to sleep with her. Ahaaa! I caught you! See, who is blushing now!"

"Das, what is he saying?" Sardar ji recoiled in horror.

"Why are you still strung in the pathos of lowliness? Look inside her and not outside. She is a devi and not an ordinary woman."

"Look inside. Hehe!! Deep inside." The guard smacked his lips and winked at Das.

"Che che!!! Sardar ji. Kardi na gandi baat. And you call me a dirty bloke." Das flinched yet kept up his fight to maintain the hierarchy by constantly pushing the guard away.

"Arre, why are you poking these bloody elbows of yours in my chest? It hurts. Someone tell this crazy guy to stop doing that."

"Das, why are you troubling the poor guard? Anyway, I want to have a cold drink. Is there any snack shop nearby?" You seem like family now. Come to Pathankot someday. We will have fun." Sardar ji looked at the guard with a certain enthusiasm, happy to have made an acquaintance of him.

"You mean girls, right!" guard said with a twinkle in his eye.

"I mean chat, pakora and tea. That's my idea of fun. It's okay, don't come. You need to listen to some parvachans. There is some problem with your mastishk, the brain."

"I am perfectly fine. There is a shop on the road outside. Get chips for me also." the guard requested.

"And a Fanta for me with masala lays." Das chipped in.

"SOMEONE CALL THE AMBULANCE!!"

"Rhea di, what happened?"

"Oye, ki ho gya???"

"Don't be so noisy. I will lose my job if someone comes right now."

"He is lying unconscious and no one is bothered about him. On the contrary, you are bothered about your chips and tea party. What is wrong with you people? Aren't you ashamed of yourself? Das, you love him like a father. You want him dead now because you smell the moolah which you are not going to get anyway. And Sardar ji, you think you can gain some leverage by conducting the last rites. You can help him in other ways if he is alive besides wanting him dead. And you, the in-charge of this place only want him dead because you don't want to go to Delhi? I don't understand what kind of civil society we portray? Call the ambulance, you dumbo guard? Why are you not listening to me? Is it a drama that I am enacting?"

"No, call the mortuary van. He is dead."

"I want to go to Samastipur. Kindly book me a plane ticket."

Das moved his arms, flying them like a bird in motion and circled Rhea, Sardar ji and guard and finally sat close to the sleeping form of the Doctor.

"And I will call all my family to the airport. I will alight from the aeroplane waving at them and they will smile. They will smile in a way they have never smiled before. And they will bring garlands and bouquets and then I will be taken in a procession all the way to my village. Like a king receives a welcome in his kingdom after winning the war I will be welcomed in my country land. My country, my Samastipur and I will be the king of Samastipur where I will get to pick and choose my bride. A girl with shimmering eyes, soft skin and a dulcet voice. She will be my queen and we will be together forever."

"That's why I tell you to complete your education. India is a country, Bihar is a state and Samastipur sounds like a village. You make it all sound so alien but at the end of the day we live in one country and yours is no different than ours."

I am amazed how the lure of money is changing equations. The Doctor is lying unconscious and no one is bothered about him. How can Das talk so casually about letting him die? The one, who brought me here despite my reservations. The one who was ready to lay his life for the Doctor has suddenly changed loyalties.

She placed her hand over Doctor's forehead and stroked it gently.

He looks so much at peace. Isn't sleep an imitation of death? Just close your eyes and forget the worries of the world. The way he is lying now. Forgotten, forlorn from the vagaries of the world, in peace with himself. Not even a flicker of stress and anxiety. How I long to relax? When was last time I was at peace with myself?

All the emotions became too overwhelming and she started crying.

All the three men looked at her. They exchanged surreptitious glances and the guard ran outside while the others stood benumbed.

"The guard has gone to fetch help. Don't worry."

****

The Medical Officer (MO) arrived in no time and smiled at everyone, nodding his head perfunctorily. He glanced at Sardar ji and glared at Das.

"Why is he looking at me, the way he is looking, Tony Singh?"

"Because you are very pretty, that's why?" Sardar ji giggled.

Rhea admonished them with a firm look in her eyes.

"No, that's not the case. The moment he entered the room he found the oddities. My features impelled him to think that I am not a Punjabi and he smells a rat here."

"Where is the rat?" Sardar ji traced the periphery around Das quickly taking a few steps and then tip toed to Rhea "Madam, be careful. There is a rat in the room. Please make sure it doesn't bite you. Das smells a rat here."

"Why is the patient on the floor? What have you people been doing with him?" the MO looked quizzically at her.

"He fell down. He was feeling a little dizzy. I tried to support him, but I could not." Rhea immediately offered an explanation.

"I presume, you are his daughter."

"Well, okay. Yes, you can say that."

"I am the long-lost son. A son, he never had. A son he always keeps on mouthing invectives at!!!"

"And I am their mama. Of the chunnu munnu kids." Chimed in Sardar ji.

The MO looked baffled and nodded his head.

"Fine, whatever. Can the family people just give the patient a breather and move towards the side?"

"Breathe...haye haye he cannot breathe." Sardar ji yelped.

Das took him by shoulder and pushed him in one corner.

"He wants to examine the patient and wants us to move aside."

"Lo ji, say nah, ek side te ho jo (Get on one side). Das, I marvel at your ability to understand all this mumbo jumbo. You have to tell me name of this IELTS center. I am impressed by your library of words. Moreover, Madam was telling me, you are not even 10th passed. I am impressed."

"Sardar ji. It's called vocabulary of words. Did Rhea di, say that to you? I must talk to her about it. She is spreading rumors about me."

The MO checked the pulse, took his stethoscope and auscultated the heart. "Everything seems fine. Looks the stress got the better of him."

"Please bring some water for him."

He splashed water on the lying frame of doctor who opened his eyes.

All of them rushed towards his side. They bumped into each other amidst the mad scramble.

Rhea elbowed the two of them jostling her way to the front.

A haggard smile appeared on Doctor's face as he tried to get up.

Das and Sardar ji took him by each arm trying to make him stand on his feet.

"Both of you leave him. You both wanted him dead. And now when he is conscious you are acting like saviors. Doctor saab, you must not believe Das at all. He is greedy and wants to acquire your clinic. I have made a small video of the same. You should kick him out of job the moment we are back in Pathankot."

"Rhea di is a liar, Dactar Sahib. She has morphed the video. She is taking some sort of badla from me for the boob pictures. I am like your son."

"See, here lies the problem. You want to be his son."

"What's wrong with it? Yes, I am his adopted son. When his own son is not there to take care of him, what's wrong with me being his adopted son?"

"You leave him. Your thoughts are contaminated. They are soiled with ill will for someone who was been your provider for years. And look, how you are repaying his kindness! Look in the mirror Das and you will see a true reflection of self. So, leave him now."

"He will fall down if I let go of his arm."

"Let him fall."

"See Dactar Sahib. Did you listen? She said, let him fall. I mean let you fall. She doesn't even care that if you would fall you might break your bones."

"Bhenchod! Stop fighting like kids both of you! I would kick both of you out of here. Rhea, he is stupid, you are sensible. But he never thinks badly for anyone. He is the boy with the golden heart. Please let it go."

The Doctor settled on the chair and indicated Das and Sardar ji to let go off his arms.

"The boy with the golden heart. I am the one. Did anyone listen?"

Das ran off to Sardar ji, ricocheting the words, "Did you listen? Heart of gold."

Then he prattled all the way to the guard and the MO and spoke in a sing song voice, "I am golden."

And then finally after completing a concentric circle he came back to Rhea who was sitting next to the Doctor holding his hand, massaging it gently all the while and looking at Das with nothing but contempt in her eyes.

"I am gold. Yes, I am gold."

She looked at him with abject hatred turning her eyes away from him.

"Rumour mongerer you are! From the boy with the golden heart you have turned yourself into gold."

****

"Can you please be quiet? He needs some rest." The MO blurted out.

The Doctor moved to the rickety bed, went into a slumber once again. He appeared calm, serene and visibly shaken.

The rest of the people found their comfy spots in the room and segregated for a while. An eerie silence pervaded in the room that accentuated the turmoil going on in the minds of the occupants.

A loud thump of boots in the corridor made them alert. They rushed outside.

In the corridor, they saw a towering figure walking in long steps with a bunch of policemen.

"The burra sahib is here. I will lose my job today. Thanks to all three of you. My wife will kick me out of the house for sure and you will land up in jail and enjoy for the rest of your life." The guard lamented.

Rhea cringed with fear, Sardar ji and Das tried hiding behind her.

"Damn! What are you guys doing? Das! Moron, leave my dupatta."

"I will use it as a shield."

"Where is your machoism??"

"Save me Rhea di. I am gold. They are coming to steal me."

"But that's a good thing, Das. You will be safe. If they put you in a jail, you will be safe for the rest for your life."

Sardar ji clapped his hands.

"Madam scored a brownie. She has a valid point. Since, you consider yourself gold, you better go to jail where you will be protected from the eyes of people trying to steal the you in you."

"The you in you…the me in me. Such a beautiful thought, Tony Singh."

"The me in me. Yes, that's it! That's the gold in me. The me in me. And some people would never be able to steal the me in me." He looked at Rhea with contempt and lifted his arms in the air and danced around her, mimicking a belly dancer.

"It is there inside me. The me in me. And there is this susu in me …I want to do susu right now. Get aside. Let me go." Das ran towards the bathroom.

"Here, he goes again. Do you think he is normal, Madam ji?"

"I have no idea, Sardar ji. He is weird, and he has been like this since my first day in the clinic. He is a little neurotic, I feel. Once we get back to Pathankot, we should buy a ticket and send him back to Samastipur. He is losing his marbles."

"Marbles, you mean kanche. Gum ho gaye. Oh ho! That's why???? Only for marbles. I will buy him new."

"Sardar ji, let go. It's no use. Not even explaining."

"By the way, do you know I am going to get into IELTS classes, the one Das goes to? I will learn all the difficult English words and use them in my talk and I will become famous amongst my friends."

"Get inside, Sardar ji. They are looking at us. Hide, hide."

Both of them immediately recoiled.

Das came out of the washroom, wiping his hands on his jeans but was again pushed back by Sardar ji.

"I am done. Why are you pushing me in there, again?"

"Madam ji, come inside, here, in the bathroom."

"Are you crazy? They will find us."

"This is the best hiding place." He pulled Rhea inside and locked it from inside.

Das tried speaking but his voice was muffled with a hand. Sardar ji gagged him, whispering sweet nothings in his ear.

"Shhh... Keep quiet."

"Sardar ji, what do you have in mind?" Rhea fumed.

"We are hiding."

"In a bathroom. All three of us. They have already seen us. What gave you this idea that we will be safe inside a bathroom?"

"I thought so. My intuitive skill."

"Let's open the bathroom door before they blow it up with dynamite and take us out." Das tried fiddling with the latch but Sardar ji pulled him on one side vigorously while he continued opening the door despite being manhandled.

"I do not want to die in a bathroom and that too with both of you."

"What do you mean by both of us? Are we untouchables?" Sardar ji whispered.

"If today, they blow up the bathroom with dynamite we would all die. Right, Tony Singh, you agree."

"Hanji, agreed. Pucca, pucca, agreed."

"And then our souls will be freed."

"Agreed"

"But I don't want to interact with your souls after death. I want to interact with some new souls, so I want to die amidst new people."

"Eh ki gal hoyi. I don't want to interact with your souls. Khota! But we toh love you. I would keep on doing so even after death. Soul to soul connection." Sardar ji enveloped Das in a bear hug.

"I know, but there are some people in the bathroom who hate the very essence of me. I am talking about them. "

Rhea who was not listening to their conversation had an ear held hard against the bathroom door.

"Madam ji, listen to me. We need to discuss a very pertinent matter. Pertinent!" Sardar ji smiled "Hai na ji, IELTS wali English. Das is teaching me."

"Oh, it's okay Tony Singh. Knowledge is an ocean and I would not die if I give you a drop of this ocean. In fact, I would let you drown in this ocean. But there are people in this bathroom who are scared to share their knowledge with anyone."

"Yes, what's the PERTINENT matter? By the way, the officer we saw in the corridor is right there in the room outside and it might be a matter of seconds before they break open this door so discuss the urgent matter soon or we will be doing it in jail." Rhea looked at Sardar ji wondering what could be more important at this moment rather than not getting arrested.

"Did I hear it right, jail?"

"Yes, jail. You heard it right. JAIL."

"Okay, one little thing. We have a serious soul issue. Can your soul interact with his soul after they blow up this bathroom with dynamite? Can you do this? Can you like him after we die?"

Rhea smiled at Sardar ji.

How can he think all the rubbish with such perfection and then utter it with a zen like calm and composure on his face? He is one of his kind. I can't believe I am trapped with two fools so far removed from the realities of life.

"Sardar ji, I think the chances are negligible. He does not have a beautiful soul and moreover it should be free and not under any obligation? Life after death should be all about setting the soul free and not getting into an endless cycle of approvals and disapprovals. If he is going to go through the same rigmaroles of people appeasing he would be more alive than dead. Now please keep quiet and let me listen to what is happening outside."

"But he says, if we have to die together, our souls should

be in perfect harmony."

"We are alive, very much alive! Do we have to die? We all are very much young. He is in his teens, I'm in my thirties and you look like..."

Rhea hesitated as Sardar ji tucked his tummy inside, straightened the creases of his shirt and looked expectantly at her.

"Well! You are young at heart and spirit and more enthusiastic about death than life. You seem to have some sort of connection with the nether world or perhaps you find the mysteries after death more esoteric."

"I am happy Madam ji, you called me young. That's a compliment coming from you."

"Young at heart." Das chuckled.

"Young ta young hi aa ji. Kyun ji. I am YOUNG."

"There is a difference. She said you are young at heart and not exactly young. There is a lot of difference. Once you start the IELTS classes you will understand these subtle differences."

Sardar ji looked baffled.

"Madam ji, you mean I am old."

"Don't listen to him. He has his own set of thinking and let him not impose that on you."

"Oye, Das do not try to misguide me. I think and act according to my own desires and not according to what other people say." He winked at Rhea "Aa theek aa Madam ji?"

"It's perfect. Don't become his puppet. Be your own person." She whispered to him.

"Tony Singh, I can see who is whispering to you. Who is trying to make you a pawn in this bigger scheme of things? I am telling you Sardar ji, beware of beautiful women. She is using you."

"Das, why are you whispering to him?"

"Because you are doing the same, Rhea di."

"Shut up! He is my team."

"Acha! Now he is my team. And when we started from Pathankot, you were like…I don't want to go with him. And now he is in my team. Look Tony Singh, people are like chameleons changing colors according to their whims and conveniences."

"What's a chameleon?" Sardar ji, narrowed his eyes and looked at Das.

"Girgit, the chameleon."

"Are you calling me a girgit?

"No, no Tony Singh. It's not about you, it's about other people."

Rhea pulled Sardar ji's arm, making him take few impromptu steps towards her side.

"We are a team."

Das pulled the other arm propelling him to move towards his side.

"My team. I found him at the taxi stand. Yeh hamari team mein hain. We are a men's team."

"No, he is in my team. We are both Punjabis. We understand each other better."

"I knew this from the very beginning that you will play this caste divide card. But no, this time I would not let him go. He is mine."

Rhea made her grip firm, tugging Sardar ji towards her side while Das pulled him the other way. He was swaying from side to side, being pulled by two opposite forces.

"Oye, chado meinu!! What nonsense!"

He opened the latch and ran out of the bathroom colliding

with the officer who was jotting out some details in his diary while the Doctor was propped against the bed.

"Aa jao Sardar ji! What was the discussion in the bathroom all about? We decided to let you people be. If you are finished you can call your friends out here."

He sheepishly nodded his head and called everyone outside. Rhea came and stood in the front while Das tried hiding behind her, holding her dupatta like a petulant child.

Doctor smiled at them.

"Look at him. He is going to the jail and he looks so happy about the same. He doesn't even know, he is approaching his end." Das whispered in Rhea's ear who tried pulling her dupatta out of his hand.

"Das, let it go. My dupatta, you idiot. Let it go. Please!"

The officer eyed up Rhea firmly. You are a Doctor, his subordinate, he told me."

"Yes sir, I am."

"And you don't know the rules and regulations! You came all the way from Pathankot with this Bihari and Sardar to kidnap your senior. What were you thinking?"

"We did not come to kidnap him. We only came to meet him, sir."

"The guard had told me all about the antics of you and your team."

"Can we get him bailed? We want to take him home." Rhea was on the verge of breaking up.

"He is under immense stress. We need to keep him under supervision for the next 72 hours. He might collapse again so you cannot take him anywhere." MO blurted out.

"We need to take him to Delhi today itself. He might turn out to be a high-end drug peddler." The officer looked displeased and flustered.

"He is not a high-end criminal. He is innocent and a victim of crime. He is a mere carrier and he has been caught unawares. You must help him out. Please try to understand."

Rhea pleaded to the stern officer.

"And we are initiating criminal proceedings against you as well for indulging in corruption by luring our men on duty and for creating ruckus and trying to kidnap someone in custody. You will be rounded up soon when we register an FIR against you."

She moved a step back horrified by the audacity of the charges. Her phone rang, disturbing the perfect calmness of the hospital.

"I am going out for a while. It's a call from home. You both stay put, right here and keep a look out for anyone entering or exiting the room." Das and Sardar ji nodded in unison. Both of them tired by hunger and exhaustion wanted to break away from what seemed like a deadly trap to them.

"Did you hear what he told, Madam ji? They are going to arrest us for a crime we never committed. And arrest me too. I, who came all the way to help you people."

Sardar ji looked morose and glum.

"I have a family to take care off. If I am jailed or arrested for something, I had no intention of getting in the first place Waheguru will not forgive me."

Das mortified by exhaustion resembled a feeble version of himself. He perched himself carefully on the solitary chair holding his legs close to his sinewy frame for comfort.

"Why don't we both just wriggle out of this situation?" He whimpered.

"How can we do it? We are both neck deep in muck. If they arrest us we are gone."

"Let's just scamper away from this place. She is smart enough to manage everything."

"Das, you love her! How can you leave her in lurch, in midst of something so dangerous? And if we go, then we prove to the police that we are guilty."

"She doesn't love me back. What is the point of loving her? And she thinks I am dumb. Look how she keeps on making fun of me all the time."

"Das, you are immature! What do you know about love? And how can she ever love you back? She is married. And even if she was not, no woman in the right frame of mind will love you." Sardar ji gave a full throttled laugh.

"What's wrong with me? I am a young hot-blooded man capable of pleasuring any woman. Age is just a number, and marriage is a façade."

"Hot blooded. Hahahaha!!!! You look anemic to me. There is a vaid in our mohalla who makes concoctions and potions. You must come and meet him. He will give you stuff that can fatten you up."

"Sardar ji, I don't want to be fat. Look at my abdominal muscles, my abs."

Sardar ji pinched his behind and prodded the bony frame.

"Ouch! Sardar ji, what are you doing? It hurts."

"All bones, no muscle. You need some protein supplements to get you in shape. Don't worry. I can be your mentor and I will guide you all the way to a fit and healthy body.

Das looked at the bulging and bellowing tummy of his mentor who seems to be fighting a constant battle to remain ensconced in the narrow domains of decency.

"Why don't you use the powerful potions to contain your own tummy, Sardar ji?"

"It's a symbol of power and valor. And it signifies that we belong to a well to do family. Obesity is a sign of prosperity and by the kripa of goddess Lakshmi my business is burgeoning. So is this flab. It's the harbinger of good fortune."

"To me you look obese and unhealthy. You seriously need to exercise."

Das looked at the two policeman who got deployed by the senior officer as he left hurriedly after giving them instructions. The guard too had left. They were sitting on the bench, next to Doctor's bed, eyeing him surreptitiously.

Das got up from his chair and the policemen no.1 starts following him.

"Why are you following me?" Das questioned him when he saw him walking behind him.

"We have orders to be with you everywhere. A police gypsy is coming very soon to escort you to the police station."

"That's alright but I am going to the loo. You want to see me doing susu in there."

"No, I will stand outside and wait."

"I don't want to use this loo. It's smelly."

"There is one at the end of this corridor. Follow me." The policeman marched in the front instructing him to follow.

Das looked dolefully at Sardar ji who sat their stoically in a reverie of his own as the other policeman sat with eyes stead fixed on him.

"Das, are you having some susu problem. You keep on making trips to the washroom or are you thinking of escaping?" Sardar ji looked at him with a questioning eye.

Escape won't come easy and the thought made Das

crestfallen.

"I would just go out for a while and run away. They are not my family so I don't have any kinship with them. I am not answerable to anyone. I have the property papers. She has ruined everything. I tried getting rid of her by circulating those pictures, but she is back again. And she is beautiful and smart, and I am falling in love with her. It's so crazy to be in love with her when I know she is like a distant star."

Meanwhile, the phone rang, and his eyes widened with a puerile glee to see the caller's identity.

"Sardar ji, it's him, it's him calling. Look. It's Jagsir."

"Who's Jagsir?"

"He's the son, the Doctor's son. He is calling me. I can't believe it! He is calling me!"

"Really!! Pick up the phone."

Das gurgled in pleasure and took the phone in one hand holding it high and started a merry dance holding on to Sardar ji, placing his hand on his waist assuming them to be a couple. Back and forth they swayed and swirled to the imaginary tunes being played in harmony.

"Oye! Stop dancing Das! Pick up the call."

"Oh! Yes, the call!"

By the time he used his fingers to punch the green button the phone had stopped ringing.

"Noooo! Sardar ji, it's not ringing any more. Ring, Ring the damn phone."

"You get carried away. He will call back and then don't start dancing again. By the way I liked that. What's this dance form?"

"It's called waltz. I saw on TV. And I learned a few steps by watching and imitating.

"You are one intelligent boy, Das but way too emotional. If only you could get hold of your emotions you can achieve great success in life."

"Arre, you are here! And I was standing in front of the loo waiting for you. When did you do susu?" the gruff policeman stood towering over Das.

"I got a call, so I did not go. Stop following me and back off."

"We have better things to do then keep an eye on some silly drug peddlers. Chalo, come on and do susu."

"I don't feel like doing it now. I have an important call coming from Germany, so I can't waste time on frivolous stuff." Sardar ji nodded in unison and added.

"The Doctor's son was calling all the way from phoren and he is the only one who can save the old man from the impending predicament."

"Okay, use the loo. I cannot get up again and again."

"Am I a kid that you are cajoling me to do susu?"

The second policeman who was watching the conversation with some sort of disinterest quickly walked up to the matter of conflict now.

"You must do susu. There was an elderly man in our village who used to control his urge to urinate all the time. And you know what happened? Do you have any idea?"

"He peed in his pants." Sardar ji blurted out.

Das was intently looking at the phone and hardly paid them any attention. The policeman no.1 had focused his gaze on Das who found it a bit disconcerting.

"Stop staring at me. I am not a drug peddler. And please take your seat. I feel asphyxiated."

"Sardar ji, this is not funny. Not at all. His bladder would burst. So, he should not hold the pee."

Sardar ji's eyes widened at the prospect of things happening inside Das' body if this impertinent pee didn't happen.

"Das, oye Das! Are you listening? Go and do susu. What will we do if your bladder actually bursts?"

"What nonsense, Sardar ji? Now you also. I don't have the urge to do susu anymore."

"But it's there. Right inside you."

"What?''

"Susu. So, get up and do it. The policeman bhajji is very right. If your bladder caves in here here there will be lot of susu in the corridor and mess for me for me to cover up. And how will Madam ji react?''

"You people are crazy over a simple thing as pee. Get lost all of you! I have to get an important call. For God's sake leave me in peace."

"You think we are idiots. Pick him up and we will strip him in the loo and make him do susu." Policeman no.1 gestured to his colleague who held on to Das and crossed his arms on his back and shackled him with handcuffs.

"Rhea di, save me. They are trying to kill me."

Rhea came running to the room after an interminably long chat with her husband and was dumbfounded to see Das in handcuffs.

"What are you doing to him?"

"We are taking him to loo?"

"In handcuffs. Take them out. He can go by himself if he intends to."

"No, Madam ji. His bladder will burst if he doesn't go."

"But I don't feel like going? Rhea di, tell these mad people to let me go. I have something important to tell you. Doctor's son called but before I could take the call, it got disconnected."

"Is everything, okay? Did your husband shout at you?" Sardar ji asked Rhea.

"Well, yes kind of! It's not good between us. But let's not discuss that right now."

Rhea tried calling Jagsir's number from his phone. The phone kept on ringing incessantly before he picked it up.

"Hey Jagsir, how are you?"

"Yeah! I am good. Are you calling from India? Do I know you?"

"Hanji, I am calling from India. How are you? How's your wife?"

"Yeah! All well. Do I know you? How did you get this number?"

"Yes, yes we know each other. How's life in Germany? Is it a good country to live in?"

Das pulled Sardar ji a little closer.

"What's going on? She is deviating from the topic. Why is she not coming to the point?"

"Yes, I would tell you. Telling you soon. First tell me, are Veterinary doctors well paid out there?" Rhea blabbered.

"Madam ji, tell him his father is arrested. What nonsense are you talking?"

Rhea placed a hand in front of the phone, "I am building the tempo. If I told him immediately he might die of heart attack."

"Yes, Jagsir I am coming to that. Okay, now listen very seriously to what I am going to tell you. It's very serious? Brace yourself. Please be patient. I am going to tell you now Jagsir, now. Yes now. It's that..."

Sardar ji and Das waited in anticipation with their mouths slightly agape. They were waiting for the reaction from the criminal son who has made his father a carrier.

"Say it! Tell that bastard, his plan has failed. He would be arrested by Indian police."

"Do you know anything about Germany, Sardar ji?"

"Yes, I do"

"Tell me then, it's in which part of the world?"

"Lage hi aa. Aa sada India te aa Germany."

"That is Pakistan you are talking about." Das grinned.

"Germany is in Europe and our police cannot just go and arrest their citizen. So, do not bother. No one is arresting anyone."

"Yes Jagsir, it's like this..." Rhea fumbled and looked at Das and Sardar ji who were whispering, "Yes, you can do it! Tell him, tell him!!"

"Yes, yes I am doing it now. Right now." She implored them with her eyes.

"I am about to say now. Brace yourself up. Your father... Hello, hello Mr Jagsir are you there???? Hellooooo."

"Madam ji, ki ho gaya."

"Oh no, Sardar ji, battery died. I need to charge my phone. Get a charger."

"Call from my phone. But tell him, tell him right away what happened without playing with words."

"I was not playing with words. I was not. I did not want him emotionally drained."

"You were thinking well of him! The one who tried to

implicate his own father. By making him a carrier, by getting him jailed."

Das curled his lips and looked completely horrified at Rhea's goodwill gesture towards Jagsir.

"Call from my phone, Rhea di."

She tried calling from his phone, but it was engaged. She felt being watched by two pairs of angry eyes. She tried calling again but this time the call would not go through and she was sweating profusely.

"This is what happens when an important call comes, and you start talking about here and there but not about the matter in hand."

"Are you talking to me, excuse me?" Rhea fumed in anger."

"This is what happens when you side with criminals. His son is the one who should be in custody and not us." Das muttered.

The two-policemen appeared again by their side and started hovering around them.

"We are asking you for the last time. Do you want to do susu, Bihari? You will be the only person responsible should the bladder burst inside you? The doctor is calling you. Go and listen to what he has to say?"

✳ ✳ ✳

11

THE SPLIT

All of them rushed from the corridor into the room.

The doctor was sitting on the bed looking dishevelled, his turban resting on the nearby table. He looked at Rhea for an interminably long time. And when he spoke his voice seemed like a distant haze.

"Rhea, mere bache I want to apologize to you first from the bottom of my heart for what happened with you at the clinic."

"But that's over. I think we should forget about it Doctor saab. Why are you even bringing it again?"

"I took it all lightly and now I feel responsible for the doings. We won't be able to meet again and I want to take it all out. You have been very brave, coming here with someone who tried to do wrong with you."

"Doctor saab, Jagsir called! He was worried about you, but I could not tell him what happened with you as the battery died. But he sounded worried."

"Nah ji nah. She was building the tempo, so the battery died down. Madam ji, tell the full thing. You kept on saying... I am telling you... I am going to tell you something really important. And eventually you spent all the energy in building the tempo. You just had to say one line...Your father has been arrested on charges of drug smuggling."

The doctor blinked his eyes and fought back the tears clouding his eyes.

"Sardar ji, somedays, the simplest things in life are the most difficult to say. The simplest emotions are the most difficult to convey. I could not make an honest confession to my son in straight words that I did not want to come and stay with him. That I am happy in my own world. I was going on with this reluctant journey and look what happened! I have no idea if Jagsir knew about the contents in the packet. I don't know if he deliberately planned it. Who can I trust if I can't trust my own son in this big bad world? I don't even think there is any use telling him." The Doctor moved his finger tips to wipe the tears that unknowingly muddled his eyes making his vision hazy.

"We cannot make him a culprit. We don't even know if he knew what was being delivered to you." Rhea whispered.

"I knew there was something wrong with the package. I knew from the very beginning. I had this premonition that something bad was going to happen."

"But that doesn't justify the drugs angle. Does it? You did not want to go. That's it. You had a negative vibe to the whole thing. How can you say you knew there were drugs?"

"I knew there were."

"No, no Doctor saab. Don't agree to something that you had no knowledge about. This will be more damaging to you, to your reputation, to us."

"There is no us. It is over Rhea! Please go back to Pathankot. This case is very sensitive. From what I have been told there is no bail. The offence is of such a grave nature that there will be immediate jail. Go back to the clinic, it's all yours. You and Das can run it."

"And what about the property, the home? Are you going to severe all relations with your son, taking away all the property from him?"

"Oye Das, pagal ho gyaan tu? What's all this property fuss about? What are you saying? We will try to save him. And we will be successful? Jallah types! He doesn't even know what to think?" Sardar ji stroked his head lightly.

"Really Das!!! You don't know what to think. You really don't know. You are thinking about the property and the clinic when we are thinking about saving his life. You are not bothered to save your annadata anymore."

"Nah nah, Madam ji. Das is not like this. He is so innocent. Look at him. Just look at him."

"Wait, Sardar ji! Das look at me. Do you have something to do with this package? Are you even remotely associated with it? Did you touch it????"

Das averted his eyes and sat on the floor cross legged.

"OMG!!! Doctor saab. Das fiddled with the package. He changed it. He took the original package and mixed it up with the drugs. Such a perfect scheme of his conniving mind to get you arrested. He knows, everyone knows in the locality that you are not on good terms with your son. And he hatched the perfect plot. Bravo Das! Bravo!!! What a perfect plot you invented. You fudged the packages, son of a bitch! You did it. All that love for Doctor saab was an illusion. You were after the money. And you knew he is all alone and he might give you all he has if the relationship with his son turned sour."

Das could not anticipate all this coming from Rhea. He sat frozen on the spot with his head hung in shame looking for a way out to escape.

"Das, look at me! Is it true?" the Doctor thundered while Das squirmed.

Sardar ji smacked Das on the head, "I knew from the very beginning you must be the one who has done that. Arrest him now, he is a devil lurking beneath an innocent face."

Everyone was looking intently at Das. He snivelled and used his sleeve to wipe his face off the sweat.

"No, I did not do anything." He blinked his eyes to drown out the fear that was lurking inside him. He crouched in a corner, his head between his legs and started quivering, shaking like a reluctant leaf that hung to last vestiges of life in the wake of a powerful storm.

"Someone please record him confessing to the crime."

"Das, you did it! I can see it in your eyes. Say yes! I will take care of your family in Samastipur. I will bring them to Punjab. Your ailing father and your budhi ma. I will bring them here and put them in my house. And the society would come to know that I care for the people. They would say... There goes the Sardar, our pride, our honour and they will respect me more for working for the destitute."

"And then you would be famous in your mohalla, in your town, in the city, in the state and who knows you might achieve national and international fame." Rhea chipped in.

"Yes, yes Madam ji. Exactly. Same to same. How did you know it?"

"Oh! Never mind. Running after fame is a bad idea. You will reach nowhere. Mark my words. You will remember my historic words."

"First of all, my parents are not destitute. They have money, little money but enough to support them. Don't try to be famous and make a hero out of yourself on behest of my parents." Das shot back.

"What drama all you people are creating? Now to whom does that package belong?" Policeman no.1 registered his irritation.

"Shush!! It's very interesting. I bet this packet belongs to

Bihari. He is the one who stealthily went to Doctor's room one day and changed it. Let's have a bet on that." Policeman no.2 winked at his colleague.

"Hmmm!!! I think Bihari is innocent. He looks so cute. I think this Doctor is the culprit. He and his son hatched a perfect plan to earn some quick money and now they are creating all this drama. Kinne di bet lani!

"We are under immense stress and you are finding it funny and placing bets? Shame on you!" Rhea admonished the two policeman who were devising ways to entertain themselves.

"Let me correct all of you. He is not my family. He is a bloody serpent. I spit on you Das. Here, take this." Doctor gurgled up a glob of spit and made a purported attempt to sully him with the mucus but unfortunately, he ended up depositing it on the foot of policeman no.1

"Oye, what are you doing? I can arrest you for this."

"I am already under arrest, bhenchod!" The doctor thundered and succumbed to a coughing fit.

"Doctor saab, you have to keep calm and don't exert yourself too much. Someone fetch him water."

"You abused a policeman on duty. Even if you get away from the charges of drug smuggling I would never let you get out for verbally abusing me."

The Doctor got up from the bed and jabbed the policeman no.1 who reciprocated with full force. In no times they were in fisticuffs, raining blows on each other.

Rhea, Sardar ji and Das were pulling the Doctor with all their might. But the tall and muscular man won't let anything dither him.

"He is not well, police bhajji. Let him go. He might get unconscious." Sardar ji bleated.

"Even if he doesn't, I will knock him unconscious."

The policeman no.1 targeted a firm blow that hit Rhea on the cheek as the Doctor dodged it successfully. A sharp pain seared through her face as she whimpered.

"STOP IT", she shouted holding her aching jaw.

The policeman let go off the Doctor who plopped on the bed again.

"I am dying. I can't get up. And if I die right now, this bloody policeman would be responsible for my death. And my darling Das, who we all believe had put drugs in my bag. And my son, of course who did not care if I am dead or alive." And he started sobbing which melted the heart of his opponent.

The policeman no. 1 straightening the creases in his shirt, patted his ruffled hair and sat down next to him.

"It will be fine. If the boy confesses that he jumbled the packages, we will put you on the next flight to Germany. You are a free bird."

"But I don't want to be a free bird. I want to be chained. I want to be entwined in the bonds of care and companionship. I want to be with people who love me. I want to be in Pathankot. My home, my clinic. Cancel this ticket and send someone else instead of me. Tell my son, to carve a father out of any man because I am not good enough for him."

"If that's the case, I am ready to go." Sardar ji volunteered.

"I am ready to go and make this terrible sacrifice. I know my wife, my kids and all of you will miss me. And the mohalla and the people I have been helping will terribly miss me. But ki kariye, jaana pena. Someone will have to dawn the mantle of being a father to a fatherless one. And I will be the one. I will sacrifice my life for you Dactar ji. Don't worry. I will go all the way to Germany. Do they serve you Punjabi food or should I get it packed from here???"

Rhea who had been hot fomenting her cheek with a handkerchief went closer to Sardar ji and placed a hand on his shoulder.

"I am amazed and impressed. Just few hours back, someone was saying that he doesn't want to get involved with all the nasty stuff and what not! Blah...blah... and now suddenly people have become so considerate that they are ready to leave their motherland and sacrifice their life."

"I know Madam ji. I have been like this from the very beginning. Sacrificing my own life for the sake of others. I like to help people and then I forget that I have a life of my own."

"You are a dhongi, an imposter, Sardar ji! Yes, you are! Close your mouth. Close it properly. Yes, like this. Go back to Pathankot and never cross our lives. That will be your biggest help."

"People misunderstand me. At the end of the day, all the sacrifices go in vain." Sardar ji retorted.

All this while Das hung his head in shame, sat in a corner of the room and did not even utter a word.

"Arrest him" Rhea prodded the policeman no. 2. "Why are you not arresting him?"

"Maintain a healthy distance. You are pushing me. Keep your hands away. You can be arrested for this." he pointed a finger at her.

"For what?"

"For taking law in your own hands."

Rhea moved her hands away when she saw she had been tugging at his uniform all along. She looked at Das and wondered.

He must have been planning and plotting for a long time. Those pictures were not an amateurish attempt to get recognition. It was a deliberate attempt on his part to get me out of the way. How mean and full of motives he has acted with? I can't believe he could go to such a length to plot against the Doctor.

"We will take him to police station. If he confesses that he changed the packages he would be arrested, and the Doctor would be freed. You can all go back."

Rhea smiled in anticipation, smacking her lips.

Mission successful. Doctor saab will be out. Das would be in. I would be the in- charge of the clinic and no more interference from him. I don't even have to bother about my dupatta any more. Wear anything, to work. No one would ogle at me, no one to bother me with silly antics. I can work and only work.

Rhea was smiling with all kinds of desirable thoughts and with the prospects of having the clinic all by herself.

Sardar ji eyed her nervously and came tip-toeing around.

"Madam ji, you seem to be very happy. What's going on your mind right now? Tell me, please."

"Wow, that's quite an investigative mode you look like you are in? Hehe…"

"I am pretty serious."

"Why are you looking at me in such a strange way?"

"I am looking for criminals around myself. Now when we know, Das had changed the packages, I can see nothing but criminals all around me. And you are a suspect as well, Madam ji."

"Why are you making such an effort? From where will I get Heroin and why will I do that? I have immense respect for Doctor saab. There is no motive for me to do that."

"What if we put it like this? You were interested to run the clinic. And you tried to get him out of his way by putting drugs in his bag."

"This is bullshit! Now you think you have graduated to the role of an investigative journalist, Sardar ji."

"If he has a motive, you also have one. You are sailing in the same boat." Sardar ji moved away and started talking with Policeman no.2

Rhea seeing them talking in hush- hush manner walked towards them in hurried steps.

"What were you talking?" she questioned Sardar ji while eyeing the policeman curiously.

"Oh, nothing. An informal chat about the case."

"You cannot talk with a third party about the case. He doesn't know anything."

"Oh, yes he can. He can talk to anyone about the case. He is giving me valuable leads." The policeman raised an eyebrow and looked at her suspiciously.

Rhea tugged at Sardar ji's arm and pulled him towards one side.

"What are you doing? Why are you spreading rumors about me?"

"I am saying all that I am feeling. You know how I like to say whatever comes to my mind?"

"I am unable to understand. We are a team Sardar ji, remember."

"If we are still a team, Das is also a part of that team. How can we leave him in the lurch? And you are out rightly saying that he is the criminal. How just is that?"

"But then he is! Look at him, sitting all huddled up in one corner. He is not saying anything in his justification. He knows he is guilty."

"Dekho, Madam ji…he is young and the dactar ji is old. We cannot trade a young person with an old one. There is no comparison. We should take Das along and leave the old man here. Let's run away from here. Let's go back to Pathankot. No one will know, we ever came here. Let the old man languish in jail . Das can repent and mend his ways."

"Sardar ji, this is crazy. What is this??? Horse trading!! You cannot substitute one person for another. Let the guilty be punished. Who are we to make inferences?"

Sardar ji pondered for a moment, shook his hands haywire and looked helplessly at Das and then at Rhea.

"There are chances you could have exchanged the packets. You are smart, intelligent and you might have done it."

He placed his hands across his chest and smiled beatifically.

"You have layers to your personality. I don't know who you are siding with or what you want to prove. You seem to love living in some kind of eternal conflict. Kindly get hold of yourself." She marched away from him.

12

DAS CONFESSES

They kept on waiting for the police vehicle, but it did not arrive. They were tired, hungry and fed up with the planning and plotting against each other. Rhea dozed off for a while and so did the others to be woken up to high pitched sounds of the policemen.

"Uth jao everyone. Get moving."

"The ambulance is for the patient and rest of you come in the police van." Police man no. 1 instructed.

Das who was sleeping on the floor holding Sardar ji's hand presented a vibrant pose. The policeman chuckled before poking fingers in their bony and bulky frames simultaneously.

"Get up, both of you. We are going to the police station." Rhea looked at their sleeping forms and got jealous to see them so carefree and enjoying their siesta.

If Das confesses today, this whole turmoil will end, and we can go back, and they can do whatever they want to do with him.

When all of them were ushered out they saw Doctor being helped into the ambulance.

Das ran and clasped his legs.

"No, you cannot take him away from us. I am also coming in the ambulance."

"Leave me, you idiot. First, you keep drugs in my bag, get me arrested and now you are doing all this drama to save me.

Police keep him away from me."

"How can you say it, Dactar Sahib! You were carrying drugs! I merely brought refined sugar and substituted it for heroin. That day, I collected the package and I knew instantaneously you were being used as a carrier."

" If that was the case, you could have told me?"

"But you would not have trusted me. I disposed of the contents of that package in the toilet and packed some powdered sugar in a brown paper. I wonder how you got arrested for carrying sugar."

"You flushed heroin down the toilet???" asked the policeman no.1 with eyes widened up.

"Edhaar aa Tarsem, look what he did? He is telling, he flushed heroin down the pot."

"You should have given it to us! Do you have any idea how much it was worth????"

"Aa dactar nu chado, eh saale nu arrest karo !!!!(Leave the doctor and arrest him) It's because of Biharis like you that Punjab is not progressing. What a waste of national resources?"

"By the way, drugs are not national resources." Rhea objected at the anomaly.

"You Bhenji, stay out of all this. Otherwise, we will slap a case against you for bad mouthing police."

"Change namune ne. Karo andar saraiyan nu. (Arrest all of them) Let me call, sir ji first. Hanji sir ji, there is a new twist in the case. What we think is heroin, is crystalline sugar! Check karlo changi taran. Je media, tak khabar pahunch gayi, badi bednami ho ni. (Check it properly. It would be damaging for us if media comes to know about the goof up.) We are arresting someone who was carrying sugar in his bag."

After taking instructions from his superior the policeman

no.1 disconnected the call.

"Ambulance is not needed. Get rid of it. Everyone comes in the van itself. We are going to the police station."

"He is not well. He should be transported in the ambulance." Rhea protested.

"Aa bhenji nu le jo ambulance de vich! (Take the lady in the ambulance!) The Doctor looks perfect."

"No, I do not want to go in ambulance all alone."

"Then you should shut your mouth and behave sensibly. We will charge sheet all of you for wasting our time and energy."

Everyone was huddled in the small police van. Rhea kept on elbowing Das who was sitting next to him.

"Please change your seat. You are touching me inappropriately."

"I am not touching you at all. There is no space. Sardar ji move a little bit. She is accusing me again."

"Dactaar ji, you move a little bit, or you come in my lap or Das you come in my lap. That way all of us will be comfortable." Sardar ji smiled. "Now, we are all fine. One big, happy family so everyone should smile."

"I am not a kid to sit in your lap. And we are no big happy family. Some people are here who wish ill for me. And who tried to implicate me in a false case."

Rhea flinched but chose not to respond.

"Das, how did you know that was indeed Heroin? I mean to say, it's only the experts who would know about drugs . What if it was something else?" Sardar ji looked at Das with a reverence who was no less than a hero to him at that particular moment.

"It had to be drugs. I know that! I came to know by the look of that person."

"And what kind of look was that?" The angry young types like this. Look here! Where you want to destroy the entire world?" Sardar ji narrowed his eyes to convey his point.

"Nah, not like this. Eyes like those of a go-getter when you are ready to do everything for the sake of money. Like this, killing eye. See this look! Can you decipher it?" Das widened his eyes and then narrowed them for a purported attempt to exaggerate the impact by his facial calisthenics.

"Yes, I got it!"

"That still makes Doctor saab, a victim though. If someone delivers him drugs that still doesn't make him innocent. That makes him an accomplice."

"Das, you are an idio! You should not have thrown it away like this. Maybe it did not contain drugs. But if you say it is powdered sugar, how can it get detected as Heroin at International airport?" Rhea looked intently at Das.

"Are you telling the truth? Hope you are not making it all up. Why should we believe you?"

"Maybe you sent that package Rhea di. You put drugs in it to implicate Doctor saab?"

"What nonsense, Das?"

"This is my point. Anyone can be guilty. Why only point fingers at me? May be Jagsir orchestrated this whole drama. Maybe he wanted to make a quick buck. Just because he is more sophisticated, and I do not match your standards does not make me a lesser mortal, Rhea di."

"Can you stop talking about my son? All of you!" The Doctor finally spoke up listening to different versions of the same story.

"He did not do it. I know it for sure. He might not like me but at the end of the day he is my son. He said it was a homeopathic medicine for a friend."

"Damn Das! You took the medicine away and put Heroin instead."

"I did not. I took Heroin away and put sugar instead."

"No one gets arrested for carrying sugar."

"Chup karo. You can give the explanations when we are at the police station." An enraged policeman gave way to an angry rant making everyone squirm.

13

THERE ARE SUSPECTS EVERYWHERE

When they arrived at the police station, Sardar ji whispered to Rhea.

"Did you get a call again from your husband?" he enquired when he saw her toying with her phone.

"My phone is switched off. I need to charge it. He must be worried but there is nothing I can do."

"I have to be back home this evening. It's my son's birthday today and we have organised a small birthday party."

"You should not have come with us. It's getting messier. You have nothing to do with this. You can just go back Sardar ji. Just leave right now. Your car must be parked where Doctor sahib was lodged. Just move now. If they record your statement, you will become a part of the ruckus."

"Madam ji, you also come with me. It's their mess. Who knows, who did what? We do not even know whether they are telling the truth. Maybe they are a team and they are doing it all in connivance."

"This is all so confusing. You are siding with me, with Das or with Doctor saab. You keep on changing your statements as well as your loyalties. To me you appear a confused soul."

Das took Doctor saab in one corner of the room. Rhea could see him talking to the Doctor who was eyeing her with suspicion. And when he saw that she was getting all worked up, he covered his mouth with his hand making it all look so dramatic, all the while looking at her from one corner of his eye.

She marched up to them, "What were you telling Doctor saab?"

"Well there was nothing to tell."

"Don't try instigating him against me."

"What is there to fear Rhea di, unless you are a culprit?" Das replied haughtily, placing his hands on his hips jutting them a little forward.

"Rhea, did you go to my room? Yes, you did! While I was packing. You came to my room!"

"Yes, Doctor saab, I did, I did come to your room. I helped you with the packing. So, what's the big deal?"

"The package was there. Right there. It was unattended in your presence."

"This is absolutely crazy. I can't believe it. You are suspecting me. You think I have link with some drug cartels." She threw her hands in exasperation and started walking away from them but then suddenly came back running.

"Doctor saab, you need to ask him how he knew the package you received had drugs in the first place. A novice can never come to know."

"Arre, by smelling it. Anyone can spell drugs by smelling it."

"Not until you do drugs. And moreover, how do we know you did not throw away the package? What if you sold that to someone else?"

"I would not have been here if that was the case. I did everything to save him."

"Perhaps, you should not have tried to save him. What was with the harmless powdered sugar? He is still arrested on charges of drug smuggling."

"Are you listening everyone? Look what she is saying! Here are the exact words. She is saying that I should not have helped Doctor saab."

Sardar ji, along with two policemen sauntered closer to the trio fomenting trouble once again.

"You don't even deserve to be heard. You wasted the precious commodity. Now shut up! Leave the girl alone"

"Waise Bhenji you are very beautiful." Smiled the policeman no. 2 eyeing Rhea lasciviously, giggling and elbowing his friend.

Das immediately stood up placing himself between Rhea and them, "Why are we here? Why are you not taking us inside?"

"It's lunchtime. Stay here and keep fighting and let us know who the culprit is. All of you are going to rot in jail for the rest of your lives. Bloody drug peddlers!!"

Sardar ji came in the forefront and said aloud. "I want to talk to all of you. I have an announcement to make. See, if we have to find who is real culprit we have to be quiet and discuss it calmly and steadily."

"Sardar ji, did anyone tell you that you are a bundle of contradictions? You are creating confusions amongst us and constantly doing some sort of partibaji."

"I am trying to see this particular problem from all the angles. I am making suspect, each and every one of you and analyzing it. This is called psychological analysis, Madam ji. You have to go in depth to get a gist of things."

"It's not working. You are creating conflicts and we are fighting. We have to strike as a team."

"Theek aa madam ji. Let's join hands."

"Okay" Rhea said.

"Okay" Das nodded

"Okay" Doctor brought his hands forward.

Everyone clasped their hands. The policemen put their hands on top of Rhea's hands and she immediately shoved them away.

"You are not part of the team. Stay away."

They expressed their displeasure.

"We also want to be part of this prestigious group. The heroine group or the heroin group" they chuckled.

"They are so sweet. Look at them. Let them join hands as well." Sardar ji smiled sheepishly.

"No, we cannot make them part of this group. We cannot take strangers."

Das placed an arm around them.

"Rhea di, we are all strangers unless we get to know each other. Stop judging people on the basis of their outer appearances. Come on friends, you are part of it. As long as everyone is working on getting Doctor saab out of this mess, you are welcome."

"Das, bhenchod! if you really thought there were drugs in the package, you should have told me the same? We could have called up Jagsir?" the Doctor fumed.

"You would have never questioned your son. You would have taken the package anyway. So, I decided to follow my own instinct."

"Point! I agree. But even if you fudged the packages how come I was arrested. If you say it was sugar in that one, how come they arrested me in the first place?"

"Yes, unless someone changed it again and substituted it with drugs."

"Who could have done that?"

"Rhea!!!!!

****

Rhea looked at Doctor saab with disappointment writ large on her face. The suspects seem to have cropped up everywhere and suspicion lurked beneath every eye. Sardar ji sat forlorn in the corner of the room, blabbering to himself while Das and Doctor had shifted to another corner, talking in whispers.

Let me go a tad closer and listen to what they have to say?

She tip-toed a little closer and the duo moved farther away throwing mocking glances at her.

"What happened? Why are you looking at me like this?"

"Nothing."

"What are you talking about?"

"We are trying to solve the mystery of the package."

"Oh! Okay. I have something to add as well."

But before she had uttered the words they had moved away, leaving her alone and she felt a tad disappointed.

The police man no.2 who had been watching everything with an amused expression lurched forward and stood next to Rhea, tapped on her shoulder lightly.

"We can be a team."

"What team?"

"Like those two have."

"I am not interested in making a team with you."

"They are implicating you in this case."

"How do you know?" Rhea eyed him suspiciously.

"See, how they are looking at you."

"They are not even looking at me. Why are you creating all

the doubts in my mind? Go away."

"You are alone, I feel so bad for you. Let me tell you that if you get involved in the case, you will not be able to get bail. We can leave you at the bus stand. Go back home. Let them sort this themselves. You have nothing to do with it."

For a moment, she looked around to see the situation she has landed herself into.

If I wriggle out of this situation right now, no one would come to know. Why I have to go through all this for people I am not answerable to?

She looked at the duo who were sulking on their own now, lost in their own world.

The crestfallen Doctor has closed his eyes and seemed to have dozed off again in a corner.

Perhaps, he is dreaming about his son and the good times that were about to come. The flight must have departed by now. He would have been on that flight, had all this not happened? Why did it all happen to him and that too at that precise moment? What if the package had not arrived? What if it was harmless? Why did it happen the way it did? If I leave right now, it might be an easy escape, but I can't just go. I can't leave him and go. Stay, I must.

"What are you thinking? My bike is parked right outside. I will ask someone who would leave you at the bus stand. Go home. I will tell them, you escaped. No one will bother."

"Why should I trust you?"

"I will hire an auto then. You must leave the police station before the incharge comes."

"No, I will not go."

"You are my daughter's age and you have to listen to me. This is not the right place for a girl like you. You must leave, right now. I have seen women get sucked up in cases and cooling their heels in the lock up for the rest of their lives. I don't want that the same fate befalls you. Come I will get you an auto." Policeman no.2 looked beseechingly at her.

He pulled Rhea's hand who yanked it off immediately shoving him away.

"No, you have something else on your mind. Don't touch me. I don't trust you. You are trying to kidnap me."

"I am not, believe me. Just leave this place. Dealing with the drugs and drug dealers will ruin your life. Make a move and go. Chalo, I will get you a drive till bus stand."

This time he grasped her from her arm and started pulling her more vigorously.

"Arre, what are you doing? Let me go. Doctor saab, Das, Sardar ji. See, he is trying to kidnap me?

"I am trying to save you, stupid girl. Come with me!"

The Doctor woke up bleary -eyed to see Rhea being pulled while she kicked frantically in all the directions.

"Oye Das, oh le gaya, Madam ji nu. Chak leya!"

"Leave Rhea di!!!"

While the policeman used all his might, Rhea was punching and kicking him. Das and Sardar ji came and grasped the man from behind. The Doctor picked up Rhea's dupatta which got trampled amidst all the jostling and handed over to her.

Das was kicking and punching the perpetrator furiously.

"Let him go. Please let him go. He was trying to save my life."

"Really! By kidnapping you. Madam ji, explain. Even you are under the fire line."

"Line of fire." Das corrected.

"Ohi, ohi. Same to same. Very good you are, Das."

"I see you have become very friendly, both of you." Rhea felt jealous at their shared proximity.

"Some one seems to be jealous." Das placed an arm around Sardar ji's shoulder and whispered something which was followed by a loud guffaw.

"Look they are saying something about you." The policeman who was lying on the floor moved uneasily and tried to get up.

"Shut up and don't you dare move." Das kicked him once more making the man wince in pain.

"Police, police. What kind of police station is this where criminals are beating the police?

"Shame on you, Das. You are beating an innocent man."

"Yes, an innocent man who was trying to kidnap you. How can you even trust him Rhea di?"

"How can I trust anyone Das? For the first time in my life I am realizing how spineless people can be? You are planning and plotting against me. We were a troika. When we started from Pathankot last night, we were a team. All three of us. And now you both have sided together, and you are trying to implicate me in this case."

✵ ✵ ✵

14

THE DRAMA UNFOLDS

"Who are these people?" The officer sprawled up in his chair asked unenthusiastically.

"These are drug peddlers."

"The girl also. Acha!!Who arrested them?"

"That one in the red turban is a Veterinary Doctor. He was arrested on charges of drug smuggling yesterday."

"It cannot be possible. We have sent the culprit to Amritsar Central jail and I have myself interrogated him few hours ago."

"What's his name?"

"Dactar sahib."

"That is his designation. What is his name?"

"He doesn't have any name. We only call him Dactar sahib." Das giggled.

"Das, shut up! He has a name. Doctor sahib please tell your name. Even I don't know your name." Rhea wondered that she did not bother to know the name of his employer.

"I am Dr Varinder Singh."

"And we arrested Mr Varinder Lal and he has already confessed. I am really sorry for this goof up. But you are lucky they did not send you to the Central jail and you were only sent at our transitory premises. But I have been told you have beaten up one of my men who is getting dressed for his injuries.

So, I am filing an FIR against you all. Arrest them for beating a policeman on duty."

"You mean he doesn't carry any drug smuggling charges now." Rhea shrieked.

"No, he was never arrested in the first place. There has been a big goof up. Perhaps they rounded him up because of the same name."

"We can sue you for this. He almost had a nervous breakdown. He missed his flight. We came all the way from Pathankot. I spent a night outside my home. My husband might divorce me for the same. We doubted each other's loyalties. Your one goof up and our lives are in turmoil. Who will pay for the mental and emotional damages? Tell me!" Rhea thundered as Sardar ji and Das held hands.

The Doctor placed his hand on her shoulder, "Calm down. It is over."

"No, it's not over. This is not fair. My life will be ruined. My husband might not trust me ever again. My in-laws will make this divorce imminent. I am going to take the police and airport authority to court and I will make sure I get press, media to know how they ruined life of an innocent girl."

She looked at Das and Sardar ji who were baffled by her outburst.

"Hanji, my wife will also divorce me because I spent a night outside home. And I will make sure each and every newspaper covers your misdeeds." Sardar ji came and stood resolutely next to Rhea.

"And I will call press from Samastipur." Das chimed in.

"Where is that?"

"It's in Bihar. That's poor IQ".

"Shut up, you idiot! No FIR. I will escort the lady, to her house and I will talk to your in-laws and your husband and if he still insists on divorcing you I would lock him up in jail. They will treat you with respect and dignity. I will make sure they do that. Are you happy now?"

Rhea smiled, "That sounds fine. But what about the missed flight."

"That's not an issue. He will get the refund or a new ticket."

"What about my wife? Will you talk to her also?" Sardar ji questioned but he never got a reply for the same.

Everyone smiled and clapped their hands. They cheered each other up and shouted in excitement.

"Hip, hip Hurray!"

"Get them some refreshments. We will start in an hour."

Rhea and team were given beverages and snacks. Everyone gorged on them hungrily and no one spoke a word.

"Sardar ji, you will get to attend your son's birthday party. Wouldn't that be great?"

"Yes, that would be wonderful. This turned out to be the most eventful 24 hours of my life. I would never forget it. Kyun Das?"

Das kept on munching the crunchy samosas. His eyes bore a vacuous expression as he nodded absent mindedly.

"I need to make some amends. I think I need to go back and meet my parents once. It's been years. Life is too short to be wasted, mourning the loss of relationships. I am going to make a sincere effort to make a difference in the lives of my loved ones. If Dactar Sahib pays me a month's advance and grant me leave I would be leaving for Samastipur as soon as we get back. I am sure Rhea di would not miss me."

"That sounds wonderful. But we would never come to know if it was really Heroin that you flushed down the pot?"

Rhea murmured.

"Let it go. Whatever it was, it's gone. Perhaps it was only a harmless homeopathic medicine. We cannot doubt Jagsir. I need to have a heart to heart chat with him and I am going to ask him to come back for a while. I cannot leave work as it keeps me connected with my profession. I guess I would stay here. God has been kind to me that I have people around me who love me and did their best to save me from a calamity." The Doctor sighed and closed his eyes.

"Should we try calling Jagsir and tell him all that happened?" Rhea proposed.

"Later. Let's get back home first. We would have all the time in the world to go through the happenings again and again. It was a nightmarish experience. Let's not discuss anything now."

Doctor and Rhea were driven in a police gypsy while Das accompanied Sardar ji in the Nano with two police vehicles escorting them.

"I never thought I would be escorted by a gypsy full of police personnel." Sardar ji glowed with pride.

"Das, do you still have that Heroin? You can get rich, super rich by selling it? How do you know it was Heroin only and nothing else?"

"Tony Singh, we should bury this drugs hatchet in Amritsar. What if they have put some kind of transmitters in the car? After all, your car was unattended for so many hours. By the way am I invited to your son's birthday party?"

"O yaara, you are welcome. And when you are back we will continue my journey with Hinglish. I mean English."

And they both laughed out loud as Das hugged the bulky frame of Sardar ji.

"Oye Mundiya, no pappiya japhiya. Let me drive."

They reached Pathankot in the evening exactly at the same time they left the day before. The Doctor and the officer had a long chat with Rhea's family. Her husband and in-laws were relieved to see her safe and welcomed her with open arms. After listening about the happenings of last twenty-four hours, they were proud of her.

The Doctor left for his clinic and asked Rhea to report for work on time, the next morning.

"No leaves, unless it is very important, remember!"

Sardar ji and Das were waiting for the Doctor and after making him comfortable and putting his luggage in his room they left for Sardar ji's home for his son's birthday party.

The Doctor, meanwhile, opened his luggage and found the package untouched. The little brown package was still ensconced in the clothes, the way he had put it there. He smelled it, but it did not give away any particular odor. He removed it and placed it in the almirah, locking it for good. He had a strong desire to open it and taste it to see if it was really sugar, the way Das presented the whole scenario. He tossed in his bed for a long time and finally lifted the covers and stood in front of the almirah. He lifted the packet gingerly, took it into the kitchen and tore open the contents. The white crystalline powder spilled on the shelf and with great trepidation he took a pinch of it and deposited on his tongue.

It was sweet. Very sweet. Tears ran down his face as he realized that Das indeed was not lying.

Early morning, he was woken up by the shrill tone of the call. He picked up and saw that it was Jagsir. He had strong urge to disconnect the call, but he could not do that. He clicked on the green button and was greeted by Jagsir yelling on the phone.

"Papa, why you never boarded the flight? I went crazy. Do you have any idea how worried I was? Your phone was switched off and I could not connect with that stupid attendant of yours. A girl calls up but never tells me the real thing. I have been going crazy!!!"

"Jagsir, what was in the package?"

"We discussed that. It is a homeopathic medicine. I told you that."

"Are you into drugs? Heroin, Cocaine… stuff like that?

"Have you gone mad? I never did drugs. I only smoke occasionally and you know that."

"What kind of medicine smells like Heroin?"

"I have no idea what you are talking about! It's crazy. Some vaid in Delhi makes special medicine for migraine. This angrez bahu of yours loves everything Indian. So, I asked a friend in Delhi to deliver at your address."

"Is it? She loves everything Indian!"

"Yes, Papa she does? She has been crying over the fact that you did not board the flight. She was looking forward to spending time with you. And she thinks you hate her because she is a foreigner. Please talk to her. I am giving her the phone. And don't worry I will send you the ticket again. You have to be mentally prepared and ready to come."

Next morning, Rhea, Das and Doctor bonded over a cup of tea at the clinic.

"You should have called Sardar ji, Your IELTS partner." Rhea looked at Das with mischief in her eyes.

"We had a blast last night. "

Das smiled gleefully. "Don't worry, he would keep on coming with his faithful Nano. He calls it his good luck car. Oh yes! Rhea di, please book a train ticket for me. I will give you the money."

"You want to go on a train. How boring Das! But I and

Doctor saab have something else in mind."

"What?"

"Here it is." Rhea handed him a print out.

"Spice jet airlines. You booked me an aeroplane ticket." He stood atop his chair and started shouting.

"I will be on an aeroplane. Yeah!!!"

"Sit down and listen. This is online confirmation of your ticket. You have to show them, and you will get a boarding pass. Go home and start packing. We wanted you to go early so that you celebrate Chatt puja with your family. You leave tomorrow morning. Ask Sardar ji to come and we will all go in his Nano." the Doctor instructed.

"Again, all the way to Amritsar."

"Yes, all the way again to drop you. And you are coming back after fifteen days. We cannot run this place without you."

Das hugged the Doctor "My dada. Thank you so much. How can I repay you?"

"By behaving sensibly."

"Das, you cannot hug me. Please keep distance." Rhea shooed him away as she decoded his intentions.

"Go now, you idiot! Tell everyone, you are going home."

✳ ✳ ✳

15

THE FAREWELL

Next day, Sardar ji reached the clinic at the designated time. He spotted Das roaming outside the clinic.

"Wow! You look handsome!"

"Rhea di and her hubby gifted me this shirt and trousers and see the Nike shoes. Dactar Sahib gifted me those." He beamed with pride.

Rhea came dressed in bright pink salwar kameez. The Doctor looked fresh, every trace of stress washed from his face. After the usual exchange of pleasantries everyone decided to make a quick move.

Sardar ji gasped to see five big bags along with some poly bags.

"How much stuff are you taking, Das? How will all this fit in my car? Chalo everyone will keep one bag in their lap or we cannot accommodate it?

"I am going after a long time. So, I can't go empty handed. There has to be something for everyone. Kyun ji?"

" I am not keeping a bag on my lap. Do whatever! I want to sit comfortably. Rhea you take care of two bags and rest Das will manage himself." the Doctor deposited himself in the front seat next to Sardar ji.

While checking the tickets the guard stared hard at Das.

"You look familiar to me. Weren't you the one who was

clutching my legs that day?"

"Nah ji nah. Some mistake. I am coming for the first time." Das tried hiding his face with his hand.

"You are the same guy. The idiot who was rounded up and taken to the manager. So where are you going?"

"I am going to Bihar. Yes, I am the one, but that day I was a different person. The one who is standing in front of you is a confident young man who is preparing for IELTS. Now please if you have seen my ticket, let me and my family go. They will be accompanying me till the lounge area." The guard snickered as he gestured him to make a move.

"Thank you very much." Das strutted passed him and so did the others.

In the waiting lounge, everyone scurried around Das.

"Das, you were damn cool! Super cool! He recognized you, but you acted so confident."

"Did I, Rhea di? I was so nervous. I thought he would make fun of me or call other guards and throw me out of the airport."

"Come on! Achha you know nah that this flight is only till Patna. Did you make arrangements to go till Samastipur?"

"All done, Rhea di. Don't you worry. I will reach safely, and I will call you when I am there."

She smiled and nodded.

"Chalo this time you go alone. Next time we will go together to Kaneda." Sardar ji hugged Das tight and kissed him on the cheek.

"Pakka Sardar ji. Please don't kiss me. I am not your girlfriend."

"We should go now. Das, Bhenchod! come back after fifteen days or I would come there and kill you." The Doctor shook hands with him and smacked him lightly on the back.

"Arre, but his flight is late. Let's stay here. Such a beautiful airport and I want to spend more time with him." Sardar ji butted in.

"I think we should make a move. Let him be on his own. He will be coming back after fifteen days. Das you take care and see you soon." Rhea followed Doctor saab towards the exit gate.

Sardar ji fished a five-hundred rupee note from his pocket and shoved towards a reluctant Das, "Keep this. I did not bring anything for you."

He smiled and took the money eventually, clutching his fingers around the grubby note.

"I should go now, or I will get emotional." Sardar ji patted his back and left.

Das kept on watching their retreating figures for a while and then cradled himself on the cushy airport chair. He fiddled with the strap of his rucksack for a long time and finally got a white paper out with some words scribbled on it. It was the will. That day when the Doctor was badly drunk and dispirited, Das had challenged him and he had willed all his property, the house and clinic to him. He had signed and the young boy from the samosa shop was made to sign as a witness to give it some validity.

He peered hard at the grimy paper that had got sullen by his constant touch. He read the words again and again. Yes, he had no doubt about it. The Doctor has willed everything to him. He had no idea how legitmate it was? But he might stand a chance if he contested it in court? He toyed with this idea for a while.

He closed his eyes momentarily, the paper still clutched in his hand. But when he opened them, he sat upright, jolted himself. In one deft motion, he had torn the will and kept on doing it until the paper was reduced to smithereens. He stashed the torn pieces in his rucksack.

He looked at the new shoes that were gifted to him by his employer today morning. He had come to the clinic wearing his old worn out shoes when he had remarked, "Das, you cannot go wearing those shoes to the airport. Go in style."

He had fished out a polybag and handed over to him. Inside were the brand-new Nike shoes, perfectly pearly white. The kind he has never seen and worn before. He had tried them on, clapping and giggling like a school girl and it turned out to be a perfect fit.

He stood and twirled around in his new shoes and did a small gig which was noticed by some passengers. A young girl reading a book, momentarily lifted her head and noticed his antics. She gave him an impromptu smile.

Das emboldened, went up to her, "Hi, I am Das and I work as a Veterinary attendant."

"That's great. I love animals. Come, sit here. I am going to Patna."

"Me too. I am going to Samastipur later."

"Oh great! They have an Agricultural University where I went to take an admission test. I think it is an amazing place."

"Wow! Finally, I get to hear some good words for my home town. By the way, I am undertaking air travel for the first time so I am little nervous."

"Oh! That is so sweet! Come with me. I will guide you. By the way I am Meeta Vashishth. Nice to meet you, Das."

She proffered her hand and he shook it with a shy smile, "Dagshman Bandhu but call me Das."

"Let's make a move, Das. Follow me."

He smiled at his guardian angel and with little careful

steps started following her as she guided and helped him at each and every step. After completing all the formalities they were sitting together ,waiting to board. Das looked at the boarding pass clutched in his hands and then he looked at her. She smiled back, "You are still nervous about this flight! Aren't you?"

"It is my first time, that's why!"

"I will exchange seat with your co-passenger. I want to sit next to you. I hope you won't mind that?"

He stood up and went next to the huge windowpane. He could see the airport apron. He looked at the aeroplanes with a childlike curiosity. They seem to hold a world inside them. He wondered what it would be like to sit in them and fly like a bird. He looked at Meeta who got busy with her book.

Life was beautiful as he looked around and saw the colors turning more vibrant. An announcement has been made and he saw Meeta waving frantically to him as she queued up in the line with other passengers.

"Come, we have to board now. Walk beside me and don't get lost."

He inhaled her fragrance as she walked in long strides ahead of him and quickened his pace to match her step.

It looked like the start of something beautiful as he absorbed the happenings in his mind. He blinked once, twice, again and again, clicking the moments with the shutterbug of his eyes to make them stay in the recesses of his mind for a life time.

✳ ✳ ✳

Epilogue

Das came back and joined his job with a renewed vigor and went for IELTS coaching classes alongside. After one year of vigorous preparation, he cleared the exam with an 8 band and won a scholarship at Berlin University in an undergraduate program. He stayed in touch with Meeta through phone calls, WhatsApp and Facebook and he is motivating her to prepare for the IELTS as well.

Jagsir has invited Das to stay with him in Berlin, until he could find a place of his own.

Doctor saab has decided to accompany Das as he thinks Das might not be able to adjust in a new country, so it would do him good to have a mentor staying with him. He decided to stay for three months with him and Jagsir after which he would come back and take care of clinic. He had firmly told his son that he would not become a carrier for any kind of homeopathic medicines or anything that is remotely covered in a brown paper.

Rhea has been made the sole in-charge of the clinic for three months. Her relationship with Mummy ji has improved a lot over the past one year. They bond over old Hindi movies and gupshup about the neighborhood.

Abhi, Papa and Kimti feel relieved and happy to see the bonding between mother-in- law and daughter- in- law. Finally, there is more bonhomie and less confrontations on the home front.

Sardar ji has sold his Nano and brought an Innova. Nano has lost its charm for him as it reminded him of those dreadful twenty-four hours that drove him crazy. He took everyone in his brand new Innova to the Golden Temple at Amritsar for seeking the blessings of the Almighty.